Mrs. Farintosh

I've long been fascinated by Sherlock Holmes's cases which occurred before I met him. In April 1883, when Miss Helen Stoner consulted Holmes, she stated that Mrs. Farintosh had recommended him. I longed to hear about the earlier case, but I had to wait, as we were immediately occupied on the journey to Surrey to aid Miss Stoner. Later, when we were on the train back to London after revealing the truth behind the deadly speckled band and its resultant rough justice, I waited a suitable amount of time, and as soon as we were settled and the wheels began to roll, I asked, "Regarding Mrs. Farintosh, who recommended you to Miss Stoner . . . ?"

"You never forget anything, do you, Watson? Oh very well. I see I'll get no peace until I tell you about that case."

"It will while away the journey back to London," I said . . . .

Early in December of 1880, just before you and I met on New Year's Day, I lived in Montague Street, around the corner from the British Museum. I wasn't as busy as I am now. I'd already retired for the night when I received a telegram asking me to come as early in the morning as possible to call on a Mr. Farintosh, who had a most urgent problem. I replied I would be there at nine, and then returned to bed without a thought as to what his problem might be.

The address wasn't far, but in the interest of time, I took a hansom to John Street, just off the Strand near the Waterloo Bridge, and stood before a narrow three-story house, built of dark brick, with carved stone pilasters and an attic. The door was

1

opened by a proper butler, whose name I later learned was Paxton, a solid fellow who looked as though he might wrestle horses, but was excellent with overcoats and umbrellas as well. "You are here about the missing tiara?"

I nodded, though I didn't yet know what the urgency was for my summons. A missing tiara sounded less urgent than a missing person or a murder.

The butler ushered me into the morning room where the entire household awaited me – fourteen people, one or more of whom may or may not have taken the tiara. I hadn't faced an audience of that size since I was onstage as Marzando the Magnificent's assistant, and never as a consulting detective. I felt like an understudy opera singer performing *Aida* for the first time.

The room was well-appointed, with floor-to-ceiling windows for the meager December morning light. They were hung with yellow silk draperies patterned with latticework. Yellow, green, black, and white were used for the rug and upholstery, and the walls were painted a cheerful yellow. A large six-sided terrarium, lush with greenery, stood on a table near the windows.

A man stepped forward and identified himself as Gilbert Farintosh, pronounced *Fairn-tosh*, a Scotsman who spoke the Queen's English. He asked me to follow him to his library, where he closed the door and turned to me in order to explain the reason for the telegram.

"My wife's tiara is missing."

I almost told him that was regrettable but beneath my services when he wrung his hands most anxiously and said,

Sherlock Holmes:
The Crimson Trail
and Other Stories

By

Brenda Seabrooke

Edited by David Marcum,

Derrick Belanger and Brian Belanger

Paperback ISBN 978-1-80424-499-9
ePub ISBN 978-1-80424-500-2
PDF ISBN 978-1-80424-501-9

Published by MX Publishing
335 Princess Park Manor, Royal Drive,
London, N11 3GX
www.mxpublishing.co.uk

Cover design by Awan

To Sherlockians the world

over who keep the game afoot

Contents

Sherlock at Work

Sherlock at Work

The thin-sliced shadow

loses itself in a bare-branched thicket,

eyes slotted against shine probe

beyond a window, a portal, a door

into hearts blackened

with evil, twisted, stained,

moated oceans of human flotsam,

ahead of the game,

sussing moves almost

before the deed is done.

Facts surface on the roiled plane

sorted, tested, amalgamated, seined

by the annealed intelligence

of his rapier brain.

"Please let me explain. I know the problem must seem trivial to you, although the tiara is quite valuable."

"It hardly seems to be as urgent as you seem to think it," I replied.

"Please. I'm neither wealthy nor titled. I must earn my way. I'm a junior in the Foreign Office. My superiors have honored me by issuing an invitation to their annual Christmas Ball. All of the women will be resplendent in their gowns and tiaras, a way of evaluating them and by extension their husbands. This tiara has been in my family for more than a century, since an ancestor brought it back from India. It may hold the key to my advancement."

I hoped that Foreign Office promotions weren't based on tiaras, but I didn't doubt it. "I assume you have searched for it already. When was its loss first discovered?"

"Late yesterday. The tiara is made of silver set with truly resplendent opals. My wife went to the locked cabinet where she keeps it to see if the silver needed polishing again. The box in which it's kept was there, but was empty."

"I see. Opals. *Upala* from Sanskrit, meaning 'precious stone'. Was the box itself kept locked?"

"It was, as was the cabinet."

"Where are the keys kept?"

"Lenora has an intricate little box with a trick opening. I gave it to her for a courtship present. Only the two of us know the secret to open it. That key and the cabinet key were both undisturbed in the trick box."

A locked box in a locked cabinet with keys hidden in a secret compartment in a puzzle box. My interest was piqued by now. "What measures have you taken to find the tiara?"

"I gathered everyone in the dining room where I thought the tiara was least likely to be hidden, because people are in and out of it all day. My wife and I then searched the servants' quarters in the attic. We found nothing. We then made our way down from floor to floor, but the answer was the same: The tiara had vanished."

"No one left the room while you were searching?"

"No. Paxton kept stern watch over the room. Only the children were asleep."

"They are how old?"

"Gil, Jr. is five, Susan is three, and little Petey is just over a year. We checked the nursery as well as their beds in case some diabolical person had hidden the tiara there. We were thorough, I assure you. We even looked under the beds to be sure the tiara hadn't been attached to the bottoms. I knew of no one I could turn to. I didn't want the police involved, or the news to reach the newspapers. I remembered hearing your name once mentioned in passing in the hallways at work, and that you are a consulting detective." He spread his hands. "And here we are."

"The difficulty of this case seems to be the time of the theft. We only know it was missing late yesterday. When was the last time your wife looked at it?"

"Sometime after we received the invitation to the ball. My wife thinks it was on the fourth. She remembers that was a Saturday, and the joint for Sunday dinner was delivered that day."

"Today is the tenth. You found the tiara missing on the ninth. That narrows the time of the theft to five days. Now I need to meet the rest of your household."

We adjourned back to the morning room where I met Mr. Farintosh's brother, Harold, two years younger than Gilbert, who appeared to be about our age, Watson. Also present was Harold's wife, Bess, and sitting quietly beside her was Mrs. Lenora Farintosh, who was younger than I expected her to be after having three children – all of them seated beside her. Her sister, Sylvia Somers, was probably around twenty-three. Gilbert Jr.'s governess, Miss Ida Ayers, was a pleasant but plain young woman of perhaps thirty-one, and Nanny Frakes was a cheerful cushiony woman of middle age.

The staff consisted of Paxton, the butler, Mrs. Bowles the cook, whose quarters both were off the kitchen 'tween floors, Mary the parlour maid, and Edith the cook's helper. From time to time, part-time workers came – window-washers, chimney sweeps, knife sharpeners, pot-menders – but none since October when the house was cleaned for the winter.

I stood near the terrarium while Farintosh introduced me to the household and explained what I would do. I watched them while I pretended to look at the scene in the glass box: Mountains covered in velvety smooth green moss, where ferns and other moisture-loving plants formed a dell with a ceramic dragon hidden in it. A circular mirror stood in for a lake with a pair of tiny glass swans swimming on it. Someone had spent considerable time on this creation.

Mrs. Farintosh noticed my attention. "My sister made that with the children."

"Clever," I said. Her sister blushed prettily.

"We did it last week," Miss Somers said. "The day it rained. Sunday I think it was."

"I put the swans in," Susan whispered from her seat beside Nanny Frakes. "On the other side."

Near the floor, seemingly stuck to the back of one of the table legs, was a bit of ferny green.

Farintosh finished relating to the household that they must tell me everything they could remember about the five days between the last appearance of the tiara and the previous night.

"No matter how trivial," I added. "I will start with Mrs. Bowles, followed by Nanny Frakes and Miss Ayers. Please remain in this room until your turn, and pray do not discuss the case."

Nobody seemed unduly alarmed at being questioned. I chose the cook first because her duties would need to be attended to soon. Mrs. Bowles was a substantial personage in a blue-print dress, covered by a capacious spotless white apron. I suspected she was a dab hand at pastries and the like. Her plain features were framed by a ruffled white cap.

"I never go upstairs 'cept on special occasions," she stated without preamble, "and there's been none since the house was turned over."

"That was in October."

"Yessir." She nodded emphatically.

"Have you heard anything about the tiara?"

"Only what's been said 'bout it missin'."

"You haven't seen anything suspicious in the five days since Saturday last?"

"Nossir." She nodded again.

"If you think of something, let Mr. Paxton know."

"I will, sir."

"Thank you. You may go."

Nanny Frakes raised her eyebrows at the door as she passed Mrs. Bowles, who gave her a nod.

"I'll be quick," I said as the door closed. Nanny Frakes was about forty. She wore a brown-print dress with another snowy apron.

"I don't know anything about the tiara. I didn't know it was missing until Mr. Farintosh came in the nursery last night, after they discovered it were gone."

"I thought as much. If you think of anything let Mr. Farintosh know. You may take your charges to the nursery now, and send in Miss Ayers."

She nodded and returned to the morning room. In a second or two, Miss Ida Ayers knocked on the door Nanny Frakes closed behind her. I'd made a list of their names and made a brief note as we talked.

The governess was dressed more modishly than the previous two – no apron, her dress of a striped merino wool with a lacy collar, a gold watch pinned to her bodice. As governess, she had more access in the house than the previous two, but she knew no more than they did.

"I've never seen the tiara and wouldn't know it if I did," she declared, her brown eyes opened wide. "This is my first year here."

"How do you find the household?"

"Gil, Jr. is a precocious little boy eager to learn. Susan will start her lessons next year."

"And the adults of the household?"

"Mr. and Mrs. Farintosh are lovely people." She refused to say more.

I asked her to tell Mr. Harold he was next, and he entered within seconds. He was a lesser version of his older brother, as if one print had been made, but the ink had faded on the second copy. His dark hair was receding, his eyes a pale gray, his nose slightly pinched. His face was marred by a thin black moustache. His shoulders mimicked his moustache's droop, sloping under his fashionable gray-on-gray coat. His voice was somewhat nasal, indicating a possible obstruction of his airways.

He, too, had noticed nothing amiss. He accompanied his wife on carriage drives in Hyde Park several times in those crucial five days. "She's in the family way," he said with obvious pride. "I'm scarcely two years younger than my brother, but he already has three children."

And also a promising career and a house on a fashionable street were the words left unspoken.

He was between positions, he said, doing a little speculating. I managed not to prick up my ears at that, because obviously living in his brother's house, without a job and a baby coming, he had need for money, but he shot that theory down in his next sentence.

"I'm not in a rush. Our great-uncle's estate is almost settled. We both have expectations, as he died without other heirs beside the two of us." He leaned back as if enjoying the inheritance in advance.

I thanked him and bade him to ask his wife to come in next. He turned at the door and looked as if he wanted to tell me his wife didn't need to answer my questions, but thought better of it and slouched out.

Bess Farintosh was a petite woman with dark brown curls, held in place by carnelian combs. She wore a voluminous gown of soft wool in a shade of russet that set off her dark eyes and pale coloring. Several years younger than her husband, she still had a fresh dewy look, even after living with him. Perhaps she, too, had expectations, or possibly she hoped her brother-in-law would be knocked down by an omnibus and the tiara and all that accompanied it would become hers.

"I haven't seen anything of that old tiara," she said in a breathy voice. "Lenora should take better care of it if it's so valuable."

I refrained from saying that she'd locked it up twice and hidden the keys well while she explained to me how she went to bed early, arose late, and nibbled dry toast until noon. "After that, if the weather is fine, my husband takes me for a drive in the park, and then I may read a magazine or a novel, or nap until dinner."

I nodded to be polite. I've no knowledge of the ways of women in the family way and didn't know if this was the usual for ladies who need not work.

"Please ask Miss Somers to come in next," I said as she slowly progressed to the door.

While awaiting Miss Somers, I looked around the library at the comfortable appointments, the leather chairs, the walls of books, the mahogany desk with ornate dagger letter opener, utilitarian inkwell, and a small globe that no doubt omitted Krakatoa, Zanzibar, Okinawa, and other islands of no importance to the Queen. The room was dark, lit only by oil lamps on sconces set into the wall. The sole outside light came from the hall through the glass transom over the door.

Miss Somers strolled in. She wore her blond hair in plaits wrapped around her head, perhaps in Viking style. Her eyes were green, and she wore a dress of the same color.

"Confound it, Watson, how do you describe all these details when you write our case studies?"

10

"Well, it isn't easy. I take notes. Sometimes I go back and fill in from memory."

"I took notes, but only to remember where they all were roughly during those five days."

Miss Somers sat demurely in the green leather chair and waited for me to finish appreciating her beauty she had packaged so well. "I am Sylvia Somers," she purred when I didn't speak.

"Indeed. Tell me of your activities during those five days from last Saturday until yesterday."

"Twice, I think, I went driving in the park with Harold and Bess. One day, I went with my sister to look at silk embroidery thread, but we didn't buy any."

"Why is that if you needed the thread?"

"I don't like embroidery, and my sister couldn't make up her mind between the greens or the mauves." She pursed her lips.

"Did you know where the tiara was kept?"

"Vaguely – somewhere in their rooms?"

"Had you seen it before?"

"She wore it at her wedding."

Interesting that she spoke of her sister as *her*, *she*, or *my sister* – never by name.

She had no more to add. I asked about the terrarium she had made with the children.

"I thought their little eyes would enjoy the greenery during the winter when there's no color, and the sun sets almost before it rises."

"Did you put it together, or did the two older children?"

"It was a combined effort. We even let little Petey put in some of the moss. I had to rework a lot of it later after they were in bed, but they had fun doing it."

"What day did you make it?"

She pursed her lips again, thinking. She must have been told that was a pretty pose. "It was Sunday, as I've already stated. Gilbert bought the terrarium the week before when I suggested it."

She had nothing to add. Like the others, she'd seen nothing, heard nothing. "Ask Mrs. Farintosh to come next, please."

Her sister hurried in a few minutes later and sat down with a swirl of her skirts. She appeared to be in motion even when she was not. "Do you have any clues yet?" she asked anxiously.

"Some things have come to mind, but I need more information."

"Watson, are you taking notes?"

"A few. I can't possibly remember all these details, and I marvel that you can."

"This is not a case that you helped to solve."

He was being generous. "I can't remember so many little things, like the fallen fern, when I haven't experienced it myself."

"You would remember that whether you experienced it or not."

"Somehow I doubt that."

"I do not."

"What kind of information?"

"Since your oldest son is five, I assume you've been married for at least six years."

"Nine. I was nineteen, Jason was twenty-two."

"How long has your sister lived with you?"

"Three years. Our parents both died within weeks of one another. My father was a lawyer in Evesham. We used the inheritance for a debut for her, but she 'didn't take', as they say. She's twenty-two now, and I don't know what to do about a husband for her. Gilbert has invited young bachelors to visit from time to time, but again nothing happened. I do wish she would make more of an effort to please."

"Are you close?"

"Not in years past, because I was older, but now that she's grown up, and we can share more activities."

"Such as?"

"She's interested in embroidery. We often go to match silks."

"Do you enjoy embroidery?"

"I hate it. I much more enjoy gardening. Gil bought the terrarium for me, but she insisted on doing it with the children. How could I say no? They gathered the moss from the scrap of a garden out back. I do think I shall add violets, both purple and white."

"Any other activities together?"

"We walk in the park."

"Did you walk much during these five days?"

"The weather wasn't clement enough this week. We were going to look at embroidery materials one day, but then rain blew up. Why these questions about my family?"

"I need to understand the background of the household. Did you engage your servants when you acquired this house?"

"Yes. My husband inherited it from his father. His mother died young. We were living here with his father when he died. There's some ancient property in Scotland, but I've never seen it. We engaged all the servants ourselves, except for Mrs. Bowles.

She was here already. When my husband's father died, his butler retired, as did the maids. Edith was engaged after we moved here. Paxton came then, and later Mary."

"And you have no reason not to trust them?"

"None at all. Paxton is the only one who even knew about the tiara. He has polished it several times. He seems pleased to be with a family who has a tiara." Her mouth curved in a fleeting smile until she remembered she might never see the tiara again. "Interesting how people value their meager holdings. I'm sure the wives of dukes and earls never even bother to count their tiaras."

"Their staffs may do that for them." I returned to the questioning. "You are quite sure no one entered your house during those five days?"

"No one."

"Perhaps some kitchen deliveries?"

"The meat delivery had been made before I looked at the tiara that day. The vegetables had been delivered earlier. They are due again tomorrow."

"What do you think happened to the tiara?"

She turned her blue eyes, clear as water, to mine. "I really don't know. I've lost sleep trying to figure out if I removed it in my sleep."

"Are you prone to sleep-walking?"

"No, not at all, but I can think of no other way it could have gone missing. Oh, Mr. Holmes, please find it!" Her eyes glistened with tears. "It means so much to him! He thinks he needs it to advance at the Foreign Office. We have enough if he never gains another step up. We could make do with fewer staff! I've told him this, but he feels it's a blot on his ability."

"Do not worry. I shall find the tiara for you, and in time for the ball tonight. Now, if you could ask Paxton to come in."

Paxton, perhaps more than any other member of the staff, knew what the loss of the tiara meant to the family, and it had happened on his watch. He was understandably worried, but in the tradition of butlers, kept his feelings to himself.

"Meat deliveries were made on that day for both the weekend and the rest of the week. In addition, vegetables were delivered. I supervised both. No tiara went out that door, I can assure you."

"I'm sure you can, but I must leave no carrot unturned."

Not only was I surprised at Holmes's levity, but also at its use during an investigation. Later, he told me he was attempting to relieve the butler because by then he already knew what had happened to the tiara.

"Yes, sir."

"Tell me about yourself."

"I was born the youngest in Alfriston on the coast. I didn't want to go to sea as my brothers did. Our father had been lost in a storm on the Channel. I was seven and frightened of the sea from that day on. At age nine, I began running errands and doing odd jobs at the pub, and later at the Mirleton, the large country house owned by the Gaylon family." He stopped abruptly.

I didn't question him further. No doubt some unpleasantness had happened, as it often does with these houses and their casts of characters. "What do you think happened to the tiara?"

"I cannot say, sir, but I am reasonably sure it didn't leave the house – certainly not through the kitchen during deliveries. Mary and Edith are two honest girls, and Mrs. Bowles is the soul of goodness."

I nodded and asked him to tell Mr. Farintosh I would like to speak to him.

"Very good, sir." He left silently as butlers do, and Gilbert Farintosh entered.

"Well, Holmes, I hope you have some indication of what happened to the tiara."

"I do, but first, I need to look over the house myself."

He nodded. "It is near the noon hour. Shall we wait in the dining room? I've ordered a light collation if you care to join us, or I could have it brought here."

"Perhaps later. A cup of coffee would be excellent."

"I'll see to it."

I waited until they were all in the dining room and Paxton brought me coffee. I took the cup and saucer with me and drank as I descended to the kitchen.

"Lord, Mr. Holmes, I wasn't expecting you," Mrs. Bowles said as she removed a pan from the mountainous stove. The kitchen was warm with pots bubbling and delectable dishes laid on the long wooden table.

I put the cup down. "Excellent coffee. I'm just getting the lay of the land, so to speak."

I walked around the kitchen, opened the door, and looked out into the courtyard. "The dustman comes once a week?"

"Twice, sir. He came on Monday, and again on Thursday, but no tiara went out of this kitchen. I check the barrels myself. There's no telling what people will drop by accident late at night. Once I found a silver comb."

"I'm sure the tiara didn't escape your eagle eye."

She stirred a pot and bobbed a curtsy. "Thank you, sir."

I took a few moments to question Mary and Edith. Neither contributed anything of value, except that the former described how she cleaned the house, specifically confirming how she had cleaned the legs of the table where the terrarium sat.

In a ragbag off the scullery, I found an interesting piece of silk. I folded it and slid it into a pocket. Mrs. Bowles' and Paxton's rooms were locked. I didn't need to know more than where they were located on the half-floor between the basement and the next (add floor.)

I climbed the servants' stairs, noting they were of better quality than many I'd seen. I started at the top floor, glancing into the rooms of the two maids with their neat possessions and pictures of family. I noted one had a photograph of a young man in a uniform in a plain frame on the cabinet beside her bed.

The next floor down held the nursery, the schoolroom, and the rooms of the governess and nanny. I didn't disturb them. Still on the back stairs, I perused the next floor, where the rooms of Gilbert and Lenora were somewhat larger and more tastefully decorated in blues and mauves. All was as I expected. I looked in the cabinet, now left open and empty of its charge, the tiara. The box was there, but locked. I looked for the trick box and found it under folded handkerchiefs. The design was Chinese, and I had no difficulty in finding the secret compartment where the two keys lay in a small velvet bag. I replaced them and moved to the sitting room. Nothing to see there. I crossed the hall to the sitting room, now by necessity a bedroom for Sylvia while Harold and Bess occupied the next larger bedroom. She must have hated giving up the bigger room. Beyond, I found a series of even smaller rooms into which the children would move when they outgrew the nursery.

I took the main stairs this time, passing through the morning room, where I prepared my revelation. I didn't bother with the drawing room, but opened the dining room door. The low murmur of voices stopped, some in mid-sentence. The longcase clock in the hall struck half-two.

"Did you find it?" Harold demanded as if it were his tiara.

"Yes," Sylvia echoed, "did you find it?"

"Would you all please assemble in the morning room? Just the family." A frown flitted across Paxton's face, quickly replaced by a bland look. Farintosh could tell him whatever he wished later. I withdrew, leaving them to follow me.

They sat in the same seating as before, in a rough semicircle with Gilbert and Lenora in the center, Sylvia on the left curve facing Harold, and Bess somewhat recessed between the two brothers. They looked at me with expectant eyes.

"I have been all over the house," I said, "looking for places where a tiara could be hidden if it weren't smuggled out."

Sylvia let out a little scream. "Do you mean some – some *housebreaker* has been inside these walls, endangering our persons?"

"I have found no evidence of that."

"Have you found evidence of the tiara?" Harold asked with a smirk. He obviously thought I hadn't.

"According to all of you, no one has entered the house, except for those who live and work here during the time the tiara was last seen on Saturday. Supplies brought to the kitchen were overseen by Paxton, who assures me that nothing left the kitchen that day and yesterday, when Mrs. Farintosh opened the box in which the tiara is kept to see if the silver needed polishing. Is this correct?"

Harold shrugged. Bess nodded. Sylvia said, "Mmm". Lenora nodded, and Gilbert said, "That is what we believe."

I took out my handkerchief and unfolded it to show a tiny frond of a small green fern. "I found this behind the leg of the able with the terrarium."

"Mary must not have seen it when she cleaned," Lenora said.

"Careless of her," Sylvia said. "You must speak to her, Gilbert."

"It was actually stuck onto the leg and completely unnoticeable in the shadows thrown by the lamps and the windows."

"I'm sure all of the debris from the making of the terrarium were cleared away," Sylvia said. "I put down newspaper before we started for that purpose, but it's possible that I missed a tiny piece."

"You didn't come here to complain about the housekeeping, I hope," Harold complained.

Sylvia smiled at him.

"No, that isn't my purpose. I'm here to find the Farintosh Tiara, and that I have done."

Gilbert sat straighter in his chair. "You have?"

Lenora looked relieved, no doubt because she felt responsible, and also the family's standing table had been salvaged.

Sylvia let out a trill of laughter. "What a relief!"

I removed from my pocket the silk wrapping I'd found in the scrap bag. As I unfolded it, the family gradually realized what it was, but I needed them to confirm. "Is this the silk in which the tiara was wrapped?"

Sylvia arose and walked over to feel the silk to identify it. "I believe so," she said as she sat back down.

I gave her a brief look to see if subterfuge were present. It was not.

"Where did you find it?" Harold demanded.

"It was stuffed into a ragbag in the pantry. Any idea how it got there?"

"Obviously the thief put it there," Harold said.

"It must have been one of the maids," Sylvia said. "I can't imagine Cook climbing those stairs unless summoned."

"Or that's what we are meant to think," I said.

"Tell us where it is, if you know," Harold challenged.

"And who took it," his wife said in a small voice. Harold gave her a sharp look.

I leaned over and opened the top of the terrarium, reached in, and started piling moss into one corner.

"Oh, you're ruining it!" Sylvia cried. "The children will be so disappointed."

"What has been unmade can easily be remade." Soon I uncovered the stones that propped up the moss. Amidst them was the tiara, the mirror of the small lake in its curve. I drew it out of the terrarium and turned it so they could see the opals like glowing moons in the silver frame. Bits of moss and fern tendrils, along with some of the dirt from the underside of the moss, clung to it.

I held it out to Gilbert. "Is this the Farintosh Tiara?"

He took it and showed it to his wife who turned it over to look inside at the engraving. "Yes," she whispered. "Oh yes! See – There is the engraved Farintosh Coat of Arms." Then she said to her husband, "Please ring for Paxton."

The butler immediately opened the door, his stoic face smiling with relief.

"Please see that it is cleaned," she instructed him, "and don't let it out of your sight."

"Very good, Madam. I will watch it as a mongoose watches a cobra."

"Well, that's a little sinister," Sylvia remarked when he'd left.

"Now for the best part," Harold said. "Who *is* the thief?"

"That I cannot say. I was asked to find the tiara, which I have done. It has been restored to the family, and Mrs. and Mrs. Farintosh may now go to the ball in splendour. It is barely half-three, which gives you plenty of time to make your preparations."

"Wait!" Bess interrupted. "How did you know it was there?" She'd been quiet throughout the revelation, and appeared somewhat worried.

"Madame, I eliminate the impossible and what remains, no matter how odd, has to be the solution. With no outsiders in the house, the theft therefore must have been done by an insider who had no opportunity to remove the tiara from the premises. The plan from the beginning, no doubt, was to do so later when the household was no longer under intense scrutiny. The terrarium was a brilliant place of concealment. Now, if you have no more questions, I'll be on my way."

No one could think of anything to ask at that point. I bowed to Mr. and Mrs. Farintosh. "Enjoy your ball tonight."

I nodded for Farintosh to accompany me, since Paxton was occupied with restoring the tiara.

I entered the hall ahead of him. He closed the morning room door behind him. "If you could step into my library a moment . . . ."

I led the way, and he closed the door quietly behind him. "Well – Who did it?"

When I didn't reply he said, "Was it the servants?"

"No."

"Then who?"

"Do you really want to know?"

"Was it my brother?"

"No, but possibly only because he hadn't thought of it yet."

"Surely not Bess."

"No."

"Then – "

"If you have properties in Scotland, I think it would be wise for your brother and his wife to go there so their child will be born a true Scot. If you have another place, your sister-in-law should go there."

"I take your meaning, sir. Thank you. I'll see to it."

His eyes looked sad, and I wondered if earlier discordant incidents, perhaps not of this magnitude, hovered around the edges of this family, and suddenly appeared more sinister in the light of the tiara's theft.

"Enjoy the ball tonight."

"Thank you. We shall." He bade me good afternoon, and I thought to myself that Sylvia accomplished something in the theft of the tiara: Gilbert Farintosh could no longer feel comfortable in his extended family, if he ever had.

"I wonder if they really enjoyed the ball?"

"Mrs. Farintosh no doubt did. I'm sure her husband went through all the motions of it, but the jealousy within the walls of his house had to be on his mind."

"How did you know it was the sister?"

"Harold spent all of his time with either his wife or at his club. That isn't to say he couldn't have done it, but I didn't think he was devious enough. He wore his stupidity on the outside of his coat.

"Sylvia's sweetness on the other hand, came with little pinches of pepper."

"Yes, but how did you know she did it?"

"It was her idea to make the terrarium with the children so they could see greenery in winter's bleakness, and she usurped her sister's involvement. The maids had assured me that they regularly cleaned the legs of the table it sat upon. One of the children had spilled some of the water for the plants on the table top, and it ran down the leg before anybody wipe it up. Mary said she wiped all of the legs all the way around. She would've seen a bit of fern.

When the household slept, Sylvia crept through the house carrying out her plan. I suspect she took the tiara Saturday last when her sister and brother-in-law were at a party to which she wasn't invited.

She hid the tiara in her room, and then had the brilliant idea to hide it in the terrarium. Lenora couldn't say no to the children. After they planted it, Sylvia slipped down late one night during those five days before tiara was found missing and disguised it as part of the mountains. A clever plan. She didn't see the tiny bit of fern, nor did she realize on the day that I visited that it hadn't been there long enough to turn brown, so it couldn't have been there the previous Sunday."

"She may have planned to retrieve it that night while her sister was at the ball, perhaps to wrap it as a Christmas gift for someone and take it and other parcels out of the house that way. With a mind that devious, one need always to anticipate such behavior before more ruin is caused."

"Holmes, you should write an agony aunt column for the newspaper! You solved the problem of the Farintosh tiara and gave advice on the domestic front. Well done!"

"Ha!" He looked out the window at the beginnings of spring, a far distance from December in London. "I found the tiara and the thief, but I can't always solve human problems."

"At least you gave Farintosh some suggestions for dealing with his relatives."

"I did, to the best of my ability. I hoped it would be the solution for him. One must consider the safety of children around such aberrant personalities."

The train began slowing as we came into Waterloo Station, and I wondered if this was the case that made Holmes wary of women, or if it had happened earlier.

"I have heard of you, Mr. Holmes; I have heard of you from Mrs. Farintosh, whom you helped in the hour of her sore need. It was from her that I had your address . . . ."

Holmes turned to his desk and, unlocking it, drew out a small case-book, which he consulted.

"Farintosh," said he. "Ah yes, I recall the case; it was concerned with an opal tiara. I think it was before your time, Watson.

– Miss Helen Stoner and Sherlock Holmes
"The Speckled Band"

The Return of Spring-Heeled Jack

As I accustomed myself to sharing rooms with Sherlock Holmes, a mystery initially arose as to his occupation. I'd noticed in the first two weeks of our acquaintance that strange visitors dropped in at odd hours. At those times, he always asked me politely if I would give them privacy. Of course I always accommodated him and took my reading material up to my room, but I wondered who these people could be that I only glimpsed in passing. Sometimes they appeared exotic, as if from a foreign land, or perhaps they were connected with the theater. Once I met a man so wizened I didn't see how he could possibly walk by himself, even with the aid of a cane. He gave me an enigmatic smile as he drifted by on his way down the stairs. To my amazement, Holmes was absent when I opened the door to our sitting room. Nor was he, apparently, in his bedroom, though I didn't open it to check. I did, however, listen carefully, but heard nothing to indicate he was in there. I retired at eleven, and the next morning Holmes was at the breakfast table when I joined him.

He often missed meals provided by our landlady, Mrs. Hudson, a widow who fussed about his health every time he went without. She seemed less concerned with my health as I gained steadily from her regular meals, and my face soon lost its hollowed look. My wound from the Maiwand battle had not yet healed, stymied as it was by the bout of enteric fever which almost killed me and left me weakened and using a cane and, most seriously, lacking in my previous energy. I was invalided out of the army, a surgeon with no practice, on a small stipend which would end in a few months. I needed to walk every day to regain my stamina, but until recently I hadn't felt up to anything more strenuous than visiting the nearby tobacconist. The steps up to our rooms slowly became less of a challenge as I pushed myself every day to go down them and back up, even if I only stayed in the house the rest of the day. I attributed any progress to Mrs. Hudson's excellent meals and vowed to walk more each day, weather permitting.

On one of these walks, on a particularly foggy evening, I met a man in front of the building. He halted to allow me to go ahead of him. As I stepped up to the door and inserted my key, I recognized him.

"Inspector Lestrade! What a terrible night to be out."

I had only known who he was for a few weeks. Before Holmes revealed to me that he was a "consulting detective", as he called it, Lestrade had been just one of the many visitors who stopped in, often requiring me to withdraw to my upstairs bedroom while Holmes used the sitting room to meet with his "clients". Only a couple of weeks before had I learned Holmes's true profession, when invited to accompany him during his investigation of a murder in Lauriston Gardens. There I had been formally introduced to Lestrade, an inspector with Scotland Yard.

He was thin with a narrow face and sallow complexion which might signal illness in some, but seemed not to be the case with him. He had a cagey look, reminding me somewhat of a ferret, and a sense of coiled energy which hid his native suspicion of the human condition – that neither larceny nor homicide was ever far from many a man's or woman's soul.

"It certainly is, Doctor."

"You have business with Holmes?" I asked, before instantly realizing it was unlikely he'd visit for any other reason. I was curious, as those were early days, and there was still much about Sherlock Holmes that I didn't know. I hoped to learn more of my flatmate's occupation, and what he did during his irregular hours.

"Possibly," was Lestrade's tight-lipped reply.

By now the door was open and I pushed it back, bidding him enter ahead of me. "Go on up. I daresay you'll be quicker than I am."

And he was. He put me in mind of a greyhound as he all but galloped up the stairs. I made my way up behind him. He waited at the door for me to enter, noting my halting progress. I knocked – and suddenly I realized it was somewhat strange to knock on one's own door, but I had no way of knowing if Holmes was entertaining one of his strange visitors.

He was not. "Come in," came the reply.

I ushered Lestrade in and followed slowly. "You have a visitor," I managed as I removed my coat, scarf, gloves, and hat. Lestrade was occupied at doing the same. I hung our coats on the rack by the door and turned to observe.

"Inspector!" Holmes said proffering the chair to the left side of his, facing the fireplace. "I wondered when you might drop in."

"Indeed. I was laid up with a case of grippe or I would've come sooner."

Lestrade took the chair. Holmes didn't ask me to leave, so I moved the wicker chair closer to the fire sinking into it carefully and trying not to make any noise. I picked up a newspaper from the floor and pretended to read it. I hoped they would forget about me and I could determine more about my new friend and his affairs.

"What can I do for you?" asked Holmes after offering Lestrade some refreshments.

"You've heard of Spring-Heeled Jack?"

"Indeed I have. He was a rough prankster who first turned up in the outer areas of London – in 1837, I believe. Periodically he has appeared in villages and other cities, but these sightings have usually been attributed to mass hysteria. He attacked women, springing at them and with claw-like hands and ripping their clothing. Women began wearing gloves with claws built into them to protect themselves, though I know of no instances where that happened. Perhaps Jack noted their defensive gloves and left them alone."

"That's about what it was. This latest outbreak – you've read of it in the press – seems to be the return of Spring-Heeled Jack to central London. He leaps down from a gate post, a plinth, some form of height, or materializes out of the thick fog and tears at feminine clothing. Like the first Jack, his face is covered, and he hides under a dark cloak.

"As I recall," Holmes said, "the earlier Jack was said to leap from rooftop to rooftop breathing fire."

"I doubt that. Merely stories, each telling becoming more exaggerated. This Jack doesn't do that. He possibly leaps off lower ledges and walls, but more likely he springs at his victims from the fog and they add the notion of heights."

"Maybe the current Jack doesn't know how the original breathed fire. Easy enough to spit folded flames of fabric from one's mouth while leaping down, and this Jack may not be able to leap from that height. He was said to be a devil, a demon, terrifying the ladies of the land."

"He did that." Lestrade nodded. "And now women all over London are afraid to go out in this thick fog for fear Jack will leap on them. He snatched kisses in the past, but doesn't seem to be doing that now. Yet the ladies remain fearful he will."

"What do you wish from me?"

"I was hoping you could help us with the case, you being a consulting detective. The Metropolitan Police thinks it's Jack returned to terrorize London after years in the shires."

"But you don't subscribe to this." It was not a question.

Lestrade shook his head.

"There are other non-police detectives in London," Holmes said.

"You work somewhat differently." The two regarded each other.

Holmes waved his hand. "Indeed?"

"That's right. You've shown that the most obvious is often not the solution."

"Nor do I leap to a conclusion based on a whim. Some may think the original Spring-Heeled Jack is back, but I suspect that isn't the case, and I've heard no facts to support such a conclusion."

"I told my colleagues you would say that," Lestrade said, "but why do you think thus?"

"For one, too much time has elapsed since the first appearance of Jack in 1837 – that's forty-four years. Assuming the original Jack was at least twenty years of age, he would now be over sixty-four, and probably more – not the age to leap off ledges and walls, or even plinths, unless he's a circus acrobat. And certainly not from rooftops."

"He seems to have dispensed with the fire-breathing as well," Lestrade said.

"Hmm," was all Holmes said.

"Have you been keeping up with the reports in the newspapers?"

"I have. Three attacks, all of them not far from here. I can't see that three ripped garments would necessitate a Scotland Yard detective to seek outside help. What do you wish from me?"

"This has been kept quiet, but last night another attack was made in this filthy fog, and the young woman's throat was slashed. We have no clues except that it again appears to be Spring-Heeled Jack's return. Will you take the case? I'll see to your remuneration."

Holmes steepled his fingers. I'd noticed he often did this when he was thinking. "The murder entirely changes the complexion of the case. I will need the details and to see the body."

"I'll arrange it with the morgue. The victim appeared to have fainted, but when she was turned over, the method became obvious. The police at first thought it was a regular murder, understandable in the heavy fog, but later in the morgue, the rips on her clothing were visible."

"No doubt made *post mortem*," Holmes said, "to tie it to the attacks, but what you have here is a case of something entirely different – a Claw Man, I would call him, rather than Spring-Heeled Jack."

Lestrade winced. "I hope the newspapers don't get wind of that. A *Claw Man* indeed."

"They will have to know of the murder. They will find their way to it on their own."

"Will you take the case?" Lestrade repeated.

"I will, but understand I work alone unless I find it necessary to utilize the Force. I'll need to interview the young ladies attacked by the perpetrator."

"That won't be immediately possible in two of the cases. The two maids have returned to the country houses to escape this wretched fog. The milliner's assistant is the only one currently available."

"She will have to suffice, then. Can you have her at the Yard this afternoon?"

Lestrade nodded and held out his hand. Holmes hesitated a moment, then reached across and clasped it. "Watson will see you out."

At the downstairs door, Lestrade wound a scarf around his neck, covering his mouth, and then he jammed his hat on until it almost covered his ears. "Will you accompany him to the morgue?" he said to me softly. "You could be helpful on this case."

"Don't you have a trained coroner?"

"We do, but you've had experience with injuries to the human body. Another pair of eyes never hurts."

I agreed to go and closed the door quickly to keep the pea soup out of the house as much as possible. I walked slowly back up the stairs. What had just happened? Had I been invited to join Holmes on another of his cases?

"Lestrade asked me to accompany you," I said on entering.

Holmes was reading. Had he heard me? I took my customary chair by the fire. The clock ticked and the fire purred, making me sleepy until Holmes suddenly slammed the book closed with a loud pop. I almost jumped under the table as memories of the battlefield assailed me. I managed to contain myself, but startled visibly. In those days, any sharp loud noise did that to me. Holmes looked at me. He must have noticed my involuntary movement.

"Like that, is it?" he said and I thought he understood what made me react so.

"Yes. Not always, but most of the time."

He nodded as if I had confirmed something. "My apologies." I could see that he meant it.

By now I was accustomed to Holmes's knack of reaching conclusions through his perceptive observations. I remembered Dr. Joseph Bell, a professor under whom I'd studied for a while in Edinburgh. He taught his students to look for clues about his patients on their person, their behavior, their speech, their dress. Ink-stained fingers pointed to a clerk. Drops of marmalade on a cravat showed a fondness for sweetness, that sort of thing.

"What do you think of Lestrade's problem?" I asked.

Instead of replying directly, Holmes countered, "What do you know of Spring-Heeled Jack?"

"I remember in my childhood, children were told to behave or Spring-Heeled Jack would come for them."

"Even in Scotland. Did it work?"

"No. We always wanted to see him leap over buildings. That's how we thought of him then. Children take what they want from stories. Strangely, he was something of a hero to us children, rather like Robin Hood. We wanted someone who could get away from adults by super-human feats. We ignored the clawing of clothing. If questioned about the matter, we probably would've denied our hero would do such a thing as claw ladies. Or kiss them until we reached a certain age, of course. A lot of boys had sore legs from all that jumping but, of course, we never made the connection." I remembered my mother heating water to soak my aching ankles and sprinkling it with mustard powder to relieve the pain.

"This Jack cannot be the original, as I told Lestrade, but that doesn't mean others haven't taken up the role. They wouldn't be as old as the first Jack. For what it's worth, I also believe the original was either part of a group doing the attacks, or there were imitators, even then. The culprits may have been a group of wealthy young men or a club with such stunts required for their initiation process. No, this is something else entirely, done under the smokescreen of the persistent fog."

"How do you propose to solve the murder?"

"We shall gather information. Come, Watson, we're off to the morgue."

I was not bothered by the visit to the morgue. I'd spent much time in them, and with dead bodies – some killed in front of me in battle, some dying in hospitals. It was the fog that bothered me today. Breathing became a chore. I tied my scarf over my nose and mouth as we hailed a cab in Baker Street.

The driver could have been a highwayman behind the scarf covering his face. He also wore a most-unusual set of spectacles which interested me. They were more like the goggles pearl divers wear in the Orient. I enquired of him if they were for bad eyesight.

"No sir. These be plain glass. Per'tecks me eyes sommat from this fog."

"Very clever."

"Where to, Guv'nor?"

Holmes told him.

I sat back and tried to take shallow breaths. This stuff was brown today, but sometimes yellow or green, hence the descriptive "pea soup" name, and it wasn't good for our lungs, as it could cause choking fits and even death in some cases.

At the morgue, we found Lestrade had left a number of documents related to the case, investigatory notes, as well as information about the three previous women who had been attacked, along with transcripts of the interviews carried out with all three. Holmes spent several moments reviewing them and, although he read quickly, I knew he would retain what he had seen.

We also confirmed that Lestrade had arranged for us to view the fourth victim, who had not survived. She awaited us, laid out on a slab.

She wasn't like the descriptions in the notes of the previous three victims who lived to tell about it. She appeared to be from a higher societal class. The reports had indicated the first victim was a lady's maid, the second worked in a millinery shop, and the third was also a maid at a great house in the area where she'd been attacked. All three provided the same description of the attacker: He wore a dark gray cloak and a mask covering his head and face.

They were lucky the slasher had been interrupted, sparing their lives. This girl, however, hadn't been so fortunate.

"Tell me, Watson, what do you see?"

The autopsy had already been performed, leaving the ghastly seams mostly covered by a sheet. Her clothing lay on a nearby table. The young lady's eyes were closed, hands beside her body. Her light brown hair had been well-coiffed, but now was somewhat disheveled in her journey after death. I drew upon what I remembered of Dr. Bell's methods and described what I saw, starting with the nearby clothing. "Her gloves are rather expensive leather, as is the case with her white fur muff. Her peacock velvet dress has a fine lace collar. Her warm cape of white wool is trimmed with white fur – ermine no doubt. That, and her fur muff, mark her as coming from a prosperous background. Her hat is missing, perhaps stolen before she was discovered." I turned my attention to the body.

"She's young, not much more than twenty. Her hands prove to be soft and uncalloused. Therefore she doesn't work with them – not as a cook, seamstress, or scullery maid. She was healthy, well-nourished, and may have had a rosy complexion, if not for exsanguination. I don't know what she was doing out in this filthy air, but it probably wasn't an errand of necessity."

"Quite right," Holmes replied. He examined a loose thread that he'd picked off her dress, placing it in a small envelope he took from his pocket. Then he gave the same attention to the mud on her shoes. I thought it strange. "As you say, her clothing tells us she was from a wealthy family, unlike the previous victims. She has been well-cared for, both in her background and her personal grooming. What do you make of the wound?"

I leaned forward. The slash on her throat had already been neatly stitched up, but I could tell that the killing stroke had been made from her left to her right. "The killer is right-handed and most probably slashed her from behind. The slashes to her clothing may have been done *post mortem*, or while she was dying, to make it look like Jack."

"Very good, Watson. You have a keen eye."

"A surgeon on a battlefield must make quick decisions. One learns to be fast."

He nodded once. "Indeed." He pulled out a magnifying glass and again examined the young lady's shoe soles. "Do you see anything here?"

I looked through the glass. "A small bit of mud."

He took out a pocketknife and scraped a bit onto a paper, which he twisted and returned to his pocket along with the knife. Next he turned the magnifying glass onto the slashes in the dress. The velvet had been torn, but the slits were fairly even.

"I have seen animal clawings in India," I offered. "Tigers, especially. These look more like they were done by a sharp knife than a claw."

"No doubt the murderer will be disappointed you weren't fooled," Holmes said, "but tell me how you know that."

"A claw would chew the cloth more. These are clean slashes that run down the warp in a straight line, as if carefully done."

Holmes smiled. "Very good, Watson. You'll do admirably."

Any praise from Holmes, as I was to learn, was high praise indeed. "Thank you. I think. Who would do such to this young lady?"

"Any number of miscreants lurking about London, but I suspect most of them would have done more to her. That wasn't done in this case and we must find out why. Why kill a young woman and mutilate her clothing after death? Why this young woman? Was it a crime of opportunity? Design? Random or targeted? When we find the answer to these questions, we will find the killer. For now, we need her identity."

"Surely her family will have reported her missing by now."

"One would think so."

The coroner's assistant, a thin, pale young man, brought us the autopsy report. Holmes and I scanned it. "See anything we didn't already know?" he asked.

"No," I said. "A healthy young lady, no evident diseases. Death caused by severing the carotid arteries, most likely from behind."

"We found this in her muff," the assistant said. He handed Holmes a folded note on thick paper. Written on it in sepia ink was an invitation to early tea from *C.B.*

"So this was her destination," I said.

"Indeed. Let's have a look at the sites of the attacks." He kept the invitation after signing for it.

We boarded the nearest Underground and made our way to the farthest site of the attacks. As we exited at Notting Hill Gate, I hoped the fog would have lessened in that part of London, but enough of it still swirled around us to necessitate the wearing of scarves. We walked to the site of the Claw Man's first appearance. According to the information we'd received, the attacker had evidently lain in wait in a nearby mews and slashed at the clothing of the first victim, Lucy Blank, a parlor maid. He caused two slits in her clothing before she managed to pull away from her attacker and run for help. The attacker ran away as well, and the attending constable found nothing at the site. The attacker was described as tall, though not excessively, and he'd worn a black cape, and a black mask over face and hair. He hissed like a wild animal, and she thought he growled as well.

The second attack came a few days later, again during heavy fog. The site was off Bayswater Road on the edge of Hyde Park. He pulled Millie Pinson, a milliner's assistant on her way home into some bushes and her clothing slashed. She described the attack identically to the first one. She confirmed the hissing, but not the growl.

The third attack on Judy Henkins, a lady's maid, occurred on the north end of the Edgware Road toward Maida Vale. The fog was so thick Miss Henkins couldn't see much, but she remembered that the attacker made the same sounds heard by the previous victims. She had indicated that he was taller than Lestrade, but not much taller.

"A tall, animal-sounding man in a cape with a black head mask who makes an even number of slits with his claw hand." Holmes summed up the meager information.

"Not much help there," I remarked.

"On the contrary, there's more information than meets the eye."

I waited for him to explain, but he sat back on the seat of our cab and closed his eyes until we arrived. The cab let us out into the street, just around the corner from the site of the murder, now rather hard to find in the darkening foggy mews. I looked about but saw no one, no constables and no horsemen, though an army could have been ten feet away and only the stamping hooves and jingling bridles revealed them. "The murderer knew what he was doing in this cursed fog," I said.

"Indeed he did." Holmes lit a Lucifer and examined the cobblestones by its meager light. A dark brown stain was all that remained of that poor young lady. What was she doing out in this dreadful fog?

"The murderer no doubt knew she would be coming this way and lay in wait. Or he may have engineered the meeting. Would you think there should've been more blood here?"

"Hard to say," I answered. "Her shawl was stiff with blood, but her dress barely touched with it."

He lit another Lucifer, moving it about as he searched for evidence of blood. "Aha! Just as I thought. Look at this."

I followed the light and saw small brown smudges on the cobbles. They went around the corner into a street that ran near Berkeley Square, a prestigious location. There, on the edge of the pavement, we found more blood. "The constables didn't look far afield," I said. "It appears that she was killed here and dragged into the mews where she might not be found straightaway."

"It does. This isn't a well-traveled roadway, but some carts and other vehicles have been along here since last night and may have obliterated any other blood spatters." He lit more Lucifers, but we found no more blood droplets.

"I was hoping to find evidence of the direction the murderer might have taken. However, he may've been smart enough to carry a rag to wipe his boots before leaving a trail. The sample of bloodstained mud that I took from the victim's soles must have adhered as she was being dragged."

We walked back to Baker Street by lamplight and glowing window light. Mrs. Hudson admonished us for missing luncheon and tea, but prepared a substantial meal for us and, after our journey, we were ready for it. After dinner, I poured myself a brandy. Holmes asked for one as well as he settled in his chair on one side of the fireplace. He busied himself filling one of his pipes, the cherry-wood, and lit the bowl. The pungent aroma of black shag filled the room.

We sipped our brandies in the quiet broken only by the sounds of the fire. I lit a cigar and perused the evening paper I'd picked up on the way back. I found the article I was looking for and read it quickly. "Still no identification of the young woman."

"That should be done soon," Holmes said. "She was too much of a lady not to be missed by now. I shouldn't be surprised if she lived somewhere near Berkeley Square."

"How would a murderer entice young lady of those establishments to go out in this fog?"

"Murderers are often ingenious. They delight in fooling Scotland Yard, outwitting decent society. I shouldn't be surprised if they aren't born that way, though no doubt some evil might be learned."

The fog mercifully lifted somewhat during the night. By morning, a thin light came in the windows. After breakfast,

Holmes proposed that we revisit the scene of the murder when the light was more propitious. I must admit the walk was far more enjoyable when we could safely breathe the air. Holmes was correct in his conjecture. We found what appeared to be a faint track of blood stains leading away from the mews, around the corner, and then alongside Berkeley Square where they eventually disappeared. Holmes studied these and made notes in a small book he took from his pocket. Then he put it away. "Let us pay a visit to Scotland Yard."

We hailed a hansom and rode in comfort. Holmes enquired of the duty constable for Inspector Lestrade.

"He's just in, not two minutes ago." He directed us to the inspector's office where a young man sat with a stunned look on his face. Lestrade was surprised to see us, but invited us to sit in the chairs before his desk. "This is Mr. Gerald Fenton. He has just identified his sister, Persephone, as the victim."

Holmes and I made suitable sympathetic comments which Mr. Fenton barely acknowledged. He was a nicely dressed young man in his early twenties, sandy hair, pale blue eyes, and a chin that wasn't as strong as it might need to be during his lifetime, despite the thin moustache he had likely grown for compensation. A goatee might have been of more use, but perhaps he could not yet manage it. "I – I thank you," he said barely above a whisper, but that could be attributed to his shock.

"Tea would be helpful," I said to Lestrade. "Four sugars." He arose and attended to it, and shortly a cup was brought by a constable. Mr. Fenton gulped it down as if his life were being saved. Perhaps it was. I have often observed the efficacy of hot sweet tea in shocking circumstances.

"Was your sister accustomed to going out alone in the severe fog?" Holmes asked.

"No, but she might if she wasn't going far. She might have been going to visit my inten – a young lady I've been courting."

"Who is this young lady." Holmes asked, "and where does she live?"

"The Honourable Clarinda Bellamy. Her father is the baron, Sir Bertram. They live in Berkeley Square. We are a scant two streets away. They are friends, and her brother has – *had* – a *tendresse* for my sister."

Tears gathered in his eyes and spilled over. He pulled out a snowy handkerchief and wiped them away. "I don't know how I shall tell my parents."

"That's our job," Lestrade said, which soon resulted in all of us climbing into a police brougham. Lestrade and I were left sitting in the pull-down seats in the corners. Though not the most comfortable conveyance when crowded so, it allowed for swifter travel in the streets and roadways.

The Fenton home was a red-brick attached house, Georgian style, to which had been added a turret on the corner which jutted out into the street, and a fence that heavily featured acanthus leaves. A proper butler whom Fenton called Marchmon took our hats and coats. Fenton led us into a drawing room, its proportions disguised with rose-printed wallpaper covered with a profusion of gold-framed classical paintings and ornate furniture in dark woods with red velvet upholstery. Mrs. Fenton was resplendent in gold brocade trimmed with black beads, and an incongruous black feather in her brown hair. Her eyes were pale blue like her son's. She seemed startled to see him in the company of unknown men. "Gerald, who are these – ?" She hesitated and swept us with another glance. " – these *gentlemen*?"

"Mrs. Fenton, I'm Inspector Lestrade of Scotland Yard." He didn't introduce Holmes or me. "I have some bad news about your daughter."

"She isn't in trouble, is she?" Her eyes went from one of us to the other, clearly wondering who Holmes and I were.

"No, Mama." Gerald took out his handkerchief and wiped his watery eyes again.

"I am sorry to inform you that your daughter is the victim of a crime," Lestrade said.

"She's been murdered, Mama," Gerald said.

"Murdered?" Mrs. Fenton, who had half-risen from her chair, fell back into a sprawl. "Murdered?" she screamed.

"Yes," Lestrade replied. "She was found yesterday, not far from here. She had no identification on her person. We didn't know her identity until your son enquired at Scotland Yard."

Holmes had the presence of mind to ring for the butler while I fanned her paper-white face. Her husband was summoned from his study, and a maid came with a *sal volatile* which I used to revive the lady, as she was half-fainting now, uttering little mewing sounds.

Mr. Fenton, upon being informed of his daughter's demise, was as distraught as his wife. Faced with their reaction, young

Gerald began sobbing. I led him to a chair and in a low voice told him someone in the family had to take charge. He didn't look like he wanted that someone to be himself, but he wiped his eyes again and went to his father, who took his hand as if it were a lifeline and said, "So much depended on Persephone. Whatever will we do now?"

"We'll go on, Papa," Gerald said bravely, and I saw his Adam's apple bob above his cravat, which seemed limp now as if some of his tears had made their way onto it. Marchmon was almost in the same state. Holmes went to a tray on a table and poured a generous amount of brandy into a glass, which he then pressed into Mr. Fenton's hand. I sent Marchmon to summon tea for Mrs. Fenton. Upon his return, Holmes took the butler into the hall question him. I could do little to assuage the family's grief other than pour brandy into their hot sweet tea and instruct the maid to stay with her mistress. After a while, I was able to join Holmes in the hall, while Lestrade asked the family some further questions.

I reached Holmes and the butler in time to hear the latter say that on the morning of the girl's death, she received a note inviting her to early tea.

"By early tea, do you mean at two in the afternoon?"

"Well, sir, it were more like half-two. It were an odd time for tea, but Miss Persephone were pleased with the invite, so I didn't say anything. I did suggest she not go, since the fog were so bad, but she laughed and said she was just going a few streets away and she could walk it with her eyes closed if need be."

"Do you know where she was going?" Holmes asked.

"I do not, but t'were any great distance, she would've used the carriage."

"Could the invitation have been from the Bellamys?"

"I couldn't say, sir, but it's possible."

"Do you know the names of any of her friends?"

"Well, sir," he lowered his voice, "the Fentons haven't lived here long. She knows the Bellamy daughter and her brother Billy, who seems to have – " His voice caught. " – *had* eyes for Miss Persephone."

"Watson, if you could get that address, please. We'll need to talk to them. I'll inform the inspector."

"It isn't far, sir. Just one street to the west."

Berkeley Square was near Albemarle Street, where the Fentons resided, but in social class it was worlds away. We soon covered the distance to where Sir Bertram Bellamy lived, on the northeast corner of the Square. As we approached the house, an imposing carriage bearing a crest turned in front of us.

"High horses here indeed," Holmes remarked. "If I'm not mistaken, that was the crest of the Earl of Oxleigh. Before you joined us," he continued, "Marchmon mentioned that the Earl lives on the Square. He intimated the Fentons would like to make their acquaintance. They may live close to the Phipps, which is the Earl's family name, but unless Gerald were to save the life of the Queen or some other daring deed, Marchmon fears that may never happen. Fenton is, I believe, a speculator in commodities. Unless the Earl were in need of a large sum of money, the

Phippses will never even know that the Fentons exist. The Earl's family is solid with diversified interests in shipping, as well as inherited land and wealth. The Fentons are barking up too tall a tree."

The Bellamy's town house was, as to be expected of a baron, twice the size of the Fentons. It, too, was Georgian, but with every appointment in perfect order. The door opened almost before Holmes's hand left the handsome knocker, itself in the shape of a hand. The butler was more imposing than Marchmon, and no doubt less chatty, but then his household wasn't in the chaos of grief.

"Yes," the solid man said, peering down his nose. The act involved drawing the upper body back in order to look at us in that fashion.

Holmes handed him a card. "Sherlock Holmes and Dr. Watson to see the Honourable Clarinda Bellamy and her brother." I hastily dug out my card.

"What might this matter concern?"

"That shall remain private." Holmes gave him an icy smile that said, "No butler will quell me," and I wondered, not for the first time, about his family history. He hadn't mentioned any in the short time I'd known him.

The butler returned shortly and ushered us into a morning room, where a young lady was seated with a book. I couldn't tell if she were reading it, or had just picked it up to give herself something to do while she awaited the two strangers at her door. Her dark hair was drawn back from her pale face. She had strong features, dark brows, a wide mouth, and rather prominent nose.

Holmes introduced us. "We were hoping to speak to your brother as well."

"He has gone out." She didn't invite us to sit, so we stood. "What did you want to speak to us about?"

"Miss Persephone Fenton."

"You do know her," I said when she winced almost imperceptibly.

"I know of her. I have met her a few times."

"Her brother Gerald has been courting you, I believe," Holmes said.

"I don't call it 'courting'. I went driving with him on a few autumn afternoons last year when the weather was fine and this beastly fog wasn't around."

"He seems to think it was more than a few drives," I said.

"Then he is mistaken. What is this about? You surely didn't come here to discuss the courting habits of Gerald Fenton."

"No, we came to ask you what you might know of Miss Fenton," Holmes said. "We are helping Scotland Yard with a case."

"As I said, I hardly know who she is. What is she to do with me? And what case?"

"She was found murdered yesterday," Holmes said. "Not far from here,"

"Oh?" She looked down at her book, suddenly shocked. "That – that's *dreadful*! Where did it happen?" She looked up.

Holmes told her.

"Why was she out in that fog?"

"Her brother believed she was coming to tea with you."

"Oh no! Why would she tell him that? I went to my sewing circle."

Holmes raised his eyebrows at her venturing out in the beastly fog herself. She seemed to understand. "It was just across the Square at Olivia's – the Countess of Oxleigh."

Was it my imagination, or did she take pride in speaking of her destination? "Wasn't it difficult to maneuver in the fog?" I asked.

"Not for me. I walked straight across to the Square fence and followed it around to the left. The Earl's house is across on that far corner."

"Miss Fenton wasn't on the way to the sewing circle?" Holmes asked.

"No. It's just a few of Olivia's friends and some of the other neighbors."

"I see," Holmes said. I saw also. Miss Fenton wasn't ranked high enough on the social scale to join the sewing circle – no doubt organized for poor children in Africa when London had its own share of poor children needing warm clothing.

A clamor sounded in the hall and a handsome young man joined us. "Clarinda, I've just heard about Persephone Fenton's murder from Deavers! And to think it could've been you, just a few streets away."

"Oh Billy!" she replied. "I shudder to think so!"

"You are, I believe, from Scotland Yard," he said to Holmes.

Holmes introduced us without bothering to correct his assumption.

Billy Bellamy was about my height, with thick dark hair and a long thin nose that gave him a supercilious look. I wouldn't have thought him upper-class enough for that look. "I'm William Bellamy," he said. "What has this to do with my sister?"

"It was our understanding you'd been seeing Miss Fenton, the victim," Holmes said.

"Our acquaintance hadn't progressed that far. I found her an agreeable young lady, but I'd no intentions in that direction, if that's what you mean."

"And where were you yesterday at two in the afternoon?" Holmes asked.

"I was at my club." He named a popular sporting establishment. "From noon until late."

"How late?"

"Very late."

"I didn't even hear your return," Clarinda said. "I read late," she explained.

"The lamplighters were turning off the gas when I arrived," Billy added.

"Do you live here with your father?" Holmes asked.

"Yes," Billy said. "Our mother died three years ago."

"Our father isn't well. I hope you won't bother him with your questions?" Clarinda had paused before her question, as if she'd been about to preface it with something silly, but thought better of it under the circumstances.

"What happened to Miss Fenton?" Billy asked. He'd been standing, but now he sank into a velvet chair.

Holmes explained.

Clarinda put her hand over her eyes and shuddered.

"Oh good God!" Billy cried out. He seemed more upset than his sister. Perhaps the social standing wasn't as important to the future baron as it was to the Honourable Miss Bellamy.

Holmes took out the note from his coat pocket and handed it to Clarinda. "Did you send this note to Miss Fenton? It was found with her."

She glanced at it, but made no move to take it for a closer look. "Certainly not. That isn't my handwriting. And I never sign anything with a *CB*. I write out *The Honourable Clarinda Bellamy*. Someone must've been playing a trick on the poor girl."

Holmes asked a few more questions. Deavers was in the house when Clarinda left for the sewing circle and when she returned several hours later. Billy's club could vouch for him if need be. Their father was bedridden with a chest catarrh.

"Do either of you know who could have sent the note to the victim?" was Holmes's last question as he returned the note to his pocket.

They both replied adamantly they didn't send it, nor had they any idea who might have.

We took our leave. "Except to see the British class system at work," I said as the door closed behind us, "that wasn't very helpful."

Holmes smiled. "Indeed," was all he would say.

We next called at the Earl's townhouse, the most imposing on the Square. His Countess was at home and would see us. She was formal with us, but did invite us to sit when Holmes told her the reason for our visit. "Oh dear. The poor girl! No, I don't know her, but I've heard of her. Someone mentioned inviting her to join us in the sewing circle, but others said not quite yet."

I wondered what they were waiting for her father to buy the Square and build a house in the middle of it, perhaps? – but I kept quiet. What did I know – a Scottish boy, a doctor from Barts, and then an army surgeon in Afghanistan?

The Countess had nothing to add to our store of information. Holmes clarified the situation after we took our leave. "Persephone's father made money in commodities, but owns no land except his London house which, though worth a bit of change, isn't the echelon to which the family aspires. Marchmon indicated that he started as a grocer's clerk. A future baron for a son-in-law would be a long step up for the Fenton family. An 'honourable' for a daughter-in-law would open doors for them. The Bellamy family pockets aren't to let yet, but with Billy gambling his nights away at his club, that could be in the near future. The Fentons may have been willing to wait for that to happen."

"Sounds contractual to me."

"Oh it is. And stultifying. Most of the population is larcenous and criminal and venal else I wouldn't have a job," Holmes said, "but the upper class is the worst. Tell me, Watson: Do you think Clarinda is a tiny woman?"

I thought of what I could see of her, seated in the parlour. "She never stood up, and her voluminous skirt hid her legs." I refused to politely call them limbs. I'd seen too many blown off and I'd surgically removed too many myself not to call body parts what they are. "Judging from her arms as she held the book when we entered, I'd say no, she isn't tiny. She may be almost as tall as I am. Why do you want to know?"

He gave me an enigmatic look just as Lestrade hailed us from the nearby police conveyance. "I sent a constable to fetch Millie Pinson, the milliner's assistant, as you asked, Mr. Holmes. She should be at the Yard now."

Miss Millie Pinson sipped tea in Lestrade's office as we entered. She was fetchingly dressed in chocolate velvet with matching toque on her dark brown hair, and a cinnamon chiffon veil thrown back to reveal her heart-shaped face. Lestrade introduced us. "Mr. Holmes wishes to ask you some questions about your attack."

She took a moment to set down the teacup then turned to Holmes. "I'm ready."

Holmes regarded her without speaking. As the silence grew, I said, "I see you're attired in a colour to defeat the fog." I nodded at her ensemble. "Even in this lighter fog, one needs to guard oneself from its noxious qualities."

She smiled. "Thank you. Most people don't understand the reasons for wearing certain colours, fabrics, or even hemlines. I wear my skirts shorter because I don't care to sweep up the filth of London's streets."

"Very sensible," Holmes said, finally speaking.

"I'm one of ten, seven of us girls. We learned early to safeguard everything we have. Including our clothing."

"Tell us about the attack."

She took another sip of tea and this time held on to the teacup. "I was on my way home after the shop closed when suddenly a tall figure leaped in front of me. He came out of the fog."

"You had no sense of anyone there before you saw him?"

"No, nothing. His claws ripped down my skirt in two places, and then, as quick as he'd come, he left. I didn't even have time to scream."

"Did you see the claws?" Holmes asked.

"No, but his hand came toward me and I felt a tug on my skirt. Twice."

"Did you notice any smells?"

"You mean the odour of brimstone?"

Holmes smiled.

"No, I didn't," she answered.

"What about scent?" I asked. "Medicants Perfumes?"

"Nothing for certain. Maybe something that reminded me of hothouse flowers."

"How are they different from other flowers?" Holmes asked.

"The scent seems more cloying."

Holmes nodded as if in agreement. "Did he speak?"

"No, it all happened in silence. I didn't even have time to scream."

"Did you hear anything at all? A whistle? Throat-clearing? A cough? A foot scraping?"

She finished her tea and set the cup down. "Well, as you know, the fog muffles everything, but at the same time you can hear more clearly. He did make hissing sounds."

"The other young ladies mentioned that hissing," Lestrade said. "They also mentioned growling sounds."

"No, I didn't hear any growls. The hissing could have come from his mouth, but it was more of a swishing sound. I work with cloth, and I know the different sounds that can make. Crinkles and rubbing sounds. Swishing."

"And you heard swishing?" Lestrade asked.

"Yes. Swishing."

"If it were cloth," Holmes asked, "do you know what it would be?"

"It wasn't taffeta or satin, velvet or linen or cotton. More like silk, but hushed. I suppose the fog could muffle it."

"Were you wearing a cape?" I asked.

"No, I wore a short coat over a woolen dress. Wool is very quiet."

"That will be all, Miss Pinson," Holmes said. "I have no more questions. Thank you for coming down. You've been very helpful."

She looked dubious, but nodded.

Lestrade summoned an officer to take her home. "If you think of anything else, please inform a constable."

When we were alone, he added, "Very kind of you to tell her she was helpful, but I can't think in what way."

"Can't you?" Holmes asked, raising an eyebrow.

Lestrade looked at me as if I might have a clue, but I shrugged slightly. "She seems to like outdoor flowers better than hothouse ones."

"I believe the fog may be worsening," Holmes said. "It wouldn't be amiss to station a constable in Berkeley Square for the night."

"You think another attack might be imminent? On the Honourable Clarinda?"

"Not with a constable on station."

By the time the police vehicle delivered us back to Baker Street, I realized again we hadn't eaten since breakfast. I was ravenous and fell on Mrs. Hudson's excellent roast chicken dinner, followed by plum cake. Brandy and a cigar by the fire and I was as comfortable as a recovering invalid could be. Holmes declined the cigar. "I think this might be another one-pipe night, but I'm prepared to extend to a second one if need be."

"A one or two-pipe case?"

"Helps me get all the strings in order."

"You know who the killer is?"

"I'm reasonably sure, but reasonably sure isn't enough."

"Do you think the killer will strike again tonight?"

"Not with a constable to keep the Square safe. The killer will not appear again as long as people are wary. In a week or so will be time for care."

He did indeed smoke a second pipe, but before its time was up, I had retired upstairs for the night with a book. I hadn't turned the page once before I fell asleep. Later I awakened, put the book on the night table, and turned down the light. I couldn't remember the last time I was this tired, I thought as I fell into sleep again.

The newspapers were initially filled with stories of the Claw Man killer in the fog, but no further attacks were reported, and the story quickly lost prominence.

The fog went away, but returned two days later. Holmes had been in and out, pursuing his own investigation. Finally, he sent a note to the countess and paced the sitting room until he received a reply. It read: *"The invitation has been sent and accepted."*

"The game is now afoot, Watson," he said as he grabbed his coat and scarf and stick. I did the same and followed him out the door.

We were fortunate to find a hansom at the door. I learned later Holmes had paid the driver to wait there until he was needed. We hurried to Scotland Yard to see Lestrade. Holmes had a plan, it seems. He dropped no clues on the way, but insisted I accompany him.

"You're sure of this?" Lestrade asked after Holmes laid it all out for him and for my benefit as well. "I don't want to be made a fool of in those exalted circles."

"I am sure. The note was delivered at half-two. It's now half-three. Half-four is tea time."

I had to admit the plan was simple, but devious and not without risk. Lestrade spoke to a constable, explaining the danger, but the young man was eager to do it for advancement. We collected supplies and left for the Earl's house on Berkeley Square. The streets were fairly empty. The heavy fog kept most Londoners inside. Holmes and I, along with Lestrade and the constable, exited the vehicle on the side of the Earl's house. We entered through the tradesman's door, but these were mere precautions. No one could even see across the street by now. Silence fell on the Square with the weight of stone.

Holmes explained his plan to the Earl.

"Will it work, do you think?" the Countess asked with trepidation.

"Indeed," Holmes replied. Moments later, he, Lestrade, and I had stationed ourselves in the shrubbery close to the front of the house. A door closed somewhere nearby.

I peered through the choking darkness, my mouth and nose covered by my brown scarf, but my eyes stung and I wished that I had special eyeglasses to protect against the fog, as had been worn by the hansom driver we'd encountered a few days before. I vowed to have some made up for me when I had any extra money.

In a few minutes, the front door of the Earl's house opened. Footsteps sounded on the steps behind us. A cloaked figure passed near us – the Countess – but didn't acknowledge our presence. I hoped she would walk slower. We didn't want her to advance too far from safety.

The figure hesitated and rearranged the scarf over her face. Beside me, Holmes exhaled. She took a few more steps toward the street, crossed it, and turned left to walk along the side of the fenced enclosure. A figure glided out of the fog behind the lady. It was the Claw Man! I could almost see a glint off the knife as he raised it to slash the Countess's throat from behind her, and for a moment, I thought that Holmes's plan had gone amiss. Before any of us could move, however, the Countess turned and grabbed the Claw Man's right hand and twisted it behind him.

The Claw Man screamed in high-pitched anger and fought back, but Holmes materialized to grab the other arm and Lestrade leaped out with handcuffs. A light bloomed at the door of the Earl's house, and he and the butler rushed out. Holmes reached up and removed a black mask that covered the face and hair of the Claw Man, revealing his true identity.

As expected, the Claw Man, based on what Holmes had revealed to us, was the Honourable Clarinda Bellamy. Even in manacles, she continued to kick and scream with rage. I have scarcely seen anyone so angry. Her identity was discovered, her plan was foiled. Lestrade summoned the police wagon and sent her to the Yard with the strictest instructions: "Do not let her out of your sight. Do not listen to her entreaties. She is the vilest murderess, and we apprehended her in the middle of trying to kill again. She is no better than a common criminal, no matter what she says."

The Countess and Earl invited us into the house. The constable, whose name was John Stevens, was asked to join us as well. He had been chosen to portray the Countess because of his average height. He was happy to remove his disguise and restore his uniform while we discussed the case.

"How did you know it was Clarinda?" the Earl asked Holmes.

"She didn't stand when we were at her house, which, while not proof, was indicative. She didn't want us to know she was tall enough to be taken for a man, and also that her skirt, being silk, hissed and might remind us that the Claw Man hissed under his cloak. She smelt faintly of flowers as Miss Pinson noted. It was not a common scent, with more gardenia than jasmine used. Gardenia is a heavier more powerful floral scent than any I've encountered and more memorable, but Clarinda didn't think about that. It wouldn't be enough to convict her, but it was enough to put her under my suspicion.

"I considered the Fenton's situation. Their dearest wish was to advance in the social hierarchy of London. This could only be achieved in their case by marriage, or perhaps saving the Queen's life.

"The Fentons played a long game. Gerald and Persephone both hoped to marry Baron Bellamy's daughter and son to raise the family's social position – but Clarinda's eye was on a higher prize than Gerald Fenton's. She wanted the Earl of Oxleigh."

"But I'm married!" he exclaimed, taking his wife's hand. "And I don't even know her."

"She comes here with the sewing circle," his wife said. "And you've seen her walking in the Square when the weather is fine." She turned to Holmes. "She really thought my husband would marry her if I were dead?"

"Her mother is dead. She lives with her father and brother, and I observed her to be a determined person. She thought she could arrange the marriage by eliminating the Countess. She would console the Earl and a marriage would ensue. This is how some people think – people who put themselves above all things, including the laws of man."

"But how did you know?"

"When I visited the places where the three slashing attacks occurred, I realized they were in order if one rode the Underground, starting with the most distant one, and working back. The attacks all happened near stations. She took a big chance with her plans for the second attack so near the first, but the fog was thick enough to warrant success. Each attack placed the Claw Man closer to the Square, which was her plan. She thought the police would think the Claw Man was playing his tricks again but had become more dangerous, moving from assaults to murder. Poor Persephone was simply a pawn. Miss Bellamy thought no one would ever suspect a woman."

"How did you know the Claw Man could be a woman?" I asked.

"I was alerted when the victims said the Claw Man wasn't unduly tall and I thought why couldn't *he* be a *woman*, and why would a woman kill another woman? The answer led me to Clarinda Bellamy – a woman who wanted something and would do anything to get it.

"In the hall as we left the Bellamy's house on the first day of the case, I saw a woolen cape. It was dark grey, but I twitched the hem and saw it was red on the other side. A woman could commit the crime, disappear into the fog while removing her face mask and turning her cape inside out. She could hide the mask in a sewing basket, or her muff along with the knife and no one would suspect her. The police would be looking for a man."

"How did you know to look for the reverse of the cape?" the Earl asked.

"At the morgue, I'd seen a red thread on the clothing of the victim." He pulled an envelope out of his waistcoat pocket. "Here it is. If you compare it to the reverse of her grey cape, you'll find it's a perfect match in color. That wouldn't be enough to convict her in court – hence tonight's charade to catch her repeating her crime – but victimless this time, of course. When her invitation arrived, asking the Countess around to tea, I knew she was ready to commit her next crime, and I put my plan into place. Constable Stevens played his part to perfection. I hope that will be in your report," he said to Lestrade.

Lestrade took the envelope. "Indeed it will."

"In the fog with the scarf over her face, the murderer couldn't tell that the figure wasn't the Countess," I said. "You used the opposite of Clarinda's trick – a man disguised as a woman."

"Brilliant," the Earl said.

"That was an exciting evening's work," I said after we were back by our fire with brandy to warm us after dinner. Holmes lit a cigar, but I passed.

"This was a case of people wanting what they can't have, though with time, I think the Fentons could've achieved their marital desires. The Bellamys would've needed money after Billy gambled all of theirs away, but Clarinda wanted more than mere money. She wanted to be a Countess."

"I suspect she didn't want to be sister-in-law to Miss Fenton either," I said.

I could see why Holmes preferred sleuthing to arguing a case in a court of law or counting guineas or plotting in the Foreign Office. I could grow rather fond of it myself.

"One thing I'm curious about: Why did you scrape the mud off Miss Fenton's shoe in the morgue?"

"As I said, it had a red-brown tinge to it that looked like dried blood. When I applied the test of my own devising to it, I proved the presence of hemoglobin. I thought when we found the killer, I could do the same with his shoes – *her* shoes, as it turned out. But I couldn't see Clarinda's feet for her skirts, and anyway, she'd most likely changed her footwear. In the meantime, if she hadn't been an 'Honourable', I could've demanded to see her wardrobe and checked all of her shoes for red-tinged mud."

"Holmes, you think of everything."

"It is my job, Watson. I'm a consulting detective. I think for everybody."

"Indeed."

The Man in the Rain with a Dog

"I'll wager you were out late last night." Sherlock Holmes was at the table in the sitting room, finishing his breakfast, while I hurried to take my place and pour a cup of much-needed coffee to start my day.

"How did you know? The damp coat or my wet shoes? I purposefully didn't put them close to the fire to dry, given how you complained of their aroma last time. 'Wet horse', as I believe you described my overcoat."

"No, not at all. 'Wet horse blanket' was the term."

"If my damp garments didn't give me away then what, pray tell, was it?"

"You really cannot deduce it? Come, Watson, how long have you been sharing my cases with me? Can you not even guess?"

Mrs. Hudson's arrival with a plate she'd kept warm saved me from having to admit I didn't know. After several gulps of hot aromatic coffee, I fell on my breakfast like a man who had just climbed the Matterhorn while Holmes concentrated on the morning newspaper.

When I finished, I asked him again how he knew I'd gone out late the previous night.

"Your book – one of those yellow-backed mysteries to which you seem to be addicted."

"Those stories are merely escape from my medical cases," I said, though truth to tell, they were quite enjoyable. "I don't see how my reading material told you I had gone out last night."

"You left it turned over, opened to your place. When I left, you were halfway through the book. If you'd stayed in, you would've finished it, because you can't put down a good yarn."

"Yes, I did go out late for about two hours."

"An urgent call?"

"It was, as are all calls in the night. Illness tends to magnify in the dark, to both the patient and the family members. In this case, the only one I saw was the patient, Colonel Thomas F. Soames. The butler, Beckley, told me the Colonel was wounded in the Crimean War and again in the Bhutan War of 1864.

"The Colonel seemed to be suffering a stroke. He appeared in a great deal of pain as he flailed his arms and legs about. I couldn't understand what he was mumbling as he rolled around on the floor after falling from his bed. The bedclothes were askew as he tossed in his agony. Often strokes are silent attacks, but this one was singularly violent. The butler was concerned for him and, failing to find his regular physician, sent a boy to locate another.

"I calmed him with an injection of salicin and opiate, and as his sunken eyes began to close, he looked at me and said, 'Free Emerald!' I assumed he was remembering something from one of his army campaigns, and he fell silent as we lifted him back into his now-straightened bed. I sat with him and watched his breathing until he seemed to be in a comfortable sleep. I instructed Beckley to have someone stay with him and send for me if his condition worsened.

"Beckley said that the Colonel was in his eightieth year, though he looked older to me, perhaps due to his earlier wounds. His body was thin and almost emaciated, his gaunt face a web of wrinkles that extended into his long neck. If he survived the night, I determined I would institute a healthier regimen to improve his overall health."

"Most commendable. One cannot say that you live an ordinary life."

I raised my eyebrows. Not ordinary, but not exciting either, not like working on Holmes's extraordinary cases. "The strange part of my night's venture came after I left the house. I exited into the mews, as I would have a better chance of finding a cab on the corner since most of the Grosvenor inhabitants kept their own coaches and cabbies seldom drive around the Square at that hour. It was now well past two. A thin misty rain fell, blurring everything in sight. As I turned up my collar, a man walking a dog on a leash, some sort of hunting breed, I surmised, spoke out of the mist. 'I trust your patient is sleeping peacefully now,' he said as the dog attended to the corner of a wall.

"'He is that,' I said. He was a tall, thin man with a woolen hat, its brim pulled low to shield his face from the rain or from onlookers. His coat was dark, as were his trousers, and he blended with the mist and shadows, as did his dog's dark coat.

"'Miss Esmeralda is well then?'

"'I can't say. I do not know her.'

"'I often return late, and Rambler here wants to live up to his name, but I walk him in the daytime as well. I live in the area, but don't know the members of this household. I often saw Miss

Esmeralda from time to time – a lovely young lady – and she always spoke to Rambler and gave him a pat, but I haven't seen her in some weeks. Months perhaps. I wondered if she were ill." He nodded at the corner of the back of the house. "Her room is on the second floor. I've seen her looking out of the window in the past. Seeing a doctor emerge from the house, well, naturally I worried that she was unwell.'

"'I didn't see her. Just the elderly colonel.'

"Just then I heard the clopping of a horse and, not wanting to walk all the way in rain that might worsen before I got here, I excused myself and hurried to hail the cab, but not before hearing him call after me that he'd seen some suspicious characters observing the house, and a furniture van making deliveries at odd times even at night. I almost called back to him that some might think *he* is a suspicious character, but I was intent in catching the hansom.

"Sometime in the middle of the night, I awoke with the thought that the Colonel might have been saying 'Free Emeralda' or 'Esmeralda'."

"Indeed," Holmes replied. "That was my first thought. When do you return?"

"Return?"

Holmes put down his paper. "You know you will be checking on your patient today, and also trying to find out who this 'Esmeralda' is."

"I thought this afternoon."

"Make it morning. As soon as possible. I'll go with you as a consultant."

"I don't think – "

"Those who live in Grosvenor Square expect such treatment. They'll think nothing if you bring along a colleague for a second opinion."

"What do you suspect?"

"Nothing as yet, but a few details of your story piqued my interest. Let's just say that my curiosity needs to be satisfied on several counts."

"Oh, very well. Let's go then." I fetched my black medical bag and grabbed my coat on the way.

"I would rather go late tonight and see the man with a dog, but that would be too difficult to explain if we had to."

I couldn't imagine to whom we might have to answer, but I let it go. All would be explained in time – Holmes's time.

The previous night's rain had left the day humid, and I was uncomfortable in my woolen coat. I opened the buttons in an effort to cool myself as the hansom wheels took us to the Square. I paid the driver and stepped up to the door, bracketed by classic style pilasters. Holmes lifted an eyebrow at the terraced house in a long row of them. "Lofty digs here. A former prime minister, some cabinet ministers, and several Lords call this Square home."

"Indeed. I can't be bothered with them unless they fall ill. Sick is sick, whether it be a cabinet minister or a chimney sweep."

I raised the knocker, a brass gauntlet, and let it fall. The butler opened the door a moment later. "Good day, Beckley, I've brought a colleague to see the Colonel – a specialist."

"Indeed, sir." He divested us of our hats and coats and Holmes's stick, and led us up the stairs.

"How was his night?" I inquired.

"Daisy, one of the kitchen maids, sat all night with him. He didn't awaken. She's off duty now, but he was still sleeping when I looked in before you came."

The patient still slept, but appeared to be in no discomfort. His breathing was regular, and his color was improved. Some of the wrinkles had smoothed out of his face. His thin hair had been brushed into place. Holmes immediately became an efficient doctor, taking out my thermometer and slipping it under the Colonel's arm. While Holmes waited, he lifted the patient's eyelids and looked at his sleeping eyes and listened to his heart. He read the thermometer. "So far everything seems to be in order here. Now, if he will awaken soon, all will be as before. Could we have a cup of warm broth here?" he asked Beckley.

"Certainly, sir. I'll see to it."

As soon as he had left the room, I gently shook the Colonel's shoulder. "Sir, we are alone here. I'm Dr. Watson who saw you last night. This is my colleague, Dr. Holmes. You told me about someone last night, but I didn't know to whom you were referring. Is Esmerelda your niece?"

The pale eyelashes fluttered when I said the name. They snapped open. "Granddaughter. Free. Free." He sighed and his eyes closed again.

"He is progressing as to be expected," Holmes said as Beckley entered with a tray containing the broth. "I recommend continuing with the treatment. Allow him to sleep as long as he wishes. When he awakens, try to get him to drink spoonfuls of the broth."

"Thank you, Doctor. I couldn't have said it better." I turned to Beckley as he set the tray on a table. "Do you wish to engage nurses for the night, and perhaps the day as well?"

"We have sufficient staff for that."

"How about family?"

"His Lordship, Lord Rocklandel, will return late today."

I nodded. "Well then, I shall return tomorrow to see how he is progressing."

"Very good, sir." Beckley saw us to the door.

Outside, the Square was busier than previously. Children walked with their nannies in the park square. Ladies chatted in twos or threes on benches, or walked near nannies pushing prams. Two gentlemen enjoyed cigars as they ambled and conversed. A young man with longish hair sat under a tree reading a book, no doubt a volume of poetry, judging by his flowing soft, pale-blue tie. A group of older boys bowled hoops. Carriages passed – indeed, a hansom turned into the street. I started to hail it, but

Holmes deterred me. "Not yet, Watson." He lifted his hat to a passing matron.

"I should like to talk to the people in the Square, but we are visible from the house's windows – and in any case, I doubt the Grosvenor Square denizens would talk to a pair of unknown men. But someone in the mews might. Let's walk around the corner and try our luck there."

Holmes hailed a passing hansom and we climbed aboard. "Where to, Guv?"

"Just around the corner," Holmes said. "Watchers," he said to me softly.

As the cab steered into the street, a furniture van from the opposite direction passed us. "I wonder," I murmured, "if that's the one the man with the dog mentioned."

The van was painted a dark green with bright red trim, with *Flournoy's Movers* written on the side in bright yellow letters. The driver wore a dark cap pulled low over his forehead that seemed to mirror his black beard. His companion seemed too thin to offer much assistance with furniture delivery.

Around the corner, Holmes directed the driver to pull past the entrance to the mews and wait there. I gave him a coin to ensure he did. He shook his head, but parked the cab.

Holmes and I walked along the mews row. The previous night's misty rain left the cobblestones and bricks refreshed. A bay horse was getting a thorough scrubbing by a stable boy, while another fetched more water from a pump for the job. A pair of coachmen, seated on a mounting block, smoked their pipes while waiting to be called into service. Somewhere in the stables, a horse's neigh received a reply.

We'd passed two stables when Holmes spoke up. "Where did you meet the man with the dog?"

"Up there." I started to point.

Holmes took my arm and turned it so I was pointing at a horse, waiting patiently to be harnessed. "Yes, I agree with you. That is a fine horse. I wonder if he works well in tandem." Under his breath he said, "Just give me the directions to Colonel's room."

"It's on this side of the house in the back, second floor."

Holmes nodded. "You were exiting the house and he was facing it."

"Yes."

He glanced over his shoulder as if something had caught his attention from the house we were directly behind. "Hmm. He had an excellent view of the back of the house. "If there is a Miss Esmerelda, that might indeed be the area of her room. Let's go before we're noticed."

"Do you think something is amiss then?"

"We shall find out. Take your bag and go back to the Square. See if you can find some young lady who might know Esmeralda."

"I'll try."

"When you're finished, take the hansom back while I reconnoiter and see if anyone knows the man from last night. I'll speak to the cabbie first."

The strollers and nannies in the Square earlier were fewer now and I didn't see the poet. As I walked up to the gate, a young lady was on her way out. I didn't like speaking to an unknown woman, but we needed to know if the man with the dog had been correct. I lifted my hat. "Excuse me, Mademoiselle." I tried to imbue my speech with a touch of French. Holmes would have thought it laughable, but I have noticed people will often try to help those who are from far away. "I am Dr. Watteau." It was the only name I could think of that was French and sounded something like my own.

She paused and looked at me. She was dressed in a blue walking suit of the same shade as her eyes. Her hair was light brown and carefully coiffed. A pleasant and pretty young lady.

"Do you know a Mademoiselle Esmeralda Soames?"

"Yes, I do."

"Have you, *peut-etre*, seen her lately?"

Two lines appeared on her forehead as she thought for a minute. "No, I don't believe I have. Not since Easter, I think."

"She hasn't been in the Square this *printemps* – or summer?"

"No. I'm sure I would've seen her. We like to go for ices in a group."

I nodded. "I was afraid of such. *Merci*, Mademoiselle. You 'ave been most helpful." I touched my hat and made my exit.

I returned alone to Baker Street. Holmes wasn't there, but that didn't surprise me. He had people to speak with, information to gather. He'd said he needed to see a man about a dog.

Mrs. Hudson was delighted that I was back, but she was also fretting about Holmes. "He misses too many lunches."

"Not as many as you think. He often has lunch out when he can't make it back here."

"I don't see any results of those lunches," she said with a snort.

I spent the afternoon visiting patients, and managed to sleep a bit to make up for the previous night, and to prepare for whatever Holmes might have in mind for later.

I heard his key as I finished my dinner. He ran up the stairs and opened the door, but instead of his usual attire, the man who entered looked like he'd never been in a house or had a meal or a bath. It was Holmes, of course, at his most disreputable.

"Your afternoon must've been fruitful," I said.

He glanced at me before disappearing into his room. In less time than I expected, he joined me as himself.

"What did you find out from the mews?" I asked as he helped himself to the dishes on the table.

"Later. We have work to do tonight. I hope you were able to nap."

"I didn't need a nap, but I did sleep a few minutes." Or longer. I knew how intense Holmes could be when on an investigation. That reminded me of something. "Why this effort? You aren't on a case."

He continued to chew as he quirked an eyebrow.

"No one has hired you to find Miss Esmeralda."

"You're right." He gulped coffee.

"Actually, it's *my* case."

"No, it isn't. You're only on the Colonel's medical case."

"True, I suppose. Then why are we looking into this Esmeralda matter?"

"Sometimes one does the things one has to. However, these events will merge. I'll explain later. Let's go."

He was out of the door before I stood up. I looked longingly at the sponge cake as I hurried after him, grabbing my bag and pulling on my coat.

Holmes was in a hansom by the time I reached the front door. "Hurry, Watson – We've no time to lose!"

"What are we doing?" I climbed in beside him and the cab moved along Baker Street.

"Have you read my monograph on the possibilities of coincidences?"

I searched my brain. "No, I don't recall that one."

He smiled. "That's because I haven't written it. Possibilities are endless. Writing such would be an infinite task not worth wasting my time. However, coincidences do sometimes slap us in the face."

"Have we been slapped? Are we about to be?"

"Not yet."

"Is this a warning?"

Holmes didn't answer until we'd exited the cab and paid the driver. Dusk was upon us now. Thick shadows fell onto the cobbles from the buildings and the Square's trees. A little wind sprang up, pushing us along the street, rustling leaves somewhere to let us know the weather was turning. At the gate to the Square, Holmes ushered me through.

Along the paths, one or two glowing cigar tips signaled the presence of gentlemen who liked to smoke out-of-doors. Perhaps their wives didn't allow it inside. "What are we looking for?"

"Men who don't belong here. A poet."

We'd just enough light to see the faces of those in the park, but none looked like the poet we'd seen earlier. We traversed the length of the inner park on one side, and then started up the far side, checking on connecting paths and benches as we hurried.

We found the man we sought, enjoying the last bite of an eel pie and a bottle of cider. He still wore his soft tie, but had removed his plumed cap, and with it his brown hair. The hair atop his head now was dark, and I saw no sign of the cap. His features, however, were the same, even more pronounced with the dark hair. His eyes were dark blue and penetrating and his mouth generous, but set in a firm line as he tried to determine the situation in which he found himself.

"Who are you?" he rasped. "What do you want? I have no money."

Holmes permitted himself a small laugh. "We don't want your money, or care for your lack of it, except where it concerns Miss Esmeralda Soames."

He dropped the cider bottle and leapt up ready to defend himself – or Miss Esmeralda. His hands folded into fists. "What about her? Who are you? What do you want from her?"

Holmes held up a hand. "We are trying to help her, and we need your assistance to do that."

"How? What do you want from me?"

"How long have you been watching the house?" I asked.

He noticed me for the first time. "A doctor? What's wrong? Is she ill? Have you seen her?"

"No," I said. "At least we don't think so."

"When was the last time you saw her?" Holmes queried.

"It was at Easter. I called at the house to speak to her guardian, Lord Rocklandel. He refused me permission to marry his ward and had me escorted out of the house. I was refused entry the next day, and every day after. I was even told not to come near the door, or I would be arrested." He dropped his gaze, but not before I saw a tear slide out of the corner of one eye.

"So, you found other ways to enter the Square," I said. "Never mind. We understand, and we're here to help both of you."

"You are disguised as a poet," Holmes stated. "How are you able to spend so much time in the Square watching for her?"

"I dress this way in case she looks out the window. She will see me because I'm dressed differently. But yes, I am a poet."

"What is your name?" I asked wondering if I had heard of him.

"Edward St. John."

"Is that how you support yourself?" Holmes asked. "Writing poems?"

"I wish it were. No, I'm a writer at *Spectify*. It's a monthly publication. I mostly write little fillers when there isn't enough to fill a page. And odd jobs. It leaves me with time to write my poems. And I'm allowed to live in the garret of the building."

I hoped our skepticism didn't show, but some must have because he added, "I'm hoping to publish my first volume of poems this month. Esmeralda was to illustrate them with pen-and-ink sketches."

"We'll help you see your Esmeralda," said Holmes, "to ascertain she is healthy and under no duress – Tonight, if all goes as I've planned." He lifted his head as if listening for something.

"Ah – I hear it now. Come, Mr. St. John. The game is afoot."

He took off in the direction of the sound of the horse's hooves. St. John stood staring at his back as he was swallowed up in solid darkness.

"Come, man. We've work to do." I had no idea what Holmes's plan was, but when he was in movement, there was no time to lose.

We followed Holmes out of the park and down to the end of the street. Around the corner stood a pair of horses hitched to a furniture moving van – Flournoy's van. A policeman held the horses' reins.

"I hope you're right about this, Mr. Holmes," said a familiar voice. Inspector Lestrade stood there in his brown suit, his ferrety face illuminated by the light of the gas jet.

"Good evening, Inspector. I'm more than right about this situation. Gentlemen, shall we prepare ourselves?"

The inspector handed Holmes a box from which emerged disreputable jackets, caps, and other accoutrements that shortly turned him and the poet into workmen on a job. I began to dread what Holmes might have in store for me. "I shall take the reins. St. John here will be my helper. Watson. You'll be the furniture."

"I'll be the what?"

"Up you go." He reached a hand down from the driver's seat and pulled me up as I scrambled to climb. "Careful there. Don't damage that leg. St. John, help him in."

I appreciated his concern for my war wound, but as I gained the inside of the van, I saw a wooden chest not unlike the kind one might pack clothing into, but also not unlike a coffin except for the rectangular shape.

St. John climbed in behind me and opened the lid. "In you go, Doctor."

I stared down at the rectangle. I didn't want to do this. "Why can't St. John go in?"

"He has to help me carry it into the house," replied Holmes.

I stepped in and lay down with my knees drawn up a bit. St. John closed the lid and all was darkness. "I don't like this," I said in a loud voice. I don't know if they heard me because just then the van began to move. It turned the corner and started up to the Rocklandel house. "*It will only be another minute,*" I told myself, but it seemed more like a month or two before the van drew to a halt. I felt the chest being lifted and carried to the front door.

We stopped and I heard blurred voices. The chest lifted and again was on the move before being set down again. I heard voices again. Holmes saying forcefully, "Then ask Lord Rocklandel!"

Before I could take another breath, the lid was raised. "Quick, Watson! Go up the stairs and find Esmeralda. St. John, go with him. Remember where her room is located, and if you have to break the door down, do it.

St. John and I sprinted up the stairs and to the back of the house. The door was latched on the outside. St. John opened it and there stood his Esmeralda, in her nightclothes and slippers. "Edward! What is happening?"

"No time now for explanations. We must hurry."

"No!" She shrank back. "Stay away! You mustn't catch this wasting disease!"

"You don't look ill to me."

"I look terrible! And I have a dreadful infectious disease. The doctor said so."

I looked around and saw no mirrors. Possibly she didn't know how she looked. "I am a doctor, and you look like a normal person in perfect health. You're a prisoner of your kinsman, Lord Rocklandel. We came to rescue you."

She looked at St. John, who nodded. "Yes, this is Dr. Watson. There's a detective downstairs. We mustn't waste any more time." He put his arm around her and I pushed them ahead of me. We went back down the stairs though for a fleeting minute I wished I knew where the servants' stairs were.

We reached the foyer just as the butler returned with Rocklandel, a large man with heavy limbs, florid features, and a thunderous scowl. "What is the meaning of this?"

Esmeralda cringed, but held onto St. Johns' hands.

"We are taking charge of your prisoner," Holmes said.

"Sir," the butler said, "the young lady is very ill. The night air could hasten her end."

'Nonsense. I'm a doctor and I wager nothing at all is wrong with her that fresh air and her freedom couldn't cure. You have kept her locked in her room without mirrors for nigh on six months. No doubt you have confined her to bed and fed her only broth and toast. That would sicken anybody."

"How dare you insinuate my ward is a prisoner!" His Lordship bellowed. His face reddened more.

"This is true," Esmeralda spoke up. "I could smell the delicious aromas from the kitchen and so longed for roast chicken, gammon, and pastries."

"She is my ward," Rocklandel said, "and I will not have the sick girl dragged from her home. Now take yourselves from my house before I resort to violence!"

Holmes looked like he would enjoy violence with this unpleasant man, but a thin shaky voice said from the stairs said, "*My* house. *My* ward."

It was the colonel, wrapped in a voluminous dressing gown, slippers on his thin white feet. .

"Grandfather, please go back to your bed. You really are ill."

"I suspect I have received the same treatment as you, my dear granddaughter, but under Dr. Watson's care, I have regained some of my strength."

"Get from my house!" Lord Rocklandel ordered.

St. John thrust Esmeralda behind him as Rocklandel advanced on them. Rocklandel pulled a pistol from the pocket of his smoking jacket.

I slid my Adams from my own pocket. "Drop that gun."

"An Adams! You a soldier! That's ridiculous." He cocked the pistol as Holmes raised his own Webley.

Shots cracked the night. I didn't know who fired besides me, but only one bullet found its mark. Rocklandel dropped his gun and clutched his upper right arm. I snatched his firearm off the floor where it fell, keeping the Adams trained on him as Holmes hastened to open the front door. Lestrade, followed by four of his men, rushed in. Holmes hurriedly told him the gist of what happened.

But from whose gun had the bullet come that was in Rocklandel?

"All right," said Lestrade. "I understand what happened, but not why."

"This man needed a doctor," I said to Lestrade. "I don't have my bag."

"It's in the wagon. I'll have it brought up."

"I'd rather you bring up a police surgeon," I said, "but I realize one might not be available on short notice at this hour."

"Let's retire to the morning room," Esmeralda said, leading the way with her grandfather between her and St. John. "Beckley: Candles, please, and some refreshments."

Beckley hurried ahead of us and lit candles until the room glowed like a ballroom. He then betook himself off to the kitchen,

Two policemen stood by Rocklandel's chair while I attended to his superficial wound, tearing open his sleeve. Another one stood at the door and helped the butler when he returned with a tea cart laden with pastries, while a fourth officer went for my bag. I wondered if Beckley were trying to make up for those months of deprivation.

If I expected Esmeralda to fall on the food like the starving young woman she undoubtedly was, I was mistaken. She poured tea and coffee and made certain everyone had been served before she allowed herself a biscuit to nibble and a cup of fragrant oolong with lemon.

Holmes stood up. "I need to ask you both a question." He addressed Esmeralda and St. John. "Is it your wish to marry? I know this is sudden, but there is a reason."

His Lordship shifted in his chair. Did he think Holmes didn't know the cause of everything that happened in this house?

"Yes," St. John said. He slid down on one knee and took something out of his pocket. "It was my mother's," he said, opening the little box. The diamond on the ring caught the candlelight and flashed a dancing rainbow around the room. "I intended to ask you the day I was barred from this house. I came to ask His Lordship for permission to marry you. He became enraged and showed me the door. Esmeralda, I love you. Will you marry me?"

For a poet he was plain-spoken, but he was also in a hurry. They'd already lost six months. To lovers, that is a lifetime.

"Oh yes! Yes, I will!"

He slid the ring on her finger.

"Excellent!" Holmes said. "There will be a special license waiting for you tomorrow, but you must be married immediately after. This is the reason for all that has gone on in this house since April when Edward St. John came to ask Lord Rocklandel for permission to marry his ward – which everyone mistakenly thought she was. To keep the colonel from interfering in his business, Rocklandel brought in a phony doctor and invalided the colonel. He applied the same measures to his first cousin once removed. That is the correct relationship, is it not, Colonel?"

"It is. He is the son of my older brother and his wife Caroline killed in a carriage accident. Esmeralda is my granddaughter, daughter of my son, Frederick and Jane, his beloved wife.

"This house was built by my grandfather. The reason behind what happened to my granddaughter and me is because of the entail put on the house by the original Lord Rocklandel, my grandfather, that a daughter can inherit this house after she reaches the age of twenty-two, but she must be married. If I die after Esmeralda is twenty-two, the house goes to next of kin – in this case the son of my late brother, *this scoundrel*, who is the *third* Lord Rocklandel." His voice drifted off. He was improving since I stopped the tinctures they were giving him, but still weak.

The constable returned with my bag. I opened it and took out what I needed. I mopped up the blood and poured alcohol into the wound. I could have used hydrogen peroxide, which wouldn't be as painful as alcohol, but I took satisfaction in the patient's groans and grimaces. I found the bullet and slipped it into my handkerchief and pocketed it. I bound his arm with a clean bandage. "That will hold him until the police surgeon can see him," I told the constables.

The colonel sat comfortably tucked into a soft blanket on a large cushioned chair. Esmeralda sat beside him and held his hand. St. John sat on the other side, holding her other hand. "My mother was named Jane," Esmeralda was saying. "She read a story about a heroine named Esmeralda Aragon, and gave me that name so I wouldn't be a plain Jane. Esmeralda is a mouthful. I prefer to be called '*Esme*'."

Holmes nodded. "The present Lord Rocklandel's parents were killed in a carriage accident. Miss Esme's parents contracted a deadly fever. She came to live with her grandfather, though the present Lord Rocklandel put it about that he is her guardian. He'd found out this house was entailed to her unless she was unmarried at age twenty-two. That was when he locked Miss Esme in her room and began giving the colonel drugs to weaken him.

"He had matters under control, but the colonel had a small stroke while he was away from home. Concerned, Beckley sent a boy to fetch a doctor, and he went to Baker Street because he'd heard of Dr. Watson, who told me about his visit to this house, and something he mentioned about a man in the rain with a dog leaped out at me. He said a furniture van and strange men called at this house at odd hours. Did such a van call here this morning?" Holmes asked Beckley.

"Yes sir, it did."

"Will you show me the piece of furniture the van delivered?" Holmes asked.

"This is *my* house!" Rocklandel snarled, attempting to stand. "I will not have you stomping all over the costly carpets with your filthy boots!" The constables pushed him down.

Lestrade and the constables searched the house until they found a dark-haired man hiding behind a bookcase in the library. They brought him to the morning room. Rocklandel turned white when he saw the man.

"Take him in," Lestrade instructed several burly men who weren't in uniform who had remained near the door. They hustled the man out.

"This is the real reason Lord Rocklandel needed to keep the house under his control. It is a conduit for assassins and saboteurs. He is connected with a network that is deployed all over Europe to keep it in a constant state of fear and unrest in order to enrich these perpetrators. Some men were brought in the same way that Dr. Watson entered – hidden in a chest. Some walked in at night, which is why the man was standing in the mews in the rain with a dog. It was he who let me know that more was going on here than the separation of two young people in love.

"I paid a visit this afternoon to certain quarters and found out a shipment of furniture was expected here tonight. Lestrade and his men waylaid the van, and its inhabitants now are locked up."

"We brought Dr. Watson in, hidden in the chest, to gain entry to the house. Our purpose was to free Miss Esme and her grandfather and clear out this nest of spies. Our work is done. I suggest, Mr. St. John, that you remain here to see that the household runs smoothly. Tomorrow you will present yourself and your fiancée at the registry office and proceed with the marriage immediately by special license. Lestrade, do you have anything to ask?"

Lestrade stood up. "I do. Who shot His Lordship?"

"Does it really matter?" St. John said.

"I rather think it does," Lestrade said. "For my report, if nothing else."

No one admitted to firing the bullet that brought down Lord Rocklandel. Lestrade turned to me. "Well, Dr. Watson, you must've found the bullet. Maybe that will tell me which gun fired it."

"No. It apparently went straight through."

Lestrade scowled. He seemed sure that I had found the bullet, but was hiding it. Still, he bade his men to crawl all over the floor and examine the wall where Rocklandel had been standing, and even the chair in which he sat while I'd attended to his wound, but no bullet appeared. His Lordship laughed as the constables ushered him out to the waiting police wagon.

A tall case clock clanged eleven times. I felt tired after all the excitement. Holmes and I were driven home in a police carriage. Upstairs, we sat in front of the fire and had a spot of brandy.

"I told you this was a singular case," Holmes said.

"You were right, but how did you know? What was it about the man with the dog that informed you, as you said?"

"I've seen the man with the dog before."

"It could've been another man with a dog. Thousands of men have dogs."

"All right. The man, the dog, the furniture van, the dark-haired men at all hours. Her Majesty has been concerned for some time with attempts on herself, on officials, bombs placed at crucial spots, that sort of thing. I knew a man with a dog was watching this house. When you told me where it was and what you saw, I immediately made the connection. It was too much of a coincidence.

"Now tell me, Watson: What did you do with the bullet you took out of Rocklandel?"

I laughed and reached in my pocket for it. "Our two bullets missed their mark. I think we may need to do some practice shooting. This small one, from a Derringer perhaps, was all I found. The bullet did go through, but it hit a piece of metal decoration on a chair. Our ears were ringing with the sound of the explosion, which masked the ping against the metal. I scooped it up in this in the confusion. Thought you might want it – but don't ever tell Lestrade."

I unfolded the handkerchief square and handed him the misshapen lead bullet. "It was the colonel on the stairs, shooting downward," I said. "Should we tell Lestrade?"

"Someday, perhaps," Holmes replied, and we toasted the colonel.

". . . I knew that you had an inquiry on hand and that you disliked the intrusion of other matters."

"Oh, you mean the little problem of the Grosvenor Square furniture van. That is quite cleared up now – though, indeed, it was obvious from the first."

– Dr. John H. Watson and Sherlock Holmes "The Noble Bachelor"

The Open Window

After I learned what work this consulting detective I shared a suite of rooms with at 221B Baker Street did, Holmes included me in his cases but with an earlier one that became known later as "A Study in Scarlet", all the credit in the newspapers went to the Scotland Yard inspectors Lestrade and Gregson. No connection was made to the world's first consulting detective who actually solved the case and that chafed me though not Holmes.

"I told you it would happen," he said.

"It doesn't bother you?"

"Only that it doesn't serve to bring in more cases."

He was correct. Days passed without a case. "Perhaps it's the weather," I offered glancing out at the choking brown fog enveloping the city.

For answer, he puffed at his pipe and glowered at the fire.

I was relieved when a caller arrived admitted by Betty. "Someone to see you, Mr. Holmes."

I marked my place as Holmes bade the rather large man take the wicker chair.

"Don't mind if ah do," he said in a raspy voice with a tinge of surprise at the invitation.

I gathered he was unaccustomed to such niceties in his dealings in life. Though his face and hands were clean attesting to a washbowl in his possession, his clothing made up of odd pieces were somewhat dusty. He may have attempted to brush them but hadn't been successful as bits of matter stuck here and there.

"Oi'm Biggers, Josiah Biggers."

"Well, Mr. Biggers, this is my associate Dr. Watson. What can I do for you? I see you are a dustman of some length of time. You were born within the sound of the Bow Bells, and were in a hurry this morning."

His look of amazement was comical. "'Ow didja figger dat?"

"Just a little hobby of mine. What brings you here so early this morning?"

"Oi been saving me quid ta get married. Oi already give Rosie a ring, that's me fiancy," he stumbled over the unaccustomed word, "and Oi was putting it down on a set of noice rooms today. Oi bin living in a crowdy place wi' other fellas an' savin' up til Oi 'ad enough. Me mates insisted on getting a pint as we was passin' Hawley's Rooms ta celebrate. Oi cudden see no 'arm in that, bein' they was treatin' so Oi went wif them. Oi was dancin' and jokin' but lef after one pint an went to pay fa the rooms. When Oi went ta pull the purse outta me pocket where Oi pinned it, nuthin were there. Some bloke done stole it. Oi needs me quid back, Mr. 'Olmes."

"How many times did you dance, Mr. Biggers?"

"Two, tree times."

"Two or three?" Holmes gave Mr. Biggers a questioning look.

" Maybe more."

"A dozen?"

"More. She were a good dancer."

"Which mate was it who suggested going to Hawley's?"

"New man since las' week. Rory seems all righ'."

"Did you tell anyone you were going to put money down on a dwelling?"

"Dwell who?"

"Rooms."

"Oi mighta done. Me best mate Curley. He mighta tol' uvers."

"Well Mr. Biggers, you've been the victim of a pair of coney catchers as they were called in times past. I suspect the new man Rory is the thief. He took you to Hawley's which hasn't a good reputation and his partner there, the one you danced with –"

"Johnna," Mr. Biggers supplied.

"Johnna kept you occupied while he picked your pinned pocket. I can't get your purse back for you but now you know what happened to it."

"S'all right, Mr. 'Olmes. Now Oi know hit's nowt o' me good mates. Oi can't pay you for yer 'elp."

"No need, Mr. Biggers. You've more to worry about such as getting meals when you've no money." He reached into his pocket and drew out a coin. As he sent it spinning toward Biggers, I saw it was a half crown.

Biggers caught it. "Oi am be'olden to yer. Oi won't deny that."

"Think nothing of it Mr. Biggers. In the future be careful with your dance partners."

"Oi don't plan ta dance wif nobody but me sweet'art."

I waited until the downstairs door closed. "Holmes, you've not earned a groat's worth from this client. How will you make a living if you pay your clients?"

"Indeed I have earned far more than a groat's worth."

"Pray tell me how."

"I'm not that generous. I'm building goodwill. The dustmen of London will be an invaluable source of information in future cases if I should need them. And Biggers has already given me information confirming my suspicions about Hawley's. I learned of a con-woman calling herself Johnna. I shall pass that information to Scotland Yard and earn some goodwill in that quarter."

"They owe you for that case you just solved for them."

"That may be. I'll not make a habit of paying my clients, I assure you. The poor man was fleeced. He came to me because he'd nowhere else to turn. He hadn't yet realized he had no funds for food."

"When you put it like that."

"Indeed. Look upon it as financing the future." He settled himself behind his newspaper until the next client called.

We'd not long to wait. Betty brought in a young woman, a maid herself from her mobcap and apron and neat brown dress as she propelled a child of about five ahead of her. His eyes were red-rimmed and he held his right arm in his left hand. A rag bandage wrapped around his wrist. The child wore clean but patched, well-mended clothing. Not a street boy then, I ascertained.

"Mr. Holmes, sir. This is Mary my friend what works down the street for the Firmans, Her little 'un Bobby burnt his wrist last week. She took 'im to the doctor and was told if it worsened to bring 'im back. She did so this morning only the doctor wasn't there. The other doctor said he was a lowcun and wouldn't see him. She doesn't have the money to take him to another doctor. Could you make that lowcun doctor see him? I don't know what that means but it ain't fair for Mary to have to pay two doctors when he said ta bring Bobby back."

Betty's breath ended in a whoosh. She wasn't accustomed to making long speeches.

"I can do better than that, Betty. We have our own physician here. Dr. Watson is a renowned army surgeon. He'll not charge another fee," Holmes added when Mary started to protest.

"Here, lad, come close to the fire." Mary brought the lad to me. "Your name is Bobby?" I asked him to put him at ease.

"Yessir," he whispered.

"How old are you?"

"Five."

"Let me take a look." I unwrapped the bandage. Yellow pus and blood smeared the cloth. His arm was seriously infected. "How did you do this Bobby?"

"Burnt it on the firespit."

"Were you turning it?"

"The cook hired 'im to take a turn on the spit. One of the kitchen kittens got too close to the fire. Bobby tried to shoo it away and tripped. His wrist slammed on the hot metal of the spit," Mary said.

"Did you save the kitten?"

He nodded.

"Well, then. You're a hero. You saved a kitten but got hurt doing it. Betty, please go down to the kitchen and boil a lot of water. Mary take Bobby down with her. I'll fetch my bag."

Bobby sat in a corner munching a jam scone when I reached the kitchen. This was my first visit and as I suspected it was spotless and in great order. Mrs. Hudson could've commanded an army regiment. "I see Mrs. Hudson has supplied you with sustenance. I'll wager it's cherry."

His mouth full, Bobby nodded. His eyes widened when he saw me open my bag. I'd been restocking it along with what the army gave me when they replaced my bag and instruments lost in the Battle of Maiwand which almost killed me. The tinctures, ointments and medicines I acquired myself.

I chose the smallest of four kettles boiling on the stove. "We'll need a catch basin," I told Betty, "and the waste water must be disposed of."

"We have a drain connection," Mrs. Hudson assured me.

I tested the water until it cooled enough for me to pour over Bobby's arm into the basin on the floor. That water turned rusty orange.

Bobby sat still as the water cleansed his wound. "Does that hurt?"

"Nossir." He gulped.

I refilled the kettle from a larger one and did the same adding a tincture of carbolic acid. "This may sting a little," I told him, "but it will kill the infection. It's like a battle, you see. The bad infection against you. You'll win because you're a strong, healthy boy and your mother takes good care of you."

As I talked I let a stream of the carbolic water fall on the wound and prepared another kettle while Betty dumped the basin. After two more kettles I determined the wound was clean. I took out a roll of bandage and cut off the amount needed. I poured carbolic on it and held it in front of the fire. When it dried sufficiently, I wrapped the bandage around his arm with the carbolic against the burn. He didn't even flinch,

"Bring him back in the morning," I told Mary as I gave Bobby a ha'penny for being brave and another for saving the cat.

"Well, Watson, I see you will lose money to my clients as well," Holmes remarked later over tea.

"Perhaps I am gaining a valuable helper as well," I said.

"We shall see."

Bobby and his mother came promptly the next morning for the dressing change. Bobby munched a sausage scone as I worked. I discovered he'd a great love of animals. I told him about the strange animals I saw in India, the tigers and elephants and birds of astounding colors as I unwrapped the bandage to discover the burn was still red but slightly less and not oozing as much. The treatment was the same and each day with incremental improvement until the skin healed.

On the last day I resolved to replenish my medical supplies. I would try Barts to see what I could find without dipping into my meager funds as my injury pension would end in a few months.

I took a cab and held my handkerchief over my face to lessen the effects of the fog. "T 'weather's 'bout to change," the driver said. I hoped he was correct. As I entered the hospital I remembered almost three months ago Stamford introduced me to Holmes there.

"Watson! Watson!"

I turned around and saw Stamford. "I was just thinking about you."

He grinned. "How's it going with Holmes?"

"Couldn't be better. I owe you one. The rooms are comfortable and the meals are excellent."

"I mean how's it with you and Holmes? You get along all right?"

"Capital! His cases are as entertaining as a night at the Opera Comique. I'm here now to try to get some bandages and supplies for my bag." I held it up as proof of my errand. "I already have a little patient." I explained to him about Bobby.

A passing nurse-in-training lingered near enough to hear my comments until Stamford took me to his lab and replenished my supplies most amply. "I owe you twice," I said.

"When you're working again," he said.

At the hospital door, I saw the same nurse. She wore a worried look. "Excuse me, Dr. Watson, may I have a word?"

It was highly unusual for a nurse-in-training to speak to a doctor. I hoped she wasn't asking me for help with a tyrant of a matron. "I'm not really in practice at the moment," I said, "my words on your behalf wouldn't mean anything."

"No sir, it's not for me."

"I see. You are a long way from home, I believe." Her speech and dusky skin told me she was from the Caribbean. "Guiana?"

"Yes, sir. Georgetown. How did you know?"

"You have that lovely lilting voice."

"Thank you. Did I hear correctly you share rooms with a detective?"

"You did. Sherlock Holmes is the name."

"Is he a police detective?"

"No, though Scotland Yard uses his services. He's a private consultant. Do you have need of his services?"

She nodded and looked at the watch pinned to her apron. "I must go."

I pulled out my card and gave it to her. "This is his address. Come when you can."

She took it as if it were a canteen of water and she'd been lost in the desert for a week.

I wondered what she could possibly need a consulting detective for as she hurried back to her duties.

Holmes perused a journal as I dozed after lunch. The cabby was correct about the weather. The fog had thinned considerably and seemed about to lift.

A cab stopped in front of the building. "A case for you?"

"Perhaps."

The knocker sounded downstairs, timid raps but Mrs. Hudson heard them. "A young lady to see you, Mr. Holmes."

The nurse-in-training I met this morning at Barts entered. I stood up and offered her the wicker chair. She sat on the edge and held out the card I gave her as if returning it.

"Keep it," I said.

"Thank you." She slid the card back into her purse. I noted she was wearing her uniform under her dark blue cape.

"I told Matron I'd an appointment. She thinks it's for a dentist. I didn't want anybody to know I was coming here. They have so many rules. A nurse-in-training may not consult a detective could be one of them."

Holmes laughed. "Who are you, nurse-in-training and why have you come to see a consulting detective?"

"I am Sarah Allman. Nora, my friend all my life and I came to train at St. Barts to be nurses like Mrs. Mary Seacoal. We read about her in a book included in a missionary box when we were ten and decided wanted to be like her when we grew up."

"An admirable ambition. Mrs. Seacoal is the Jamaican nurse who helped the troops so much in the Crimean war," I explained to Holmes.

"I know Mrs. Seacoal and her work. She utilizes herbs and comfort in her treatment. Nurse Nightingale stresses order and protocol."

"Yes, in Georgetown we use herbs and botanicals but we needed the training of a hospital. We were accepted at Barts and all was well. Then two weeks ago on her time off, Nora went to Twinings to buy tea for my birthday the next day. She hurried and had just enough time to get back before curfew but heavy rain fell. She took a cab but was an hour getting to Barts. She was late and Matron dismissed her from training. We implored Matron to give her a second chance. We explained what happened.

"Nonsense, she said. Nurse Jackson could've walked back to Barts in fifteen minutes from the Strand. She said Nora was gallivanting with men and now lying about it and if I wasn't careful I would be next. Mr. Holmes, she wasn't lying. It happened just as Nora said.

"Last week she sent word she found a job sitting with sick people. It isn't much but she has a room. The patient was some important man and he died and now she's been arrested for murder and theft. Because of me, she has no future."

A tear slid out down her cheek.

"What do you want a detective to do, Miss Allman?"

"She didn't murder anybody or steal anything or tell any lies. I want someone to find out how the patient died and clear her name."

"Do you want me to reinstate her at St. Barts also?"

"Yes. If you can."

She pulled a white handkerchief from somewhere and twisted it in her hands.

"What tea did she buy for you at Twinings?"

"Earl Grey. It has bergamot in it."

"Ah. And that makes it better?"

"Yes." Firmly.

"We must try some. Do you have a photograph of your friend, Miss Allman?"

"I do," she said rummaging in the purse under her cape and handing Holmes a small photograph. "We had our likenesses taken when we arrived to send our families and one for each other."

"Charming," Holmes said and passed it to me.

The girl in the photograph wore her neatly braided hair wrapped around her head in a coronet. Sarah wore hers in a figure eight on the nape of her neck. Nora was smiling in the picture and looked happy.

Sarah glanced at the clock on the mantelshelf. "I must go," she said gathering her cape around her.

I accompanied her downstairs. "She's lucky to have a friend like   you.
"We are lucky to have each other." She turned to me. "Much depends upon our training here. People held fetes to help pay for us to come. They are depending on us to return and train nurses there. We are the first from our faraway jungle country."

"I understand. Your friend's case is in good hands."

Holmes was already in his Inverness and hat when I returned to the sitting room. "Get your things, Watson, we've work to do and not a minute to lose."

I grabbed my hat and coat. "Where are we going?"

"Scotland Yard to see out client."

A few flurries of snow blew into the hansom as the driver navigated the streets of London. I couldn't complain. Anything was better than brown fog. We traveled the two plus miles to 4 Whitehall Place more quickly than I expected. Holmes paid the driver and we entered the headquarters of Scotland Yard, the London police through the striped doorway under the third-story clock. I'd heard tales of the origin of the name but nobody knew with certainty. The rear entrance opened onto Great Scotland Street which may have been the site of a palace or house where the Scottish royalty stayed when they came to London or it could have been where coaches left and returned for Scotland. Or a Mr. Scott may have owned the property but as Holmes says, what matters is who owns it now.

Holmes introduced himself to the officer on duty as Sherlock Holmes, consulting detective here to see his client, Miss Nora Jackson.

"Consulting what? Never heard of such." The man's normally florid face reddened more when Holmes handed him his card.

"You must be new. Is Inspector Lestrade about or Gregson?"

"Holmes, Watson. What brings you here?" Lestrade was somewhat sharper than his colleague Gregson though it was not apparent looking at the wiry, rodential man with quick dark eyes in a nondescript brown suit, waistcoat, and hat which he removed.

"Lestrade. I'm here to see my client, Miss Nora Jackson."

"The murderess. What do you think you can do for her? We caught her red-handed."

"That remains to be seen."

"What led you to suspect murder?" I asked.

"Found a bit of feather in his nose. From smothering with a pillow, you know."

"What was the autopsy report?" Holmes asked.

A furrow tracked on Lestrade's brow as he remembered who solved the Study in Scarlet case. And who took credit for it. And who maybe didn't order an autopsy in the suspicious death of a lordship. He had the grace to look slightly abashed.

"There's still time for one," Holmes reminded him.

"No need."

"Indeed. It will be necessary in court. My client?"

"Come this way. No harm in you talking to her." He pressed his lips together as if he knew Holmes wouldn't take on an obviously nonpaying client if he didn't have reason to believe her innocent.

Nora Jackson looked like her photograph but her face was swollen from crying. She wore her nursing uniform. Apparently she'd not been given time to change.

Holmes and I entered with Lestrade following. "I wish to speak to my client in private," Holmes said.

"Very well. But make it quick."

"This young lady's life is at stake. I shall take as much time as needed."

With a grimace, Lestrade left us. Nora Jackson stood when we entered. Now she sank down on the ledge that served as a bed and chair. We remained standing.

"I'm sorry. I don't have any money to pay for a – did you say consulting detective?"

"I did. Never mind about a fee. This is my associate Dr. Watson. Your friend Sarah Allman consulted us."

She turned to me. "A real medical doctor?"

"Yes. Of late an army surgeon."

"To help me?"

"Yes," Holmes replied. "Now tell us what happened. You were working for a family called Despard, I believe. How came you there?"

"You know about nursing school? My dismissal?"

"I do indeed. I shall address that as well but first let's clear up this charge."

"Lady Despard sent for me on her husband's doctor's recommendation."

"Did you know this doctor?"

"No. I'd had one overnight job sitting with a patient of Dr. Reeve. He went away to a meeting in Scotland I think. Dr. Vincent is acting as his locum."

"Do you know where Vincent regularly practices?"

"Somewhere in Yorkshire. He told me he was a distant cousin to Dr. Reeve and liked to get away to the city when he was needed.

"I stayed two nights without mishap. The patient slept at night. I'm not there in the daytime but the kitchen maid Carrie sat with him then and she told me he slept all day, too. Last night he convulsed and died."

"Were you in the room when this happened?"

"Not at first. The doctor were there and he sent me to the kitchen to get hot water for an infusion and to have a cup of tea to fortify me for the night. It were around eleven then. When I returned the patient were agitated and the doctor tried to calm him. He gave me orders while he held the thrashing patient. His lordship moaned and made noises I couldn't understand. The doctor told me to prepare an infusion of the herbs on the nightstand. I did that. He held it to his lordship's mouth and it seemed to soothe him. He fell into a deep sleep.

"The doctor said he should sleep all night and left his patient in my charge. I sat in a chair where I could see him clearly in lamplight. He seemed comfortable and I don't recall him moving much for the rest of the night. Carrie came in at seven. She asked me if he passed a good night. I said he did but when I took his pulse, he were gone.

"The doctor were sent for. He said his lordship was still alive and tried to arouse him but he convulsed again and died."

"Were the police called?"

"No, sir. Her ladyship were distraught. I helped prepare the patient and stayed with the body until the undertaker came. The doctor attended to Lady Despard. And then I went home to my room. Later the police came and searched my things. They found a gold ring in the bag I carry with me on cases. They said I murdered Lord Despard with a pillow. They arrested me and locked me in here."

Tears slid down her cheeks. She had no handkerchief. I handed her mine.

"This ring," Holmes prompted, "had you seen it before?"

"No, sir. It were one of those with a seal on it like a man wears on his pinky. The police said the safe in his lordship's room were opened and robbed of jewelry and money. They wanted to know who my accomplice was. I said I didn't have one. They asked how I opened the safe. I said I didn't. I didn't even know it was in the room. They said it were behind a picture of boats in Venice. I remember staring at the boats during those long nights but I never knew a safe was behind them.

"They asked again who my accomplice was. I said I didn't have one. Work alone do you one of them said. I said I work at sitting with patients who are ill. I don't know how to open a safe and I didn't have an accomplice.

"Why then was the window open? they said. I said I didn't know it was. The doctor might have opened it to give his patient fresh air. Why would he do that, they wanted to know with the choking fog out and anyway his patient were deceased.

"I said I didn't open the window. I would never open it to that nasty fog unless the doctor ordered it and he did no such thing."

I nodded approvingly. People shut themselves in their houses and only go out when necessary during those brown fogs when breathing was painful.

"Do you know the circumstances of his lordship falling ill?" I asked.

"They said he was at his club and took sick there. They'll hang me, won't they?"

"I think not," Holmes said. "We must go, Miss Jackson."

"He'll sort it out. He's the best," I said, disliking to leave her alone in that dismal cell.

I was rewarded with a wan smile.

"This is more than a simple case of robbery or even murder, I suspect," Holmes said when we gained the street.

"What do you mean?"

He smiled and called for a cab.

Number 1 Sutheley Square lay in Mayfair, the wealthier part of London, once the site of the fair in May. Holmes enlightened me. I'd never had occasion to visit in this area when I was at Barts. The house stood alone unlike the others nearby. Built in Georgian style of dark brick dressed with stone, No. 1 rose four floors behind a brick and wrought-iron fence draped with black bunting. More bunting swooped from all the windows linking them in scalloped rows and a wreath of black feathers hung on the door crowned by a fanlight. The butler answered the lion-head knocker as if waiting behind the door ready to fling it open.

Holmes handed him a card. "Sherlock Holmes to see her ladyship."

The butler took it with two fingers of his white-gloved hand and glanced at it. "Consulting detective. Her ladyship has no need of a detective." He started to close the door.

"That, my good man is not for you to decide. I've just come from Scotland Yard and she needs to see me."

"I shall see if she is at home."

He shut the door and left us standing on the stoop. I regarded the mourning wreath. "This must have cost a bit." I blew on the feathers to reveal the iridescent sheen of purple and green.

The door opened as I bent slightly to blow again. The butler looked askance at me. "Her ladyship will see you."

"Interesting sheen on the feathers," I said as I followed Holmes into the hall draped with black and up the black-draped stairs to a sitting room where her ladyship awaited us.

Lady Despard sat in a regal chair with lions carved on the sides, her husband's chair I surmised as a more ladylike chair in rose velvet upholstery sat empty on the other side of the fire.

"Pray tell me why I need to see," she paused, "a consulting detective?"

No mourning crepe for her, the black silk dress rustled slightly as she raised her hand to touch a black and white cameo brooch at the high neck of her gown. A black silk cap topped her brown hair. Her sharp eyes were a bright blue, her face unlined and I wondered if she were considerably younger than her late husband, perhaps a second or even third wife. She did not invite us to sit. "Which of you is Sherlock Holmes?"

"Your ladyship, I am he. This is my partner, Dr. John Watson, late of the Fusiliers."

"Late of? Were you cashiered?"

"No. I was wounded at Maiwand and invalided out of service. I am aiding my friend while recuperating from that and enteric fever." I deliberately left out a prefatory ladyship. Her haughtiness was irritating to one who had taken a Jezail bullet for king and country.

"My condolences. Your husband was murdered..." Holmes began.

"Yes, yes, by that wretched girl from the Indies. We know that."

"Not by Miss Nora Jackson but by another," Holmes finished.

"I think not. My husband's ring was found in her baggage."

"The murderer made sure of that. Why would this girl lately come to London keep a signet ring in her bag while disposing of the remainder of the jewels and whatever was in the safe?"

She let go of the cameo and waved her hand. "Who knows what these people think?"

"These people?"

"Thieves. Robbers. Murderers."

"If this young woman wanted a piece of the jewelry for herself why would she not have kept a jeweled piece? Why a signet ring that clearly belonged to his lordship with no doubting its ownership?"

"It looked shiny?" she offered.

"Shinier than a glittering diamond bracelet, a glowing emerald ring, a smoldering ruby necklace? No, your ladyship. The signet ring was chosen by the killer to connect Miss Jackson with the theft and the murder. Perhaps the thinking was that his lordship awoke in the midst of the theft while the safe was being opened and she killed him to prevent him incriminating her. She had time to pick her souvenir among the baubles or perhaps she did it at home while waiting for her partner to come for the loot or perhaps settle with her. No money was found in her room save what she earned. So why the signet ring?"

"So you think she wasn't working alone?"

"No, I think she was only working as a sitter for an ill patient."

"Then why was the window open?"

"Miss Jackson said she would never subject an ill patient to the brown fog on the loose that night," Holmes said.

"Quite right," I said. "It can cause an ill patient to worsen within minutes. No doubt the murderer opened it to make you think an accomplice was waiting outside."

"Who first noticed the open window?" Holmes asked her.

"Why, I don't know." She fingered the cameo again.

"Tell me the sequence of events that morning, if you will," Holmes said.

"The sitter notified the butler his lordship was - was gone."

"Who told him?"

"Carrie, the day sitter."

"What was his next move?"

"He told me he went to his lordship's room and ascertained he was indeed deceased and then he reported to me."

"And what did you do?"

"I went to his room to see if it were true. And it was."

This last sounded bleak. It was the first sign that she had lost her husband. Perhaps she had feelings after all. Or perhaps she knew what was called for and was supplying it.

"Word was sent to the doctor who came immediately. He signed the death certificate, death by natural causes. He then waited with me until the undertaker arrived and saw his lordship off."

"Where were the two sitters?"

"They went to the kitchen for sustenance. Nora was paid and dismissed. Her services were no longer needed. Carrie returned to her regular duties."

"When was the theft discovered?"

"After – after my husband was taken away I put the death certificate into the safe in his room. When I opened it, I discovered the safe was empty. All the money and jewels were gone. And the window. That's when I noticed it was open. I sent somebody to close it."

"And that's when you called Scotland Yard?"

"Yes. They immediately went to Nora's room wherever it is and found the signet ring in her things. Do you really think she didn't do it?"

"I know she wouldn't do it. All she ever wanted to be was a nurse. It was as important to her as having a title."

Her ladyship had the grace to look slightly ashamed. I took the opportunity to relate to her what happened to nurse-in-training Jackson.

"She would never risk her position over a signet ring," I said. I explained about the fetes to raise money. I'd seen many dedicated nurses. These two from Guiana were among them. "To them nursing is a vocation."

"What led the police to suspect murder?" Holmes asked.

"With the safe robbed, they went to the mortuary and found a feather on him. They concluded he had been smothered with a pillow."

"Was the signet ring kept in the safe?"

"No, my husband wore it all the time but when he was taken ill, the doctor removed it in case his hands swelled and I placed it in the safe."

"While the doctor was there?" I asked.

"Yes, but he was busy with my husband."

"With your permission I would like to look around outside," Holmes said.

"Very well." She rang a bell. "Wilson, show Mr. Holmes outside to the window underneath the bedchamber where his lordship...."

119

I put my hat on and followed Holmes downstairs.

"You do not need to accompany us, Wilson," Holmes said at the door. "Merely tell us which window was open the night his lordship was murdered."

"Her ladyship said to show you and show you I will." He marched out the front door and around the side of the house.

We followed him into a small park-like area planted with evergreen trees and shrubs to a window in the middle of the house footprint. "There." He pointed to a window on the second floor.

Directly below that window lay a bulb bed with a few leafy things visible. We studied the bed and surrounds. Nothing had been disturbed since the raking. "When was the gardener last here?" Holmes asked.

"Not for some weeks due to the inclement weather."

"Was the window open or closed when you went to his Lordship's room with Carrie?"

"Closed. Now, if you've seen what you wish to see, I shall return to my duties."

"Indeed. We shall look farther afield in case the bundle rolled."

The butler turned on his heel and left us. Holmes waited a minute then said, "Quick, Watson, we must find the kitchen."

We sped around the house to the trade entrance and kitchen. Holmes knocked on the door. It was opened by a young house or scullery maid. She was thin inside her uniform, her light hair almost hidden by a plain white mobcap. "Yessir?"

"Good day. I'm Sherlock Holmes. I would like to speak to a Miss Carrie, if I may."

"Who is it?" called a low voice.

She looked over her shoulder. "It's two gentlemen, Mrs. Cook. They wants to speak t'me."

A stout cook not yet middle-aged came to the door. "What do you want with our Carrie?"

Holmes gave her his card. "We need to ask her some questions about the death of his lordship and see the room where he died."

She took the card, squinted at it then gave it to the thin young woman. "Wot kind of questions?"

"About the state of the room that night."

"See that you don't tarry."

Carrie led us to the servants' stairs.

The stairway was narrow and dimly lit. In contrast the bedroom was large and well-appointed, comfortable yellow velvet chairs by a black marble fireplace, handsome hangings. We checked the bulb bed below the window. "Was it open when you came on duty this morning?" Holmes asked Carrie.

"I don't rightly remember, sir. The room were dark. The fog were awful bad. I wouldn't've noticed. I talked with Nora a bit and then we checked on his lordship and discovered he were daid-like. I ran to get Mr. Wilson while Nora stayed with 'im. Mr. Wilson sent the kitchen boy for a jarvey. It were quick in coming. He sent me for the doctor."

"Was this Dr. Vincent?"

She nodded.

"What happened when you knocked on the doctor's door? Did you wait long?"

"No sir. T'were not at all long. He reached for his bag and we hurried back to the 'ouse in the cab. I were sent back to the kitchen."

She looked anxious. "Ought I to 'ave done sumpin else?"

"No, indeed, you did quite right. I'm a doctor," I told her.

She seemed relieved.

"Can you show us where the safe is?"

She pointed to the painting which Holmes opened as if it were a cabinet door to reveal the safe. He tried its door. Locked.

"I think we've seen everything we need to here," Holmes said. "You've been most helpful. One more thing. Were Lord and Lady Despard a happy couple?"

"I wouldn't know, sir. She's his second wife."

"Any children?" I asked.

"From his first wife, God rest her soul. Two boys away at school."

Dusk fell while we were inside. "Time to call it a night," I said hopefully. My stomach was empty. We missed tea. I didn't want to miss dinner as well.

Nevertheless since we were close by, Holmes insisted on stopping at the doctor's office. He gave the address to the driver and in a short time we were facing a brick building with a sign denoting Dr. Reeve's practice. Holmes asked the cabbie to wait. We rang the bell. No one answered. A man walking a bulldog told us the doctor was out seeing patients. The doctor lived on the premises. Not quite Harley Street but close.

"An excellent arrangement," I murmured knowing I could never afford to open a practice in this neighborhood.

The next morning, restored by two excellent meals with sleep in between, Holmes and I again stopped by the doctor's premises. He answered the door himself. Holmes gave him a card, introduced us both and asked for a few minutes of his time. "We're aiding Scotland Yard in a case."

"I'm rather in a hurry. What is this about?"

"The unfortunate demise of Baron Despard."

"Come in then." He closed the door but didn't offer us a chair.

"A Sussex man from your accent. I understand you practice in Yorkshire," Holmes said.

"Yes, there was an opening and I took it. Practice is slow in the small town and I often act as locum for physicians who need to travel for short times."

"Where did Dr. Reeve go?" I asked.

"I believe he went to a meeting in Paris and planned to enjoy himself before returning. Medical practice can be intense as you know." He nodded at me.

"I do indeed."

"What happened that night?"

"I'd not yet retired when I heard a loud rapping on the door and the bell ringing. I opened it to a footman asking me to come quick, his lordship was took sick, I believe, was the way he phrased it, at the Lusio Club.

"I donned my coat, grabbed my bag and went to the club. The patient was vomiting, gasping and agitated. I gathered from his mumblings he fell ill while dining there."

"Was he still at table?"

"No, they carried him to a small anteroom and placed him on a sofa which was for the purpose of removing sick or inebriated members to spare the others."

"Were any other diners taken ill?"

"No, only his lordship. I had the staff call for a brougham and help him to it. I sent a messenger ahead informing his household to be ready. I put a cold compress on his throat to ease the nausea on the journey which was short. The household footmen aided by the butler carried him to his chamber where I could make him comfortable and assess the situation. I ruled out appendicitis and other organic ailments. His symptoms were those of a man who has eaten something disagreeable. I introduced an emetic. When that didn't work, I repeated the dose, this time with results and he fell into a deep sleep. I stayed the night with him. In the morning I told Lady Despard to hire a night sitter with some medical background though not necessarily a trained nurse as I expected him to sleep during the nights he was recuperating. I gave them a list I found in Dr. Reeve's desk and they chose Nora Jackson. Carrie of the household would sit in the day. I expected a man in the prime of life such as his lordship to fully recover."

"And he did not?" Holmes prompted.

"He did not. Over the course of the next two days he was incoherent, mumbling, rambling. I tried sitting him in a chair but he could not remain upright. I suspected he suffered a stroke in the violent throes of whatever beset him."

He anticipated my next question. "Yes, I certainly thought of removing him to a hospital but Lady Despard did not wish it. 'With your help we can attend to him here, she said.'

"He seemed more comfortable on the third day but he worsened in the night and I was called. I did what I could to relieve him of stress and pain and finally he fell into a restful sleep and I left. In the morning the day sitter Carrie came to my door and I rushed over to find his lordship slipping away and nothing I did could keep him here. I called to his wife and she held his hand as he went. It was a sad case. I wish I knew what he had imbibed or eaten that day at the Lusio or elsewhere but he hadn't been able to tell us."

"Yes, knowing the agent would've determined the treatment," I said, "but without knowing, your treatment seemed to the best possible under the circumstances."

"You say he was still alive when you were called to him." Holmes asked. "Nora and Carrie thought he'd already slipped away."

"To the untrained, his thready pulse might have been undetectable but yes, he was still breathing though shallowly when I arrived and for nearly half an hour after."

"What did you do when he was gone?" Holmes asked.

"While Nora and Carrie prepared his lordship for the undertaker, I comforted her ladyship and filled out the death certificate. When the undertakers arrived I took my leave and returned to my waiting patients. Which I must do now," he ended as a well-dressed lady alighted from her carriage, escorted by a young woman in nursing uniform.

Dr. Vincent ushered us out and walked down the steps to greet his patient. "Lady Barrington!"

We followed and watched the party until the door closed behind them. "A smooth manner, wouldn't you say?" Holmes observed.

"Indeed. He knows which brass to rub."

"I need to send some telegrams. Take this photograph to Twinings and find out if Miss Jackson was there when she said she was. You have your notes?"

I patted my jacket pocket while Holmes hailed a cab. I decided to walk as the day held a hint of spring and I'd been feeling a bit stiff and achy. A walk would do me good but halfway to the Strand I wished I'd taken a cab myself. The hint of spring turned into a rumor and then a memory as a shower manifested itself. I took a cab back to Baker Street and was finishing a cold luncheon plate when Holmes arrived. He refused luncheon and puffed furiously at his pipe by the fire as the rain intensified and I was glad not to be out in it.

Holmes received telegrams during tea. "You seem to have good news," I said as I buttered a scone.

"If news of murder is good, then I suppose I have."

"Not recent murders, I hope." I took a hurried bite in case he was hared off on a murder hunt.

"Not in the last two days."

I waited for him to elaborate but he was not so inclined as he ate heartily of scones and sandwiches. I reported what I learned at Twinings. "As to the Despard case, my money is on the wife."

"Come, Watson, she will have to step down when the older son marries. She'll be the dowager step-mother then," Holmes said. "Despard was worth more to her alive than deceased."

"Yes, but until then she will have control and could make another advantageous marriage to a man closer to her age. Maybe she already has one in mind."

He glanced at me over his forkful of ginger cake. "You have a devious mind."

"I'm a Scot."

He laughed as Mrs. Hudson entered with a fresh pot of tea.

"I'm glad to see you're enjoying yourselves," she said, pouring.

"Thank you, Mrs. Hudson. Excellent tea."

"Luncheon was good, too," she began but was interrupted by the sound of wheels.

"Finish up, Watson, our carriage awaits."

"Pray enlighten me."

"In due time."

Some enlightenment lay with the police vehicle at the curb and its passengers, Lestrade, a sergeant and Nora Jackson looking as if she had hope again. The destination soon became apparent as we headed toward Sutheley Square. "Wait down the street," Lestrade instructed the driver.

Wilson was again on the other side of the front door. "Her ladyship is in the drawing room."

Lestrade left his sergeant in a small anteroom as we went up the stairs. I was beginning not to be surprised at the way Holmes conducted his business but in her ladyship's drawing room I was amazed to see not only a curious Lady Despard in her black silk but Sarah Allman and the matron from Barts. Miss Allman introduced us.

"You were at Barts I believe," the stern-faced Matron Montrose said to me.

"I was."

"Where do you practice now?"

"I was invalided out of the Fuseliers after the Battle of Maiwand and enteric fever. I am still recuperating."

"Hmph."

We were soon joined by the clerk at Twinings, a man in a waiter's uniform, and a man who looked like a jarvey. After a noisy ascension of the stairs in walked none other than Mr. Biggers. Holmes nodded at him. Biggers laid his finger aside his nose and I wondered what he knew that Holmes hadn't told me.

Holmes asked everyone to take a seat and looked at his watch as Carrie slipped in and quietly took a chair. "The doctor is late."

The downstairs doorknocker sounded and in a few moments Dr. Vincent joined us. He looked around the room at the assembly and made to retreat. "Come in, Dr. Vincent. You are just in time," Holmes said.

"I was told her ladyship was in need of my services."

"And well she might be. Please take a seat. Inspector Lestrade of Scotland Yard has asked all of you to come here to clear up some misapprehensions about the death of Baron Despard and clear Miss Jackson's name. Thank you, your ladyship for allowing us the use of your drawing room."

"I want to see the murderer of my husband punished." She stared hard at Nora Jackson.

To her credit, Miss Jackson stared back without cringing or flinching.

"On the face of it, this was a simple case of a young woman stealing a ring in a crime of opportunity but in fact it is not simple at all and isn't a crime of opportunity but a diabolical one that was carefully planned and orchestrated by one person who was not Miss Jackson.

"Lord Despard, in perfect health, dined at his club on Thursday last at which time he became ill. A footman summoned the nearest doctor, Dr. Vincent who was standing in locum for Dr. Reeve. The doctor took charge of the patient and removed him from the Lusio Club to his home. He believed he could care for him there as well as at a hospital. Is that true, Doctor?"

"That was my thought, yes."

"And mine," Lady Despard said.

"You stayed the night and in the morning gave Lady Despard a list of sitters for the nights as might be needed. You recommended the first name on the list because she'd had some nurse's training. Is that correct?"

"Yes."

"Miss Jackson seemed a reasonable choice, therefore. Is this how you remember it, your ladyship?"

"Yes." Her voice was low and controlled as if she were steeling herself.

"Miss Jackson sat with the patient at night, Miss Carrie Pelton, released from her kitchen duties sat during the day." He looked to her ladyship for confirmation. She nodded.

"During that time the patient slept. Did he ever regain consciousness?"

Miss Jackson said no and Miss Pelton concurred.

Holmes turned abruptly to her ladyship. "Did you not consider calling in another doctor?"

"I – well yes, I mentioned it to Dr. Vincent but he assured me his lordship was making progress and needed to rest. 'Sleep is the best thing for a stroke victim,'" he said.'" She brought her black handkerchief to her eyes.

"How did you discover the robbery so soon, your ladyship?"

"The doctor gave me the death certificate. After he left, I opened the safe to put it in and discovered it was empty."

"Is it possible your husband had emptied the safe?"

"No. Before he left for his club that Thursday, he put some securities in the safe and also my ruby necklace."

Holmes nodded. "Tell us, Miss Jackson, what happened on Sunday night."

"The patient was asleep when I came on duty at seven of the clock. I gave him his ten 0'clock infusion and soon he became agitated. I told the butler and he sent a footman for the doctor. The doctor came immediately and gave his lordship another infusion. The patient quieted and slept peacefully. The doctor sent me to the kitchen for hot water and told me to have a cup of tea while I was there as this might be a long night. When I returned he mixed another infusion and told me to administer it if the patient became restless. He left at three and soon the patient moaned. I gave him the infusion and he fell asleep. In the morning at seven Ca-Miss Pelton came on duty. I couldn't find the patient's pulse. The doctor was sent for."

"Did her ladyship sit with her husband?"

"Yes she did but that were private-like between them. The doctor signed the certificate and gave it to her. I stayed until the undertakers came."

"Was the window open at any time?"

"No, sir. The fog were bad."

"Thank you, Miss Jackson. Miss Pelton, was the window open when you went on duty that morning?"

"No, sir."

"Inspector Lestrade, was the window open when you were called in on the robbery?"

"It was."

"Dr. Vincent, was the window open when you were called in that morning?"

"I don't remember. My concern was for my patient. I'm certain it was closed. I wouldn't subject a patient to that toxic fog."

"Inspector, did you find any evidence of an accomplice waiting outside for the thief to toss down the ill-gotten gains?"

"No."

"And you assumed since a robbery had taken place in that room, his lordship had been murdered as well?"

""It seemed a possibility. After we found the feather, we found the signet ring in Miss Jackson's possession."

"A ring she denies ever seeing before. A ring assumed to be shinier than the glittering jeweled pieces also stolen."

"Why else would it have been in her kit?"

"She wondered the same thing. When did you confirm murder had been done?"

"We found a bit of feather in the nasal cavity. And the autopsy confirmed."

Holmes raised his eyebrow slightly. "Confirmed suffocation or some other cause of death?"

Lestrade had the grace to look down. Only Holmes and I knew he was late with requesting the autopsy. "Some other. The feather had been placed there likely after death. The cause of death was poison. And heroin. And opium."

"A lethal cocktail. And you still suspected Miss Jackson?"

"We are open to other suggestions for the murderer's identity."

"This was a meticulously planned murder-robbery, but not the only murder and most likely not the only robbery. We are concerned with the murderer of Baron Despard. Are you satisfied Miss Nora Jackson did not commit this murder, Inspector?"

"At the present time, I am. She is released from custody."

Holmes turned his attention to one of the men I didn't know. He was a thin man of middle age with receding hair. "Mr. Lathem, you are a waiter at the Lusio Club?"

"I am."

"Were you on duty the night his lordship became ill?"

"I was."

"Did anything odd happen that night besides the illness?"

"I noticed a waiter I didn't know. Then his lordship fell ill and I didn't see him again."

"Thank you. Mr. Arnold, is this the young lady you sold tea to one afternoon two weeks ago at Twinings on the Strand, Miss Nora Jackson?"

"She is. She bought our finest Earl Grey because she said it has bergamot in it."

"What was the weather like?"

"Just as she left, rain poured down. She said she must hurry back to St. Barts. I helped her get a hansom."

"Mr. Flinders, do you have something to add to this inquiry?"

Mr. Flinders, the jarvey stood up, cap in hand. "I do indeed. There's often a rotten apple in a barrel and Lon Turman is a rotten jarvey. We'd suspected him of taking fares for a long ride so's he could charge more. E's been removed from the ranks of London cabmen and warned to leave London."

"Thank you, Mr. Flinders. The cabman Tugman noted Miss Jackson was a nursing student and probably didn't know her way around London. He took her on an hour-long ride, causing her to miss curfew. Are you satisfied, Matron?"

"Well, I, I never thought of such an occurrence."

"I trust she will be reinstated," Holmes said.

"I am not sure of the protocol –"

"Then refresh your memory, Matron. My husband was a patron of the hospital," her ladyship said. "Mr. Holmes, you have explained the circumstances of his lordship's death but you have not yet told us who the thief-murderer is."

"Haven't I, your ladyship? The window in his lordship's room was closed according to two witnesses and then when the police arrived, it was open. Isn't it evident to everyone?" He looked around the room.

I had my suspicion and I suspected Lestrade did as well. I was loathe to accuse another doctor but I didn't have to.

"Dr. Vincent," a voice said.

Mr. Biggers. I wondered what he was doing here.

"I did not. I swore an oath to do no harm as a doctor," Dr. Vincent said with a great show of indignation.

"That might carry more weight if you were a doctor. I suspect you never finished a course of study because you were forced to leave, possibly St. Bartholomew's and you've been killing doctors connected to that institution and now have started on the patrons of the hospital."

"You have no proof of that."

"I don't but Mr. Biggers does."

"A dustman. What does he know of the matter?" Scorn curled the doctor's lip.

Mr. Biggers stood up looking even more like a dustman than before. I suspected Holmes had told him to exaggerate his appearance. "Mr. 'Olmes asted me dis morning' to take the route where ta doctor 'as 'is practice. I swapped wif me mate and imagine if you will wot Oi found in me sifter from the rubbish at the doctor's place." He looked around the room, then opened his hand to disclose a green poison bottle, the raised skull and crossbones clearly visible across the room.

"I suspect a thorough examination of Dr. Reeve's cellar will reveal a recent grave. And of Dr. Vincent's practice in Yorkshire where according to local police, the door has a closed-until-further-notice sign on it. When the cellar is checked, I fear we'll find the real Dr. Vincent."

The doctor jumped up and pulled a gun from his bag. "Don't move," he snarled as he backed toward the door. The weapon appeared to be a Colt six-shooter.

With the Colt trained on us, he reached back with his left hand and opened the door.

Before he could exit the room a vase crashed onto his head. The doctor went down without firing a shot. I relieved him of the Colt. "Excellent aim, Wilson."

"Thank you, sir. I was hoping to get the chance to do that. Something about that fellow rubbed me the wrong way."

"Butlers are excellent judges of character," Holmes said, overlooking Wilson's snobbish judgment of us.

"Why did he drag it out making his lordship suffer? He was a kind man."

"Vincent intended to murder him that first night but changed his plans when Lady Despard opened the safe to put away the signet ring. He discovered what riches were at hand. He needed to keep his patient unconscious until he could open the safe."

Wilson shook his head in disgust.

"What put you on to the doctor?" I said over one of Mrs. Hudson's scones

"Two things. The open window. The doctor thought the confusion would obscure who did that. And the ring. Why a simple gold ring?"

"Because it was the only piece easily linked to the victim."

Holmes cut a piece of ginger cake. "By now, the fake doctor believed he was actually a doctor. He made a mistake in refusing to see young Bobby."

"That was Vincent?"

"Yes. I suspected him early on after Mary confirmed Dr. Reeve was the Firmans' doctor. Why wouldn't he see Bobby? I also suspected Vincent was the waiter at the Lusio Club who put something in Despard's food to make him sick. Lestrade believes St. Barts' dismissed him. Something to do with theft. Scotland Yard is still collecting information but as many as ten doctors connected with Barts may have been murdered. He posed as a patient and emerged as the doctor with the victim's identity. Despard was the first of the patrons."

"An ugly case."

"Most murders are."

"Most aren't done by masquerading doctors."

"No but they're often done by people who want to blame others for their flawed characters. Vincent outsmarted himself by opening the window and planting the ring. If Miss Allman had no accomplice, why was the window open? And why would she keep the one piece that could tie her to his lordship?"

Downstairs the knocker banged briskly and Mrs. Hudson announced Mr. Biggers.

"I'm 'ere ta pay me debt."

"Nonsense. I didn't get your purse back for you. The fee doesn't exist. Anyway, you repaid me by finding that bottle."

"Tea?" I offered.

"Don't mind if I do."

I poured him a cup and filled a plate with everything on offer which was handsome indeed to make up for the luncheon we missed. I wagered Biggers missed his as well.

"That were a lucrative street you put me on to, Mr. 'Olmes. Oi found some pricey brass pieces h'and a noice vase. Ere's yer 'alf crown."

Holmes slipped the coin into his waistcoat pocket.

"Oi got me purse back, too. "

"How did you do that?"

He ducked his head. "You should know, Mr. 'Olmes."

"I do, indeed. You and your best mates waylaid the culprit that night and retrieved what was left of your purse."

"Hit were mostly there. That Johnna dolly got her cut and Hawley, no doubt."

"Have you not heard? The police closed down Hawley's not long after your visit," I said.

"Did you do that, Mr. 'Olmes?"

"I put in a word at the Yard. Johnna will not be fleecing anyone for awhile. Nor your former mate."

"You got your money back," I said after Biggers departed.

"I did, indeed. We can return somewhat to the way life was before the murder. Miss Jackson is back in her nursing classes. Lady Despard's valuables were returned though her situation is greatly changed. Lestrade's case was solved. Little Bobby's wrist is healing."

"And a vile murderer was caught. Did you receive remuneration for this case? Let me guess. Goodwill from Barts."

"No doubt."

"Credit for the solution?"

"Well-"

The downstairs doorknocker sounded again. Mrs. Hudson announced Wilson bringing a packet from Lady Despard. He was persuaded to stay for a brandy and was a most engaging fellow away from his butlering duties.

"Do you plan to open it this week?" I nodded at the packet still lying unopened on the table after Wilson took his leave.

"I already know its contents."

"And they are?"

"A flowery letter and a cheque."

"How can you be so sure?"

"Open it."

I did. He was correct. The letter was written on thick cream paper with a crest on it. "How did you know?"

"The clues are always there, Watson. You merely have to look for them. If Lady Despard were only writing a note of thanks, she would've posted it or had a footman deliver it. She sent her butler which meant something more was in the packet."

"Another surprise?"

"Not entirely. She was not my client and owed me nothing but she benefited from my solving the crime. The family will now be free of rumour and innuendo."

"I meant the butler. Who would've guessed at his affability?"

"Ah. The butler. He gained fame as the butler who bashed the murderer. A hero in the butler's club. When he retires he can write his memoirs."

The way to gain fame for Holmes's exploits lit a flame in my brain. That night I sat down and wrote the first story of the world's first consulting detective.

***

The Vampire Matter

The weather that October was most peculiar with cold gale force winds in the middle of the month followed by cyclonic winds and abnormally high tides on the west coast of England. "I see the Great Western Railroad Tunnel was flooded in that six-foot wall of water up the Severn," I said.

Holmes made no reply. I looked up from the newspaper. "Holmes, did you hear me?"

Still no reply. He stood by the window, intent on something in the street below our shared sitting room on Baker Street where I dwelt recuperating after my return from Maiwand over two years ago. I still felt the effects of my battle wounds but they were fewer now and my invalid's pension would soon end. I needed to think about opening a medical practice of my own instead of working temporarily as a locum for doctors who are called away.

Before I could speak again, Holmes said, "I heard you and flooding in a tunnel so close to the mouth of a river governed by tides is not unexpected but perhaps can be overcome with better engineering. I am watching Lestrade on his way to our door and wondering what brings him here so early in the morning."

It was not early to some at half nine, I started to say when the doorknocker sounded downstairs. Holmes moved to the fireplace as the Scotland Yard inspector saw himself up the stairs, knocked and entered. Holmes and I worked on a few cases with Greg Lestrade, a sallow, ferret-faced man of medium height and dogged intent.

"Good morning, Inspector. Sit you down. What can we do for you on this raw morning?" Holmes leaned an elbow on the mantel. I folded my paper and put it aside but remained seated.

Lestrade had been here often enough to know not to take Holmes' chair though it was currently unoccupied. He pulled up a cushioned wicker one just as Mrs. Hudson entered with a coffee pot and tray of cups.

"You'll be catching your death in that wind," she said in explanation, "and 'tis almost elevenses."

"Excellent, Mrs. Hudson, and I see you've brought some of your tasty biscuits, as well. I've been up since before dawn and though I breakfasted at home this will be most welcome," Lestrade said.

She set the tray on the table and with a smile left us to help ourselves.

"To what do we owe this visit?" Holmes said, stirring his coffee.

"It is assuredly not social." Lestrade tightened his lips in distaste. "I've been tasked with engaging the two of you on a case that is probably not a case but because of the terror involved must be dealt with."

I looked up as I reached for a biscuit. "Terror?"

"What, I wonder, could be so dire?" Holmes said.

"What do you know about vampires?" Lestrade asked with a perfectly straight face.

"What!" Holmes's laughter coincided with a swallow of coffee. Both exploded out of him.

While he mopped up the damage with one of Mrs. Hudson's napkins, I answered for him, "Some bats are actually blood-sucking vampires. Three species living in the Americas feed on the blood of animals. At times they may also bite humans if no animals are around. Their bites are not painful but they can carry rabies which results in death."

Holmes finished his mopping up and laid down the napkin. "I trust there is more to this fascinating subject that relates to our isle than South American fruit bats."

"Indeed. What do you know of human vampires?" Lestrade said.

"Stories of vampires have been around since the thirteenth century but they are tales, no more," Holmes said.

"Indeed they are," Lestrade said, "but unfortunately people tend to believe in them. There's been an outbreak of vampire accusations near the Welsh border. A farm family believes the deaths of two daughters were due to vampire activity and now the village believes it is spreading. The local constabulary can do nothing to stop it and, in fact, may actually believe it himself. We've been asked to send someone to staunch the flow. Scotland Yard wishes to engage your services in getting to the bottom of this matter and who better than you Holmes, backed up by a medical man?"

Holmes raised a quizzical eyebrow at me. "What do you say, Watson? A little westerly excursion?"

"How can I resist?"

"I thought you might see it that way." Lestrade pulled a folder with railway tickets peeking out of the top and handed them to Holmes. "If you hurry you can make the 11:05 to Bristol. Your destination is Hiselton near the Welsh border."

I was already on my feet and moving to pack my grip as Lestrade took his leave. I suspected I would need my medical bag as well though not much could be done for rabies victims beyond trying to relieve their anxieties and make them comfortable.

Within the hour we were ensconced in a compartment enjoying the lunch Mrs. Hudson hurriedly made up for us as the train headed out of Waterloo Station toward Bristol where we changed for the spur line to the village of Hiselton.

As we exited the Hiselton station, a knot of men roared at something in the high street. Holmes dropped his grip and broke into a run. "Hurry, Watson, we need to save a life."

Two men held the arms of a frightened young woman while others pushed at her and snatched at her. One produced a rope while others shouted, "Over here! Drag her over here! Keeton's got a rope! Let's 'ang 'er!"

I dropped my grip but held onto my medical bag in case it was needed. With my free hand I removed my revolver from my pocket. Holmes had his out as well and as soon as we were close enough to see what the fracas was about, he let off a shot into the street away from the brawlers but close enough to give them pause.

The sound slowed those holding the girl I now saw more clearly, a slip of a girl. I brandished my pistol but didn't waste a shot unless needed. Those on the far side edged away from the men holding the girl as they discerned we were both armed with revolvers and meant to use them.

"You, men, let go of the girl. What do you think she has done?" Holmes snapped out in a curt tone.

"She be a vampire," one of them growled.

"What's your name?" Holmes asked, training his revolver on the man.

"I be Varney, sir." He let go of the girl. The other man did the same and moved backward into the thinning crowd behind him.

"Who be you?" Varney asked.

"I am Sherlock Holmes, sent by Scotland Yard to prevent just what you were about to do. What is wrong with you?"

"This gurrl is a vampire, sir," Varney said but he seemed less certain and stood with his arms by his sides. "She kilt the Owens daughters."

The other men stepped closer to him, braver now that they'd been reminded of the girl's crime.

"And how did she do that, pray tell?"

"Sucked their blood out."

"Sucked 'em dry."

"Til they died."

"Where is your constable?" I asked authoritatively to remind them I backed Holmes.

"He's out looking at some sheep sucked dry last night."

"And you think this girl killed the sheep?" Holmes asked.

"Maybe not her but some of her vampires."

"They's a nest 'a them close by."

"They sucks everything dry, then they moves on."

"Ta tha next victims."

The speakers kept their distance but one burly rough took the girl's arm.

"Watson, the girl."

While Holmes held his revolver on the quietened mob, I put down my medical bag and reached for the girl's arm. I could feel her shaking as I drew her away from the man holding her other arm. He stuck his chin out and tightened his hold but when I pointed my revolver at him, he let go and stepped back. The men waited to see what would happen next. I thought they were thoroughly cowed by the might of our weaponry but one cannot turn one's back on a mob. Slowly we backed away toward our grips left in the street. Holmes picked up my medical bag as I had the girl in one hand and my revolver in the other.

"You're safe with us," Holmes said in a low voice. "My friend is a doctor. We'll take you to safety. Where is the inn?"

"Up there." She nodded her head at the street opposite the mob.

"Turn around and take the girl to the inn," Holmes said to me. "I'll follow with my revolver trained on the street."

"I don't think they'll go against two revolvers," I said. "They may be stupid but they appear to lack a death wish."

"Watson, your humour amazes me."

We backed slowly, stopping only to pick up our grips. We passed several mercantile establishments albeit small until we reached the Holly Man Inn with its sign of a spirited man wearing a crown of berried holly swinging in the wind. We entered the porch of the ivied grey stone inn at the same time another man rushed up and embraced the girl. "Ivy, m'girl, they sent me on a fool's errand. They said Muggins was broke down with the shipment of mash on the Bristol road but he warn't."

"I'm safe, Uncle Will, thanks to these two gentlemen." Ivy smoothed her green cloak pulled awry by the mob.

The man noticed us and our still-drawn revolvers. "I thank you for being here to save my niece. Who are you gentlemen?"

"I am Sherlock Holmes and this is Dr. Watson. We were sent by Scotland Yard to look into matters in Hiselton."

"And a good thing we arrived when we did. Those scoundrels were about to hang this young lady." I returned my gun to my pocket, the better to handle my bags but Holmes kept his in evidence.

"Come in, come in and tell me. I'm William Cole. Welcome to my inn."

"You should have a reservation for us made by the Yard," Holmes said.

"Indeed I do. Received a telegram early this morning."

Holmes gave me a look. I knew what it meant. Lestrade had been sure we would accept.

Innkeeper Cole pulled pints for us as Ivy told him what happened.

"I was just crossing the street, Uncle Will, when two men grabbed me and the street filled up with them yelling in my face. They said I was a vampire sucking blood from their families. I never sucked any blood 'cept a pricked finger. I don't even like black pudding, I don't."

"Why do you think the men focused on you?" Holmes asked.

Mr. Cole answered for her. "She's not from here. She were my late sister's niece by marriage. Got no family left. She came in the summer to live and work at the inn."

"I didn't have nowhere to go but the workhouse or the streets." She looked ready to cry. I felt around for my handkerchief but she pulled herself together. "An' I look different."

Indeed she did with those green eyes and red-gold curls held back by a green kerchief.

"I'm not staying here with these people," she declared.

"Where will you go?" I asked.

"I been walking out with a lad who bicycles over from Wales. He has a two-hundred acre farm, free and clear. Why do they think I'm a vampire?"

Holmes raised his eyebrows. "To the village you're a stranger and you have those remarkable green eyes and brilliant hair, all reasons for the mob's behavior but what started them off?"

"Someone in the mob mentioned a sheep killed by vampires. Said that's where the constable was," I said.

"A ruse to get him out of town just as Muggins' accident was. It wasn't a spur of the moment act but a pre-planned one," Holmes said.

"What do we do now?" Cole asked.

"First, Ivy you must not leave the inn until this is resolved. Next, we shall await the return of the constable," Holmes said.

"People are edgy hereabouts," Cole said.

"Indeed," Holmes said. "And why is that?"

"Bad weather. Wet fields. Poor crops. It will be a hard winter without enough food. They need something to blame."

"Or somebody," I said.

We signed the register and followed Cole up to our rooms while Ivy went to the kitchen to prepare a meal which proved to be excellent. Holmes was already at table when I joined him.

"What are our plans?" I asked as we enjoyed brandy by the inn fire.

"We're here to stop anything from happening as we did on arrival."

"Any clues to what we're to expect?"

"Today's attack on Ivy, we hope, will be the worst. With Scotland Yard here, it's doubtful they'll try again but we must remain wary. I've told Cole to lock up the inn early tonight and Ivy to remain in her room until morning."

"I'll sleep with my revolver at hand." I wasn't sure I would sleep at all. I was still feeling the effects of fighting for a life though only with words this time. With revolvers to back up the words, I felt the rush one gets in battle where only luck will keep one alive. Luck was here today for Ivy but what about later? We needed to get to the heart of the matter.

Ivy seemed to be less terrified in the morning light as she served us breakfast. A brave pink ribbon held back her glowing curls. "Will there be anything else, sirs?"

"That will be all," Holmes said.

She lingered as if undecided about a matter then pulled an envelope from her apron pocket. "Would it be safe for me to post this now?"

Holmes looked at me. I didn't think the miscreants would be as brave early in the morning knowing we were both armed but one can't be too careful with another's life. I shook my head slightly.

"If you wait until we finish our breakfast, we'll escort you to the post office and back," Holmes told her as he buttered his toast.

"Meet us at the door at half-eight," I said, scooping marmalade onto my toast.

"Oh, thank you, sirs." She skipped back to the kitchen as if we had removed a load of firewood from her shoulders.

"Whom do you think she has written to?" I said.

"Oh her young man, no doubt. The lad with the bicycle and the farm."

Holmes was proven right when Ivy met us at the door. She'd removed her apron and wore an old grey kerchief and cape of the same shade. Her green one from yesterday was, no doubt, damaged by the mob. She walked between us holding her letter with both hands as if it were fragile.

"It's to my friend in Wales. His farm isn't that far away but it's over the border. I wasn't sure how to spell vampire. Is it pier or pire?"

"Which did you use?" Holmes asked.

"P-i-r-e."

"You are correct."

"Thank you. I didn't want Sam to think I didn't learn my lessons in school. He wouldn't want – well he reads books."

"What is Sam's surname?" Holmes asked.

"Surname?"

"Sam what?" I said.

"Jones. Samuel Jones. It's from the Bible."

The day was brisk and I tightened the wool scarf Mrs. Hudson knit for me last Christmas. 'Blue to match your eyes,' she said. Holmes's was navy.

"Good morning, Mrs. Crumley. Stamps, please for my letter," Ivy said.

The postmistress peered over her spectacles and raised an eyebrow as if Ivy shouldn't be posting a letter. Her gray-brown hair was gathered in a tight bun on the back of her head. She wore a knitted mustard checked shawl over her ample figure.

"Indeed." She took the letter and weighed it. "That'll be four pence. It will."

"That much? I only have two."

Disappointment weighted Ivy's shoulders and she looked about to cry.

With a percussive sound as loud as a shot, Holmes slapped a tuppence onto the counter as I reached for my pocket.

"I trust the mail will go quite soon without delay. " He raised his eyebrows at the postmistress.

"As soon as it ever does." Mrs. Crumley stared back at him.

He took Ivy's arm. "Come, my dear," and they swept out of the shop. I followed but at the door I turned and saw Mrs. Crumley hold the letter up to the light to look at the address.

On the street a few passersby either stared at the three of us or turned away in seeming disgust or perhaps fear. Holmes patted Ivy's hand tucked into the crook of his arm. "Ignorant fools," he said.

I don't know if any heard him but he wouldn't care if they did. Holmes didn't suffer malignant fools well. Nor did I but as a doctor, I tried to be more understanding of their fears and reactive behavior.

We returned Ivy to the safety of the inn and left for the Owens farm which was within easy walking distance. "Bring your medical bag," Holmes reminded me. "It may be needed."

The dark stone houses of Hiselton seemed to huddle unusually close together as if for protection against something unknown. Perhaps that image was too fanciful but it seemed to fit the village today. Above us in the opposite direction, a fine manor built of Portland stone looked down on the high street and I wondered what, if any, interaction existed between them and the local people beyond work.

Our brisk pace soon brought us to a crooked lane. A wobbly sign hung from a cross-piece between two posts told us we'd reached Mere Farm. "Mere indeed. It could mean a small farm but I think in this case it means shallow pond or wetland," Holmes said.

The road bed had been raised by some means until it was almost a bridge though unlike a bridge it was solid underneath with soggy land on each side of us. A thin, disconsolate cow slowly ate something brown on this late October day. "That soggy field is bad for its feet," I said.

Around another turn, a few shorn sheep huddled in a clearing. They stared balefully at us.

"Late shearing," Holmes said. "They may not make it through the winter."

Dark trees blocked sunlight save at high noon. "I think I would cut some of these trees and let light in here."

"You would and I would," Holmes said, "but perhaps there are reasons for leaving them. They certainly give privacy to the family living here."

"Farm families I'm familiar with welcome visitors and neighbors but I suppose the trees allow blockage from winter winds."

"Always looking for the best, Watson. Admirable of you."

"More likely hopeful," I said but Holmes stepped up his pace and was now at the door of a dismal grey house with wispy grey smoke emitting from a single chimney. A few chickens scratched around in the dirt. The remains of a kitchen garden lay on one side of the house and behind it a field of late corn seemed to shiver in the wind.

Holmes rapped on the front door without reply. He knocked again. We heard some muffled noises within and suddenly the door was flung open. A cadaverous man stood there.

"Mr. Owens?" Holmes asked. "Charles Owens?"

"That's right. Who be ye?"

Holmes introduced himself and me. "We've come to speak to you about the loss of your two daughters. May we come in?"

My heart sank. I didn't want to go inside that close, dark house where the family huddled around a smoky fire. I'd no need to examine this couple to diagnose them but I went through the act so they would understand me when I told them their fate. I started with Mrs. Owens, a thin pinched-faced woman in a grey woolen dress wrapped in a voluminous brown shawl. I bade her to remain seated and took her temperature. As expected, it was above normal. I listened to her heart and looked at her throat. I was just finishing with her husband with the same dire results when a young woman came in from the back door carrying a basket of eggs.

"This is my niece Nell. She come ta help my wife with the chores after our last daughter was kilt by that vampire."

"How long was that?" Holmes asked.

"Vinnie died in the spring. Josie died in late summer. 'Bout three month it is now."

His wife nodded and wiped away a tear.

"Why do you think vampires killed your daughters?" Holmes asked.

"Stands to reason, don't it?" Mr. Owens said. "They was pale as snow from vampires sucking out their blood."

"Did you see actual puncture marks?" I asked.

Mr. Owens nodded. "I did."

"What did these marks look like?" Holmes asked.

"Like somebody poked holes in their necks." Mr. Owens nodded again but Mrs. Owens looked away.

"Did anyone else see them?' Holmes persisted. "A doctor. The minister. The constable?"

"No, nobody but they was there. I saw them," Mr. Owens insisted.

I examined Nell and to my great joy, she seemed healthy. Perhaps she had a chance.

"Nell must return home this very day," I said. "Bring only what you can carry and leave the rest. You must go now. We'll help you find transportation."

"But she ain't been here a month," Mrs. Owens protested as Nell gave us a frightened look and ran up the stairs.

"Mr. and Mrs. Owens, I am sorry to give you such grave news. You both have tuberculosis. Consumption. That's what caused the deaths of your daughters, not vampires. Nell seems to be free of it if she leaves now."

They stared blankly at me. "No," Mr. Owens said. "They was kilt by vampires."

"No vampires," Holmes said.

I nodded in agreement. "My advice is to sell your place and go live on the southwest coast where winters are milder and the sea air will invigorate you."

"Does that mean it will cure us?" Mrs. Owens asked, hope trembling in her voice.

"Sea air can work wonders," I said, not wishing to commit myself as to their fate.

"How did we catch it?" Mrs. Owens asked.

"Likely from the animals. They'll have to be destroyed. I'll inform the constable. The money realized from the land sale should keep you comfortably for a long time. Until this can be done, I advise you not to eat any food from your animals. They likely are carriers of the disease."

"Not no vampires?" Mr. Owens asked as if it were better to be bitten by a mythical creature than attacked by microbes.

Nell returned with a cloth bag of her things. She donned a blue cloak hung on a peg by the door and we left the Owens to discuss their arrangements. Nell had questions about the illness and I answered them as we walked.

"There's no cure?"

"None that I know of and I keep abreast of medical matters. You show no symptoms of it but stay away from close contact with people for a month."

"Not even church?"

"Especially not church. Eat fresh vegetables, walk in the sunshine and you should remain healthy."

I directed her to wash all of her clothing when she reached her home and dry it on the clothesline and to take a bath herself.

"But it's only Wednesday."

"Nevertheless, you need to do this so you won't bring infection home to your family. Take your meals alone, outside as much as you can and keep your distance from everyone."

At the inn I bade us all to wash our hands thoroughly at the outside pump using carbolic soap from my bag and I gave her a cake to take with her. I arranged for a meal to be brought to her outside where a small table and stool were set up in an alcove between buildings and then to return home. We would inquire about conveyances but she said it was an easy walk of five miles. She would be there long before suppertime.

After we'd eaten, I said, "Well, this vampire business has been put to rest. I'm certain none of the Owens(') daughters were bitten by a vampire. The parents are most definitely in some stage of

160

tuberculosis and I'm certain that's what killed the daughters. No need for us to remain here."

"No, but we've missed the last train to Bristol. And Ivy will be safer with us at the inn until her young man comes."

"You think she's in danger then?"

"People may prefer to believe in vampires before disease."

"The tuberculin bacillus was proved by Robert Koch last year but there are still those who believe evil spirits must be driven from the house at midnight on New Year's Eve by the banging of spoons on pots."

"Koch doesn't believe human and bovine tuberculosis are the same disease. I noticed you do," Holmes said, extracting a cigar from his vest pocket."

"I have examined the bacillus myself from sheep, cows, and humans. I see no difference." I took out my own cigar and lit it from a spill on the mantelshelf, passing it to Holmes.

We stood smoking in front of the fire. I had the feeling Holmes was waiting for something to happen. I noticed he'd left his stick leaning against the fireplace. We'd not long to wait. The inn door burst open, kicked by a bulky man who could've passed for a blacksmith. Two lesser men accompanied him. Through the window I saw a knot of others, likely the same ones we'd met yesterday.

"Where is she?" he demanded in a booming voice.

"She's not here, Lunk. Leave my premises," Mr. Cole said, managing not to quaver.

"We don't b'lieve you. Men, search the inn."

Holmes stepped forward. "Did you not hear the innkeeper? He said she is not here."

As Lunk reached for Holmes, he received a thump from Holmes' stick. I'd not seen him reach for it. Holmes could be as fast as a striking snake. "Mr. Cole asked you to leave. I suggest you do so," Holmes said raising his stick.

"You –" he lunged for Holmes who suddenly wasn't there but a policeman's baton was and it delivered a harder blow than a stick. A uniformed constable took Lunk's arm and led him to the door. "Lunk, he's from Scotland Yard. Do you want police swarming all over the place? Now go on home and sleep it off. The rest of you disperse. I don't want to hear any more of this vampire stuff. The Owens' daughters were not killed by vampires. I'm not telling you again. The next to cause trouble will be locked up. Now get yourselves along about your business."

The constable introduced himself when he returned from dispersing the men. "George Freeman." He joined us for a cup of tea and a cigar from Holmes. "These are hard-headed men."

"Many work at difficult jobs which do not require them to think," Holmes said. "If they did think, they probably couldn't continue doing what they do. Too often they have to be shown."

"Why didn't you pull your revolver?" I asked Holmes.

"I didn't want to put bullet holes in the inn."

"Where's the girl?" Freeman asked.

"I sent her to our rooms with instructions to stay there with the door locked." Holmes drew on his cigar as the constable lit his. He was a youngish man still in his twenties, stocky, of medium height with dark brown eyes and thick sandy hair.

We told him of our visit to the Owens farm. He shook his head. Hiselton had taught him much about the vagaries of men already.

Cole joined us. "Will you be wanting to exhume the Owens girls to prove they were not killed by vampires?"

"That may be complicated," Holmes said. "I didn't bring it up with the Owenses. They had enough to deal with this day. The order will have to come through the Ministry of Justice. The parents will have to agree to it and the burial authority as well. We may not need to resort to that but I'll start the process with a telegram to Scotland Yard."

"You gentlemen leaving tomorrow?"

"We shall see," Holmes said.

"We hope Ivy's young man will come for her by then," I said. "With her hair color and being a stranger to the town, she is a perfect target to explain the otherwise unexplainable deaths of the Owens sisters so close together."

"Men have long assigned a supernatural reason for the invisible cause of disease. So many microbes are being discovered, they are confused. They fall back on old superstitions and folk beliefs," Holmes said.

"The girls were unnaturally pale living back in those wet dark woods. Consumption would make less sense to some of the more backward villagers than death by vampire," Freeman said.

"If a woman's bread fell flat in the baking, it was easier to say an old woman put a spell on her oven than to admit she made a mistake, especially if her husband was handy with his fists," I said. "Many, both men and women, but mainly women were accused of witchcraft for causing a bad harvest, a broken bowl, or any misfortune."

"And it's easier to say a dragon ate a young woman than admit she's in the family way and left to avoid bringing dishonour onto her family," Holmes said.

"This is not the first time Hiselton has had a case like that. It was before my time but the girl, a maid at the manor didn't run away. She was shunned for awhile but managed to marry, I believe," Freeman said.

"The groom, a pig farmer, as rough and crude fellow as you'll ever meet was no bargain but she remained in the village," Cole took over the narrative.

"What happened to them?" I asked, curious.

"The maid died in childbirth a few years later. The boy was raised by his stepmother until the father died. Joe Tilley was his name. She left Hiselton with the boy. Later I heard she married a naval man in Chepstow."

"What happened to the son?" I asked.

"I don't know. Most likely he went to sea with his stepfather," Cole said.

Freeman stood up with reluctance. "I thank you gentlemen for the tea and for your help in diagnosing the killer of those two young women. I will see the animals are put down at the Owens farm and urge them to sell out and retire to the seaside on your orders, Doctor."

"Good luck with that," Holmes said.

We walked to the train station for Holmes to send a telegram to Lestrade, starting the process for exhumation.

After a hearty dinner, we finished our evening with a cigar and a brandy. The taproom held a few men but none were recognizable from the afternoon's. Holmes and I retired early to get a start in the morning.

We were awakened before dawn by screams in the street and a hammering on Holmes's door and mine. "Mr. Holmes! Dr. Watson!"

I pulled on my dressing gown, stepped into my slippers, and grabbed my Adams before I opened the door. Holmes was already in the hall talking to Mr. Cole.

"She's not here," Holmes said, "nor in the Doctor's room either."

I nodded.

"She's gone. Ivy's gone and there's a mob out there."

"Did you look in her room," Holmes asked him.

"Yes, I assumed she was hidden with one of you gentlemen."

"We told her to lock herself in her room after supper was served and if anyone tried to get in, she should pile furniture in front of the door," I said.

"What's happening in the street?" Holmes asked.

"I don't know. My first concern was for Ivy. I unlocked her door and her bed hadn't been slept in. I came straight up here."

He turned and ran down the stairs with us behind him. Ivy's door was open and her room was empty. "She's gone. They've taken her out the window."

"Not necessarily. Did you hear anything?" Holmes said.

"No."

"The mob didn't come after her then. Those men are not capable of stealth. You found her door locked without evidence of interference. No furniture is lying around. Her clothes seem to be missing and personal things as well," Holmes said. "She may have left with her young man."

"But she only mailed the letter to him yesterday," I said.

"Nevertheless, he may have heard of the troubles in Hiselton from someone passing and come for her," Holmes said. "Now I think we need to find the cause of that screaming."

The front door of the inn was barred for the night. Cole opened it and we looked out into the street. A pale sun appeared almost over the tops of trees and houses, sending watery light into the street. A few people stood about looking at something lying in the middle of the road bed almost in the same spot where we rescued Ivy from the day before.

Unmindful of our dress with only Mr. Cole in trousers, we moved closer, peering over the shoulders of several workmen and one woman in a sunbonnet, a basket of laundry over her arm. "It's that vampire," she said. "That same girl vampire. You should've hung her yestiddy." She turned around and saw us. "You kilt this man, you did."

"What makes you think this man was killed by a vampire?" Holmes asked in a reasonable tone.

"He ain't got no blood."

"Let me see." I tried to break through but the men around the body pushed back

"Let him through," Holmes said. "He's a doctor."

"He don't look like no doctor."

"He's in his nightclothes," Cole said.

The crowd parted and I knelt to examine the body. The man lay on his stomach. I turned him over. The crowd gasped.

His neck once, no doubt, ruddy now was as white as paper as were his face and what I could see of his arms and hands. Twin puncture marks on the side of his neck where the carotid artery lies seemed to be where the blood drained out.

"He was killed elsewhere and brought here for display," Holmes said and I nodded.

"How you know that?" someone said.

"If he'd been killed here some blood would be visible," I said. "The average human body circulates nearly five litres of blood."

"The vampire done kilt him here," the woman insisted. "Sucked all his blood out with his fangs."

"Nonsense," Holmes said. "Look at the wheel tracks on each side of the body. He was pulled out of a cart which continued along the street. The tracks are slightly deeper on one side than the other." Holmes followed the tracks in the dirt of the high street. He returned within minutes and reported the tracks disappeared into a patch of woods at the edge of the village.

Constable Freeman joined us along with other villagers. "What do we have?"

"We got ourselves a real vampire. Not no consumption like that doc said." the woman thrust her chin toward me. Her eyes were close together in a face no longer young but probably not as old as it looked.

"Let's go get that vampire," a young man said and, as if he released the doors to a chute, the crowd rushed to the inn.

"Stop them, Freeman!" Cole said as he ran after the dozen or more led by the stocky man.

"It's all right," Holmes said. "They won't find her."

"Where is she?" the constable asked.

"She left in the night," Holmes said.

"Let's move the body out of the street," I said. "I need to examine him further."

"Do you know his identity?" Holmes asked.

"Yes, he's a farm worker. Drifts around where he can earn a little to keep him in drink and a bed. Old Billy Bates. He doesn't have any family here. If he has any somewhere else, I don't know where to find them. He's been staying at the Marsden place."

Freeman assigned four men to carry the body to the doctor's office on the side of his stone house facing the inn. Dr. Peters was finishing his breakfast, reminding me we'd had none, not even tea and were still in our nightclothes. Freeman explained what happened including the charge of vampirism. Peters snorted at that and took his time drinking the last of his coffee after offering us a cup. We declined reluctantly as we hoped that would speed up the examination of the dead man. He took two final gulps and stood up. "Now what do you have for me? A murder, you say? Surely not in Hiselton."

We entered his surgery. I was pleased to see his instruments were steel-handled instead of the bone or wood many doctors still clung to despite Dr. Lister's proof of the adherence of microbes.

One glance at the body and the doctor was in no doubt as to the way Bates had entered his present state. "Bled out," he said.

We needed to know how. None of us accepted the vampire theory.

On removal of his clothes, we discovered Bates was stabbed in the back. His shirt, however, was intact without even a tear. "He must've been hung up to get the blood to drain out of the stab wound," Peterson said.

"Not the most efficient way to do it," I said. "It must've taken a long time without the help of a pumping heart."

"Someone wanted us to think he had been sucked dry by vampires. They went to pains to hide the stab wound perhaps thinking it wouldn't be seen. He was redressed in an undamaged shirt after the blood drained out," Holmes said.

"What about the fang marks?" the constable asked.

"Added after the body had drained," I said.

"Looks that way," Peterson agreed.

"Constable, go to the inn and bring the mob here to see for themselves the cause of death," Holmes said.

"Did you attend to the Owens daughters during their last illnesses?" I asked as we waited.

"No, I've only been here since early September. I came as a favor to the Uffingtons at Severna Manor. They're trying to find a young doctor to locate here. I was in the process of winding down and closing my practice in Bristol to take a professorship at Exeter."

I nodded. Exeter was a new arts and sciences university open only thirty-two years. Peters could shape the curriculum to more acceptable beliefs. No more filthy surgical aprons used over and over without washing. No more germ-bearing instruments or unwashed hands.

We heard the mob before we saw it. They filed around the table and quieted at the sight of the undressed man with the stab wound in his back. Someone had plunged the knife in deeply, most likely into a body inert from drink or dosed with laudanum. "This is what killed Mr. Bates," Dr. Peters said. "No vampires were involved."

The constable pointed to the gash. "He was stabbed here."

"And this is the place of exsanguination," I added.

"What's that mean?" one of the men asked.

"It means the place where the blood drained out of the man after death," I said. "When he was stabbed, his heart stopped pumping. The blood stopped flowing. The body was probably hung to let gravity finish the job after death. Then it was cleaned, redressed, and the puncture marks were made in his neck to make you believe a vampire had done it."

"Somebody kilt old Billy."

"It were a vampire done it," the woman said. Mary Putney who took in laundry and sewing, the constable told us later. "Why else would it have holes in the neck?"

"To fool you," the constable said.

"Humpf. Cain't fool me," she said.

"So folk'd think it was vampires?" one of the men said.

"That is correct," Dr. Peters said.

The crowd seemed mollified at that point except perhaps for the laundress who still shook her head, insisting it was vampires. Holmes and I left the constable in charge and returned to the inn with Cole. "Will you be going back to London today?"

"No," Holmes replied for us. "This vampire business has taken a new turn. It is no longer necessary to get that exhumation order. A genuine murderer is responsible for that poor man's death."

When we were dressed and breakfasted, Holmes went to the train station to send a telegram to Lestrade and a few others. Freeman sent one to Bristol as well but the constabulary there decided to let the representative from Scotland Yard continue to handle vampire matters with the local constable. Lestrade concurred with a terse reply, 'All yours'.

"It's obvious someone wanted to kill this man and went to great lengths to make it look like a vampire murder," Constable Freeman said, joining us at the inn.

"Indeed," Holmes said, "but why now? The Owens girls have been gone for several months."

"Poor harvest. Strange weather. Two close deaths in one family. They need something to blame," Freeman said.

"Dragons, witches, vampires. Take your pick," Holmes said.

"Why do people murder any time?" I said.

"Greed. Love. Money. Hate. Revenge. Someone wants something. Our job is to find out what and who. This man has lived around the village for awhile. Why would somebody wait until now to kill him?" Holmes said.

"What harm has he done to anyone?" I said.

"None that I know of," Freeman said.

"When was the last time he worked for anybody in the area?" Holmes asked.

"Let's see. He did a little harvesting, a little timber cutting, some charcoaling, some hog-killing…"

"Do you know whose hogs?" Holmes interrupted.

"That would be J.D. Marsden's hogs. He leaves after hog-killing. It were early this year because feed cost more than he wanted to pay. He's not the only hog farmer harvesting early this year. Most likely Bates was looking after the place for Marsden and staying the winter."

"We need to have a look at the place. Watson?"

Freeman stayed in town to keep an eye on things. Holmes and I followed Freeman's directions to the hog pens at the Marsden place, well out of the village. Under the killing tree we found blood too fresh to be earlier hog killing. And we found cart tracks that looked like the ones straddling the body when we found it. The tracks disappeared in the layer of leaves on the lane. Holmes measured them. "Same distance."

We reported our findings to Freeman at the inn where he was having a warming cup of tea. We joined him and I pulled out my flask to add medicinal brandy to our cups.

After a few sips, Holmes said, "This is a real murder made to resemble a vampire's feeding."

"I hope the villagers are convinced of that," I said.

"I don't see the point of it," Freeman said.

"Don't you?" Holmes raised his eyebrows.

"The murderer knows we're on to his tricks. He won't try any again." Freeman set his cup down with a clink.

"Nevertheless it might be prudent to advise the people of Hiselton to stay inside well before sundown," Holmes said.

Freeman looked worried at the thought of another murder but he left to spread the word.

Holmes checked for telegrams at the train station while I indulged in another cup of tea.

Cole hadn't seen or heard from his niece since the night before. I was concerned something dire had befallen her.

Holmes was not. "No doubt something has but that doesn't necessarily mean it's dire."

The day, as befit the village's mood, was raw and gusty with chips of ice in the wind. Holmes sat by the fire and smoked several pipes. I hoped he'd brought along enough shag to last until tomorrow. This might be a long night.

At sundown, Holmes and I took a turn around the village. The houses were shuttered against the coming night. Wind skirled and eddied around the streets catching leaves to whirl away into the dark. I burrowed into my scarf against the bitter cold and pulled my hat down. No one walked on the streets but us and a small brown dog that soon trotted around to the back of a house to take up its post for the night.

"'Tis a night fit for the undead to walk," Holmes said.

"Is that a quote?"

"No, merely an observation. Someone has gone to great lengths to set this up."

I stared at him. "Do you mean you think this has all been planned?"

"Planned, orchestrated and executed but to what means we do not yet know."

"That's terrible. If we know something is about to happen, we should…"

"What? Tell everyone in the village something is about to happen but we don't know what? Essentially we've already done that. The die is cast but only the caster knows what it will be. We've taken all possible precautions."

We turned to go back to the inn. Above the town Severna Manor glowed like a lantern. "Did anyone warn the manor house inhabitants?" I wondered.

"Freeman did. He said they have guests staying the night. Lord somebody and his family and a cousin of the Uffingtons. They were warned and agreed to keep everyone inside. We've done all we can do."

We turned in early after a supper of steak and onion pie but I found sleep difficult. I went over the events in Hiselton and finally fell asleep on the third listing.

Holmes woke me at first light. He gave no explanation. I dressed hurriedly and joined him for a quick cup of tea with Cole who looked worried. "Mr. Holmes, I fear you will find my niece…"

"Not Ivy, Mr. Cole but something bad, I suspect."

"What do you mean?" Cole wiped an invisible speck off the table.

"I mean this has all been prelude to something. Today we may find out what."

Night mist clung to shadows and hollows but the wind had dropped. We met Freeman returning from checking the north end of the village.

"All is well on this end," he said.

We accompanied him up little crooked lanes and winding streets that led to dead-end farmhouses. Smoke was beginning to emerge from chimneys as we regained the high street. Freeman turned to go back to the constabulary.

"Aren't you checking Severna Manor?" I asked him.

"No need. Nobody would bother those folk."

"I daresay a cup of tea would be welcome now but we must be thorough," Holmes said.

With a shrug of disapproval, he rejoined us as we walked south to the gates of Severna Manor.

"Severna. For the river?" I asked.

"That's right," Freeman said.

"What led to the manor being named after the river? You can't even see it from here," I said.

"A streamlet flows down the backside of the estate and runs into the Severn. It's a connection, I guess," Freeman said.

The manor slumbered behind closed gates. We could only see the top of it over the thick woods.

"Nothing here," Freeman said.

"The Uffingtons deserve the same attention the village received from us. We need to check the drive to the house," Holmes said. "Watson, your eyes are better than mine. Is that something at the curve of the drive?"

"Only in reading," I said as I peered into the darkness afforded by the trees. "It's possible something is there. We should check it."

Freeman thought we were seeing a puddle but he knocked on the gate-keeper's door.

"All right, all right, I'm a'coming'," said the elderly man, pulling up his suspenders as he opened the gatehouse door. "Constable, is it? Be they expecting you at the house?"

"Open the gate, Rucker."

We rushed past the startled man and reached the bundle. As we feared, it proved to be a body white as paper with twin puncture marks on the neck.

"Oh lordy, it be one of them ghost men kilt by a vampire." Rucker crossed himself.

"Do you recognize him?" Holmes asked Freeman.

"Yes, it's Gerald Uffington, the son of Lord Ardsley."

Rucker moaned. "I better tell the folk at the house."

"No, you fetch Dr. Peters," Holmes said. "Watson."

Cart tracks came out of the woods and straddled the body before going back the same way. We turned Gerald slightly. He was dressed in nightclothes and slippers. I pulled the robe and nightshirt up and found the stab wound that likely killed him and from which his blood had leaked but not here.

Holmes examined the drive toward the house and the frozen grass on each side until we were joined by the doctor and several men from the town stable. "Is it the same as the other?" Peters asked.

Holmes nodded. "Constable Freeman, come with us to tell the family."

Peters directed the men to move the body to his surgery.

The morning was silent and a mist clung to the great woods that ringed the manor house before opening to a vast expanse of snow-covered grass. We didn't speak on that solemn journey to tell the lord of the manor we found his son and heir murdered on his driveway.

The butler answered the door. "Yes? The trade entrance is-"

"I am Sherlock Holmes sent by Scotland Yard. This is Dr. Watson and you know Constable Freeman. We're here to see his lordship."

"Very well." He stood back and we entered the spacious hall crammed with statuary, bouquets of hothouse flowers and ceramic ware, vases and such. "May I take your coats?"

We shed our coats and gave him our hats. He led us to a small room off the hall where his lordship saw those who were not tradesmen but also not of his class. Paintings of animals hung on the wall between bookcases. An imposing mahogany desk stood at one end where his lordship could sit and receive tradesmen who stood before him in supplication.

We were not invited to sit.

"May I say what this visit is about?" the butler asked on return.

"A family matter," Holmes said.

"Very good, sir."

We'd not long to wait before his lordship joined us. He was a tall man with graying hair and moustache, and blue eyes, an older version of his son. He wore a knee-length velvet smoking robe over a loose-collared shirt and trousers hastily donned with one leg caught in his boot top. "What can I do for you?"

Holmes introduced us. His lordship nodded at the constable whom he'd met at least once before. "We have sad news to impart," Holmes said. "Your son Gerald has been found on your drive, deceased."

For a moment the man didn't react. "This is outrageous. My son Gerald is still abed. It is hardly eight of the clock. If this is a joke – constable, I shall report this."

Often the loser of a loved one will bluster or rage to keep the calamity at bay but eventually, the truth sinks in as it did with his lordship. When his anger seemed spent, I

took his arm and led him to a chair. "Holmes, some restorative, if you please."

Holmes anticipated and had the brandy at the ready from a tray on a chest against the wall.

This was a sad way to begin a day but as a doctor it was not unknown to me, nor to Holmes. Freeman was still a young man and until this week he'd never been involved in a murder case.

He had no defenses and looked as if about to cry. He may have known Gerald. They were of an age.

"Where-where is my son?"

"He is at Dr. Peters surgery."

"I want to see him."

"We'll take you to him," I said.

"We will need to speak with the people in your house later," Holmes said.

Lord Ardsley nodded as he went to the door and asked Yates the butler for his coat which he put on over his smoking robe. As we left for the doctor's surgery, Holmes instructed the butler not to tell anyone in the household of the death of Gerald Uffington.

"Very good, sir."

"How long has Yates been your butler?" Holmes asked him as we walked down the drive.

"I don't know. Six months. A year."

"How did you happen to employ him?"

"Our previous butler, Denton, died suddenly in his sleep. Yates heard about it on the butlers' grapevine and applied. He had excellent references. What's this all about? You don't suspect Yates of killing my son?"

"We suspect everybody."

"It was some riffraff living rough around the village. Find him."

"We intend to," Holmes said.

The crime followed the previous murder without exception even for the son of a lord. The victim, stabbed in the back and hoisted somewhere to bleed out, puncture marks made with an awl most likely, the body redressed in this case in night clothes and slippers and arranged in the drive to the manor not far from the gatehouse. The gate keeper heard nothing. He swore he'd slept soundly through the night until Holmes and I awoke him.

We agreed to let his lordship make arrangements for his son's funeral and return to the manor to inform his family and guests and give them time to dress and break their fast. We left him in the keeping of Freeman as we returned to the inn and informed Cole while we ate a hurried breakfast ourselves.

"Why would someone kill the young lord and an itinerant worker?" Cole asked.

"It does seem odd," I said, thinking of London murders. "From the top and bottom of society."

"Victims of a single murderer are usually of the same class or station or connected by job or family or business. It is unusual for victims of the same crime method to be so far apart in their social stations with no apparent connection but as we shall see, it makes perfect sense within the context of Hiselton." Holmes buttered the last scone. This brisk weather gave him more appetite than he usually exhibited when working on a case.

Holmes lit a morning cigar as we walked back to the pig farm. Nothing was changed since the day before except animals clawing the site of the blood from yesterday. We found no fresh blood, no wheel tracks. "They must have another staging place," Holmes muttered.

"They?"

"Certainly. These are crimes involving more than one person, possibly as many as three."

"Do you know who and why?"

"I'm close to knowing who. Why will follow but I have my suspicions." He would say no more than that but walked as if lost in thought though Holmes was seldom lost in thought or terrain. I suspected he'd received some intelligence in those telegrams he sent earlier.

A crowd gathered outside the surgery, angry and afraid. Mary Putney with her basket on her arm shouted, "That vampire done struck again!"

"It kilt the lord's son."

"Do something, Mr. Holmes," a calmer man begged.

"Something is being done," Holmes said. As we passed Mary Putney, he glanced inside her basket and turned abruptly. "Come along, Watson, we are needed at the manor."

At the edge of town, instead of continuing through the manor gate he turned and led me around to a side street where a small house of tumbled stones, was barely staying together. "Freeman said this is where Mary Putney has been living for several months."

"You think she was part of the killing?"

"I do. We need to find proof."

We walked around to the yard of what had once been a small farm and found in a collapsing shed, a cart of the right size. Holmes measured the distance between its wheels. It was the same as the one was used in Bates' murder. Holmes pushed it and the tracks looked the same as the other tracks we'd found at the pig farm and on the high street. He examined the wheels. The dirt clinging there looked like all the other dirt in this village. "It's the same cart," I said. "I'd swear to it."

"Most likely but this proves nothing. Anyone could've left the cart here."

In a disused animal pen we found fresh blood. "Again, anybody could've spilled blood here to frame a single woman," I said.

"True. Stay here. I'll get someone to come for the cart."

"Who do you think is involved besides Mary Putney?"

"I don't know their names yet." He would say no more.

Presently as arranged a lad came from the manor, a knife boy called Clem who wheeled the cart through the tradesmen's gate while we returned on the driveway. At the manor we met Freeman with Inspector Ellis and four uniformed policemen who'd just arrived on the train from Bristol. Holmes filled him in on the case until he knew as much as I knew. Holmes, no doubt knew more but didn't tell us except to say it was an elaborate scheme.

Holmes plied the door knocker shaped like a large fist. Yates opened the door. "They're waiting for you," he said. He showed us into a large drawing room gracefully appointed in rose and shades of green where the family sat in solemn sorrow, Lord and Lady Ardsley, their daughter Jane of age, and their guests, Lord and Lady Beecham, their son Percy and Lord Ardsley's cousin, Welland Combes. Welland slouched against the back of a chair and looked to my eyes somewhat hung over from drink. All wore black or grey clothing except Percy in brown. Lord Ardsley made the introductions. "You will be needing to speak to the staff?"

"Not at the moment," Holmes said. "Yates may stay. He may prove useful to answer some of my questions."

Yates took his station at the door.

"When I was asked by Scotland Yard to come here to put down the rumors of vampirism in the Owens family, the case seemed to be a simple one of ignorance, fear, and hysteria. On arrival we protected a young woman from an angry mob accusing her of vampirism. Their intention was to hang her. With her safe, we turned to the problem that brought us to Hiselton. Dr. Watson determined the cause of the deaths of the two young Owens girls to be consumption and we sent their seemingly healthy young niece back to her home.

"We thought our work finished, but we waited to hear from Scotland Yard if we needed an exhumation order to prove the Owens girls died of consumption. In the early hours the next morning, a man was found murdered with two puncture marks on his neck. He had been exsanguinated by the stab wound in his back. The victim was identified as Billy Bates, an itinerant worker who had been helping at a pig farm outside of the village and staying there for the winter as caretaker. This pig farm was once the dwelling of a man named Tilley whose wife died in childbirth. He remarried and his second wife raised his young boy. When the father died suddenly, the stepmother and son left the village after selling the pig farm. Marsden, the current owner of the farm is an absentee owner and not involved in the case.

"We realized more was going on here in Hiselton than hysteria. Yesterday Constable Freeman went to every house in the village and asked the inhabitants to go inside before sundown, lock their doors and stay there until morning. The instruction was passed to your butler, Yates." Holmes paused and looked at the butler.

"I didn't see any need to pass on the instruction," Yates said. "If anyone were to leave the house after I locked it, I would know about it."

"Of course," Holmes said, "but sometime during the night, Gerald Uffington left his room and went out into the park where, it seems, the murderers attacked him and left him in the drive to be found, another victim of the so-called vampire."

Lady Ardsley gasped and put her black-bordered handkerchief to her face. His lordship patted her hand.

"My apologies," your ladyship," Holmes said with a bow. "If you would like to leave now…"

"No, I wish to hear what happened to my son." She spoke more firmly than I suspected she felt.

"I never heard him leave," Yates said, looking miserable.

"Of course you didn't because you killed him as he lay sleeping in his bed, drugged no doubt. You and your partner carried him outside to a waiting cart and pushed him through the trade entrance to the house nearby where Mary Putney was living. You stabbed him in the back, just as Billy Bates was stabbed and the blood exited the wound. You punctured the carotid artery area, redressed him in his nightclothes, put his slippers on his feet so it would look as though he'd gone for a walk in the night and returned through the woods. You left him on the first curve of the drive where he would be seen but only barely from the gate."

"Here now, I did no such thing!" Yates shouted.

Holmes ignored him. "You forgot one thing. His slippers were new and hadn't been on his feet outside the house. They were clean. If he had walked down the wet mud of the drive where grit, rocks, and leaves would cling to the soles of the slippers the evidence would be visible there. "Constable?"

Freeman opened the parcel he had brought with him and showed the clean soles of the young lord's slippers.

"Your next mistake was to think Mary Putney wouldn't fall under suspicion. The first time I saw her, she was carrying a basket with neatly folded mending and washing in shades of red, blue, and yellow to deliver to customers. The next time I saw her, she was carrying the basket of deliveries with neatly folded garments in the same shades of red, blue, and yellow. I suspect she was the source of the vampire rumor. Constable?"

Freeman brought forth the basket with the selfsame garments neatly folded.

"Mary Putney left this behind in the house she was renting as she made her escape earlier today soon after the crime was discovered. Police are on the lookout for her. And, Yates, you and your partner made one more mistake. You left behind at the cottage the cart you used to push the two victims into place where they would be discovered and thought to be killed by vampires. The cart still has fresh blood in it. You didn't bother to try to hide it thinking Mary Putney would trundle it back to the pig farm where it would pass unnoticed as it almost was but she hadn't time for that last important part of the cover-up of this reprehensible crime."

Yates bellowed his innocence. "It was not I! Your lordship, I would never harm your son. I have no reason to harm him."

Holmes ignored him and looked at Inspector Ellis. At his nod, Holmes continued. "It was a diabolical plan. The paleness of the Owens girls may have given the killers the idea to use vampirism. Stir up fears about vampires in the villagers. Intensify it with the first murder and then commit the second important one. Gerald Uffington was your target from the beginning."

Someone in the Uffington family gasped.

"That ain't true. I had no quarrel with him. Somebody else musta done it." Yates's precise diction slipped.

"Somebody else was involved. Would you like to name him, Yates or shall I?"

"I don't know what you're talking about. This is all lies. I never murdered nobody."

"Then why were these bloody gloves left in the cart? They appear to be your butlering gloves with your initials stitched inside each one, JYT for Joseph Yates Tilley. "I checked the parish records and found a Joseph Yates Tilley born to a Mary and Joseph Tilley twenty-eight years ago. I suspect this isn't the first time you've killed, led into it by your vicious father whom you also most likely murdered from the reports by a pillow smothering him when he was drunk. That's when you and your step-mother now known as Mary Putney sold the pig farm and left the area. Was this present plan yours or your partner's?"

The room seemed to be holding its breath. Then Yates let his out. "It were his. I knew about the village and the girls dying of consumption. I met him in a bar by chance in Bristol. I recognized his name when someone called it out. We talked. He wanted to kill his cousin and inherit the entailed Severna Manor."

"And his name?" the inspector said sternly.

Yates tightened his lips and stared at the inspector.

"Constable Freeman," Inspector Ellis said.

Freeman pulled out his handcuffs and snapped them on Yates. "Joseph Yates Tilley, I'm arresting you for the murders of Billy Bates and Gerald Uffington."

"We suspect the previous butler met the same fate as your father, but two murders will be sufficient in this case," the inspector said.

"The partner would've been in better position to murder the previous butler," Holmes said. "Your accomplice supplied you with glowing references. Are you ready to name him?"

With cold steel encircling his wrists, Yates-Tilley seemed to collapse. All his bluster and bravado were gone with the appearance of the bloody gloves. "Welland Combes."

The Uffington family gasped all but one. He ran to the window followed by cries of stop him, get him, kill him, and clap him in irons until he jumped out, shattering the glass.

"Grab him!" the inspector yelled down to the constable waiting by the bloodied cart. The four constables made quick work capturing Welland Combes as he struggled and cursed them.

"The scheme was all Combes's idea to inherit Severna Manor. Stir up old fears of vampirism using the consumptive deaths of two farm girls, orchestrate a vampire murder and then turn on the real quarry. I regret we were unable to prevent the murder of the young lord." Holmes again bowed to Lord and Lady Ardsley.

His lordship thanked us while his wife couldn't stop her tears. Lady Beecham took her hand to console her. Lord Beecham stood by Lord Ardsley and Percy held Jane's hand.

I looked at Holmes. He nodded. Our work was done. We took our leave of his lordship and the inspector.

At the inn, we packed and went down to the taproom. We'd time for a cold collation before catching the train to Bristol. The taproom was filled with men congratulating us on finding the killers, condemning the nephew.

"I knew all along it warn't vampires," said the blacksmith.

Others shook their heads at such foolishness.

"These beliefs almost led to the death of an innocent young woman," Holmes told them sternly. "Let that be a lesson to you. Don't take the law into your own hands."

"Maybe they did," Cole said. "She disappeared. Maybe one of them killed her."

"Coulda been the murderers," the blacksmith said.

"No. She is well. I would put it in White's betting book if there were time. Those murderers wanted their victims found," Holmes told them.

Just then the inn door opened and Ivy walked in followed by a stalwart young man with dark hair and a firm gaze. She held up her hand for everyone to see the wedding band on her ring finger. Amidst congratulations she introduced her husband to Holmes and me and thanked us for saving her. "Sam came for me as soon as he heard the news from a traveler. We couldn't risk a light in case someone were watching the inn and had to hurry. I didn't have time to leave a note. We were married this morning by special license. I hope you weren't worried, Uncle Will."

"I was," Cole told them, "but Mr. Holmes seemed to think you were safe and that was good enough for me."

"How did you know, Mr. Holmes?"

"A simple deduction. The bushes were rather beaten up under your window which was opened from the inside, not jimmied. Your clothes and such were missing. And, of course, we didn't find another body."

We were just in time for the Bristol train. "I wish we'd been in time to save young Gerald," I said as we settled into our seats.

"Yes, if I'd realized sooner the manor was involved, perhaps we could've saved him but look at it this way, Watson. We saved two young women and the murderers are in gaol."

"What about Mary Putney?"

"I suspect she won't be caught for this crime but if she commits others without her smarter stepson, she may be."

I contented myself with that as we approached Bristol. "If she'd returned the cart to the farm, would you have suspected her?"

"I would. One of those telegrams told me Combes was a wastrel. With young Uffington out of the way, he would've inherited the manor and title."

"Proving it would've been difficult without the cart."

"Very difficult. I wonder if Mary did it to remove her stepson from her life. Maybe she feared him. He had most likely already killed his father, the previous butler and, no doubt, others. She may have feared him. Did you notice a resemblance between Lord Ardsley and Yates?"

"Now that you mention it, yes. They have the same blue eyes. You didn't say anything to Lord Ardsley?"

"He has enough sorrow to bear."

"True. He didn't need to know one son murdered the other."

"Or his half-brother murdered his son."

"We'll never know. Pray the Uffingtons never come to that realization."

"Pray also Yates doesn't reveal his true father. His mother no doubt told him and he grew up resenting his social status."

"The sins of the father," I said, "or the grandfather."

As we prepared to change trains in Bristol, I hoped this case would be the last one involving vampires. I knew it would not be the last one involving the wicked ways of sinful men.

**

The Christmas Card Case

Several days before Christmas, the grey sky spat gritty snow over London. I saw the last of my patients for the day before noon. I hadn't established a practice yet, but when my monthly pension ran out from my battlefield wounds at Maiwand, I filled in for doctors who needed to be away from London for a time. In the days leading up to Christmas, I was working for a Dr. Daniels in a poor but respectable area of London. I dressed burns, sewed up cuts, splinted limbs when needed, or placed them in plaster casts. I listened to hearts hardly able to continue and prescribed what I could to help the patients get on with their lives. One such hadn't appeared for her appointment. I was concerned for Miss Lucy Meers and resolved to look in on her during the holidays. I found her address in Dr. Daniels's files and copied it into the little book I carried with me always.

On my way back to Baker Street, I mailed the last of my Christmas cards to colleagues, patients, and friends, and also a package to Millicent Watson, my late father's second cousin twice removed, in Scotland. I assumed she was still living since I hadn't heard otherwise. This year's gift was a selection of teas from Fortnum and Mason. It wasn't exactly a case of *in loco parentis*, but I sent something every Christmas since my parents were gone. Cousin Millicent was my one last connection to family. She must have been close to ninety by then and lived with her late husband's great-niece.

Wind blew a flurry of flakes into my face as I turned the corner into Baker Street and hurried to 221 where, since the previous January, I had shared rooms with a singular fellow who styled himself the world's first consulting detective. I was still discovering bits of information about him, and I wondered if I should purchase a token gift for him. I had the feeling he didn't celebrate Christmas, just as he'd ignored Easter. He cared nothing for the acquisition of the material objects that most people pursued beyond the practical. Case in point: He kept his pipe tobacco in a Persian slipper nailed to his side of the mantelshelf after he'd acquired it in a case last summer *. He had an affinity for smoking and drinking, and a gift of either tobacco or brandy wouldn't be amiss. I stopped in the tobacco shop and bought a box of Habaneros. For Mrs. Hudson, I already owned a small blue vase given to me by a patient, and with my limited resources, that was the extent of my Christmas gift-giving in 1881.

Holmes was in and Mrs. Hudson had prepared an excellent mid-day meal for us, eaten in silence after my one or two attempts at conversation were answered with a single syllable. I gave up and repaired to what had become my chair on the left side of the hearth, with Holmes taking the right.

The fire in the grate snapped and hummed, lulling both of us into a postprandial torpor following the excellent lunch. The mantel clock ticked agreeably. Holmes lit a cigarette and rose to stand by the window, watching the weather. I didn't have the energy to light one and join him.

"I'm glad I don't have to be out in this any longer," I remarked. I'd seen patients all morning and felt a comfortable slide into sleep that awaited me.

Holmes laughed and tossed his cigarette into the fire. "Don't get too comfortable, Watson. I suspect our situation may change in one or two minutes, if not sooner."

I'd not long to wait to see if his prognostication would become actual. I'd found this often to be the case with the world's first consulting detective. His powers of observation were acute. He noticed minute clues that enabled him to construct scenarios of occurrences, and sometimes he even seemed to see them in the air that were no more substantial than a winter snowflake.

Today seemed one of those times when a knock at the street door brought our landlady to our sitting room.

"A lady to see you, Mr. Holmes."

"Show her in, please, Mrs. Hudson."

At that moment she ushered in a young woman in her late twenties, about our age. She was dressed for the weather in a dark blue walking suit with snowy lace at the throat, and a hooded cloak of the same hue which removed the necessity of a hat or bonnet. Her hair was a rich shade of chestnut, styled in the French way.

"This is Mrs. Ingoldsby."

"Please sit by the fire and let it take the chill away," Holmes said, indicating the basket chair. As she perched on the edge of the seat, he drew up his own seat.

"You are Sherlock Holmes?" She had a pleasant voice, but seemed perturbed by something.

"I am. This is my colleague, Dr. Watson. How can we help you?"

I nodded at her.

She produced a velvet bag and rummaged in it as she told us. "I really don't know if it's anything. My husband says it's just one of those things that happens. People come and they go. That's just the way of things."

"And your husband is?"

"Jarred Ingoldsby. At the Foreign Office."

"Indeed. May we offer you a brandy on this raw cold day?"

"No, thank you. The fire is sufficiently warm."

"Does this concern your husband?"

"Oh no. Well, I don't think it does. No, I'm sure it doesn't."

"Is it perhaps blackmail?"

"No, nothing sinister. In fact it may be nothing."

"It must be something to have brought you here."

"Tell us about it," I said in my best doctor-to-patient tone.

Holmes looked amused as if he recognized what I was doing – as I'm sure he did. He often seemed to know what people were thinking and doing before they were aware of it themselves.

"Every year on the sixth of December, my husband and I receive a Christmas card. There's never any name on them. The handwriting is unfamiliar to either of us. But this year, no card has appeared. I'm concerned that something has happened to the sender. I wouldn't like to think this person has fallen into something dangerous, or died without us ever being able to reply because we don't know who it is. I realize it's late, but I've been busy with our daughter and twin sons, and also my husband's obligations." She finished looking in her dark blue bag and drew out a thick bundle of postcards tied with a green ribbon, which she handed to Holmes.

He took the cards but didn't look at them. "The sixth of December – it may have significance. That's the day celebrated in Holland as St. Nicholas' Day – the night before Sinterklaas and his helper would have brought toys and sweets to good children who left their shoes outside the door awaiting his gifts. Does your family have a Dutch connection?"

"No, not that we know about, on mine or my husband's side. We're completely mystified every year as to who sends them, and why that date, and we've racked our brains to try to find the answer. It's become our Christmas mystery."

Holmes took the bundle and removed the ribbon. The fire settled into a warm purr as he studied each card. Mrs. Ingoldsby watched him anxiously. By then, I was becoming familiar with his methods. He examined the front of each card, and then the back. When he'd looked through all of them, he glanced up.

"Can you tell anything?" asked our visitor.

"Oh yes, several things. They were all sent by the same person – either a woman, or possibly a man imitating a woman's handwriting. I would venture that it was most likely a woman. The writing itself is excellent rounded copperplate. The writer learned his or her lessons well, and most likely early in the Queen's reign. The author used proper black ink and a quill pen.

So we know she is most likely an older woman, perhaps of limited means. What does this suggest to you?"

"Why . . . I don't know. She could have been a neighbor, I suppose."

"Indeed. Someone you or your husband knew in the past. But who would be intimate enough to send you unsigned cards?"

Holmes then perused the scenes printed on the cards. "I'll consult a stationer, but I believe these cards were printed quite some time ago. If you look at the women's clothing in the illustrations, a frothy polonaise bustle style is shown. By last year, this bustle had subsided into the princess line named for Alexandra the Princess of Wales who popularized it. The horizontal waistline has disappeared into a smooth long-line look involving tucks and darts, with volume appearing lower."

"Why Mr. Holmes, you amaze me!" Mrs. Ingoldsby cried. "You know more about the style of women's dresses than I do."

He amazed me, too, but I dared not say it. I hadn't even noticed that bustles had completely disappeared from the world in 1880 – though I was busy in a war during much of that time. Good riddance in my opinion.

Holmes smiled briefly. "It is an important part of what I do to know styles. No doubt many bustled dresses were remade to fit the new style. The point of this discussion is that these cards depict women in out-of-date clothing. Sometimes depictions do this on purpose, but Christmas cards tend to represent the immediate present, or go much farther back to the days of Jane Austen, or even classical times. In those cases, the depictions wouldn't show a decorated tree, since those were first introduced by Queen Charlotte at Windsor Castle in 1800 and didn't become popular until Prince Albert surprised Queen Victoria with one in 1840. Only then did the custom spread."

The clock on the mantel chimed four times. Mrs. Ingoldsby abruptly sat forward and gathered her cape. "Oh, I must go. You've provided me with a great deal of information already, Mr. Holmes. Will you look into this matter for me, as small as it is?"

"Certainly. I don't believe I've ever had a case involving Christmas cards."

Mrs. Ingoldsby gave him her visiting card. He glanced at it and slid it into a pocket. "I'll be in touch."

We both stood and I escorted her downstairs to the front door where a cab awaited. I helped her into it. "I do hope my problem isn't too trivial for Mr. Holmes's time and attention."

"It isn't," I said, as if I knew. Even after a year of knowing him, and occasionally assisting in his investigations, I wasn't entirely sure yet what intrigued Holmes and what he considered trivial. Clearly kingdoms wouldn't topple over these Christmas postal cards, but the affair might lead to something bigger than it seemed.

When I returned to the sitting room, Holmes had found his magnifying glass and was studying the cards inch by inch. "What do you think?"

"I think from the little we have gleaned that some soul wished to keep up a connection with her betters – perhaps she was a former servant – but was too timid to put her name or address on the cards. It was enough for her to send one every year."

"Astute of you. You'll be a detective yet."

Was there a touch of jest in his tone? "It isn't so different from diagnosing a patient's illness and finding either a cure or relief from pain."

"That simple, is it?"

"Yes. It is that simple."

"You're right. You are already a detective of sorts, though not as versed in ordinary clues as you are in observing medical clues. If someone comes in with a hollow cough, your first thought might be tuberculosis. A closer look, however, plus some palliative medicine to enable the patient to sleep without coughing, might reveal a case of grippe."

"You are correct. You might make a doctor yourself."

A smile flashed over his mouth and then was gone. Was he making sport of me? If so, I think that I gave as good as I got.

"You did, Watson. You did."

I didn't quite know how to take this – or how he knew what I'd been thinking. "Brandy?" I asked to change the subject.

"I hear Mrs. Hudson with our tea. Perhaps later."

Later that evening, after a joint of sirloin accompanied by tender peas, carrots, and potatoes in beef gravy, we finally had our splash of brandy and Holmes returned to the stack of cards.

"The first Christmas card was printed by John Callcott Horsley the artist for his friend Sir Henry Cole in 1843. It merely said '*Merry Christmas*'. The custom caught on when illustrations were added and postage was dropped to a penny, and then to a half-penny, along with the cost of the cards as well. I suspect the sender thriftily bought up a packet of ten several years ago, after the holiday had passed, and when they subsequently cost even less – perhaps three pence instead of five. It was then that the idea was born to send them to someone from the author's past and better days."

"You can tell all of that from simply looking at the cards?"

"Certainly not. Some of that I remember from when it occurred. And at one time I needed knowledge about Sir Henry Cole for an investigation – that fact was still in my little brain attic."

"Indeed."

"Look at the pictures and tell me what you see. Describe the cards to me."

He handed over the stack. I looked through them one by one, spreading them out on the recently cleared table. First I sorted them according to pictures. "These are mostly scenes of Christmas morning, it seems. The first one is a pair of robins perched on a berried holly branch with snow on the ground. The rest have scenes of Christmas trees, most with children in them. This one has an older woman with the children, and two have a fireplace behind them. The fireplaces differ, and the trees slightly as well. This one has cats and rabbits around a decorated tree. This one is the same, but instead with cats and mice."

"Small differences. The cats and rabbits aren't wearing clothing, while the mice are."

"True. The final card shows Father Christmas watching children dancing around a decorated tree."

"Excellent. You've categorized them. What differences and similarities do you see?"

"The card with robins depicts no children or decorated trees or Father Christmas. All of the other cards depict a decorated tree. Nine have human figures in them. All ten have some seasonal greenery, either a tree or holly."

"Again, excellent. Is there anything else that they all have in common?"

I looked at each card carefully – too carefully.

"Come, come, Watson. How can you not see it? Why isn't it jumping out at you? Or flying in circles around you?"

I gave him a blank look. "They all depict Christmas . . . ."

I looked again at each card. Holmes became impatient.

"The birds, man. The little red birds."

"Oh that. They're so small I can hardly see them."

"In your defense, I did use the glass to spot them, but they can be seen by the eye. Each card has a tiny red bird tucked away somewhere. On the Christmas trees in different places, or almost hidden in the holly on the robin card."

He handed me the magnifying glass and instantly the tiny birds jumped into view. "Yes, I see them now."

"Observe, they were all hand-drawn and colored with some sort of dye instead of ink – possibly beet juice. If you hold the cards a certain way in the light, you can see the slight indentation made by the quill."

"Someone was sending a message."

"Possibly. If so, we must find out what the message is."

"However will we do that?"

"We'll start with the postmark. These cards were all mailed at the Houndsditch Post Office. Our sender must live near there – at least up until last year when the last card was sent – as these have been consistently sent from that post office for years. Tomorrow I'll pay that office a visit."

In the morning, I had no patients to see. Dr. Daniels had returned from his journey and, as I had no new assignment, I accompanied Holmes to the post office. "If anyone remembers the cards, it's most likely to be the postmaster," he said.

No patrons waited in line and we had the building to ourselves. The man behind the counter, who confirmed he was the postmaster, looked old enough to have been there for some time.

Holmes took the bundle of cards out of his inside pocket. "I hope you'll be able to help us. I'm Sherlock Holmes, and this is my associate, Dr. Watson."

The rather stooped man with gray hair brightened. "Dr. Watson? It's you then, is it? I'm Jonas Case. I came to you when you was *loco*-ing for Dr. Samson."

Indeed, I couldn't recall every patient that I'd seen while serving as a *locum* in various practices all over the city, but I did remember this one. "Mr. Case – of course! You had a bad case of grippe."

"I did. That medicine you give me fixed it right up. What can I do for you gentlemen, ah Mr. – "

"Holmes," I said quickly. "Sherlock Holmes. He is a consulting detective, and I'm assisting him in an investigation."

"How do, Mr. Holmes."

"Fine, thank you, Mr. Case." He lifted the cards. "We're trying to locate the sender of these. They were sent from this postal station on the fifth of December every year for the last few years – until this year. Do you recognize them, or remember who might have sent them?"

The old man took the cards. "Not many as sends Christmas cards in these parts." He flipped through them, looking on the side with the address. "Don't have writing on the greetings part." He then turned them over and recognition brightened his pale face. "But I do indeed know the sender. It's Mrs. Ava Beale. Lives nearby."

"Would you happen to have her address?" I asked. "She may be ill since she missed sending a card this year."

"I do. She lives over on Wirthy Lane. Round the corner, not far. I'd show you myself, but I can't leave."

"Thank you, Mr. Case," I replied. "I'm sure we'll find it. Take care of those lungs now. Get out and breathe fresh air when you can." I tipped my hat, as did Holmes, and as we left, new customers came in to buy stamps.

"Around the corner, he said." Holmes headed around toward the nearest turn. After some searching, we found it. Wirthy Lane was a mean little street. Some of the houses had small upstairs balconies that jutted overhead above the street, blocking any sunlight that might be trying to reach the place. After several enquiries we found the house in question, a rickety shamble of a building whose origins lay several centuries in the past. We were told that Mrs. Beale lived upstairs in half of a balcony that someone had enclosed a century or more ago. We climbed the inner stairs carefully. They shook with every step.

When we arrived at the street side of the first floor, Holmes knocked on the door opening onto the landing. "Mrs. Beale? Mrs. Ava Beale?"

No reply.

"Mrs. Beale, my name is Sherlock Holmes, and with me is Dr. Watson. We're here about the Christmas greeting that you failed to send this year."

"How do you know that?" came a weak voice.

"On each card for ten years you drew a red bird – possibly this was meant to represent yourself, as your name '*Ava*' means '*bird*'. Mrs. Ingoldsby, of the family that received the cards, has engaged us to find you and see if you're all right. She's worried because no card arrived this year on St. Nicholas' Day."

"Oh!" The low cry could have been a sob of happiness, or despair or relief. The door finally opened and a tiny frail bird of a woman stood there, clutching a frayed shawl.

"Please come in," she almost whispered, "though this is no place you would like to be."

The sliver of a room was icy, and would have been impossible to heat, despite the fact that someone had papered over the many cracks in the walls. Mrs. Beale hadn't done much to keep it warm, besides setting a charcoal pot on a square of bricks. A north-facing window let in pallid light, and I suspected before our arrival that the poor woman had been wrapped tightly in the neatly folded blanket lying upon the corner pallet bed.

Mrs. Beale may have been pretty in her youth, but the difficulties of her life had aged her. With only one chair in the room, we stood to talk. I was worried that she might keel over simply from the exertion of speaking with us. "As a doctor, Mrs. Beale, I must insist that you sit while we speak."

I took her arm and settled her on the plain wooden chair, and then busied myself looking for tea things. I found a cup and a battered kettle, but no tea – or any other foodstuff for that matter. I shook my head at Holmes and opened my empty hands to show there was nothing to eat or drink in this room. Clearly this was unacceptable for human habitation.

"We shall consult Mrs. Hudson. Come, Watson, not a moment to lose."

"Is there anything you want to take with you?" I asked her.

The woman was shocked that, within seconds of our arrival, we were preparing to leave and take her with us. "Just a chest," she replied. "There. It serves as a table."

Holmes lifted and half-carried her out the door and down the stairs, leaving me to struggle with the small trunk, which proved far heavier than I had expected.

"I don't think I can walk far," Mrs. Beale said when we reached the pavement.

"We'll get a cab," Holmes replied.

"Not likely in this neighborhood," I muttered.

"You there, lad," countered Holmes, gesturing to a small ill-dressed boy watching from across the street. "Find us a cab and there's a coin in it for you." He held up a sixpence with one hand while the other supported Mrs. Beale.

I set the trunk close to my feet, just touching my leg. In this neighborhood, an inch farther away and it would be whisked away before I missed it. I took off my overcoat and slid it around Mrs. Beale just as a strong gust of wind armed with snow grit nearly blew us away.

The boy returned within minutes. "Ee's comin!"

Holmes gave him the sixpence and, noting his raggedness, something extra. I heard the coins clink.

Almost immediately, a hansom turned into the street. Normally hansoms carry two passengers, but Mrs. Beale hardly made a third person. Even so, we fit snugly inside which wasn't bad considering the coldness of the day.

Once inside the hansom with the trunk at my feet, Holmes unwound his muffler and tossed it to the boy. "Take care now," he said as the cab drove us away.

Presently Mrs. Beale spoke. "This is the warmest I've been since my husband died."

Holmes looked at me over her head. "We'll see that you will be warm from now on."

I nodded. Somewhere in London, we ought to be able to find a place for her. Mrs. Hudson would have some suggestions. If not, then perhaps I could ask some of the patients that I'd seen and come to know. The lady was not going back to that terrible room.

"Agreed," Holmes said, nodding my way.

This time I wasn't surprised he'd discerned my thoughts. How could I have been considering anything else? We couldn't help everyone in need in London, but we could help Mrs. Beale.

"Upon my soul!" Mrs. Hudson said when she saw our visitor. We explained the details of the investigation, how we'd located the poor woman and the conditions in which we'd found her. Our capable landlady took over and soon Mrs. Beale was filled with hot soup and crisp scones dripping with butter. She'd had a bath and now wore some of Mrs. Hudson's things until hers dried from the quick washing that the maid gave them.

Mrs. Hudson tucked the little old lady under a shawl in front of the fire in her own sitting room and then climbed the stairs to report to us. "She's had a dreadful time of it, poor thing. Her husband was a clerk for a company cataloging libraries. The last place he worked, over fifteen years ago, was at the home of Lord Belding, in the library at Sheldon House. It was extensive and required a number of years to sort out. During that time, Mr. Beale was given the use of a cottage and he brought his wife with him, letting their own cottage out for rent for the time. Mr. Beale was a deal older than his wife, and they never had children of their own, and neither possessed any other family. While they lived in the cottage, Mrs. Beale became fond of the Belding children, taking them on picnics and what-not.

"That's when she met Mr. Ingoldsby. He was a ward of the Belding family after his parents were killed in India. She was especially close to him during the time she spent at Sheldon House. Years later, she saw his name in the newspaper and started sending the Christmas cards, although anonymously. They were a connection to her past, and it made her happy to do so."

"Thank you, Mrs. Hudson," said Holmes. "I believe you've discovered the remaining questions related to the matter, and you've been most kind as well."

"I couldn't have done otherwise, poor soul. She isn't to go back to that room. She can stay here until we find a place for her."

Holmes didn't look surprised. Nor did I.

I took my bag downstairs to Mrs. Hudson's sitting room to make sure that Mrs. Beale was well and to determine if she needed any additional medical attention. Her pulse and heart rate were a trifle weak, but that was to be expected. She had a normal temperature reading. Holmes came down as I was finishing my examination and waited impatiently until I was done.

"Now Mrs. Beale, please tell us the rest of your story – after you and your husband left Sheldon House."

"We went on as before. With the extra money from the long let of our little house, my husband was able to purchase a small annuity for our old age only he died not long after and I was left. I stayed in the cottage for another year or so, taking little jobs of sewing or caring for others as I could, but as costs rose, I was forced to sell my home and seek out rooms, nice at first, but then meaner and meaner, until I fetched up in Wirthy Lane." She heaved a great sigh, as if letting out the very misama of that dreadful place.

"And then what happened?" Holmes asked.

"At the end of every month, I always go to the bank to receive my annuity check and cash it. Two months ago, a pair of ruffians lay in wait for me. They were rough and took all of my money. Last month, the same thing happened again. I managed to buy enough food to last me with the little I'd saved back from previous months, but my rent is due on the last day of every month, and after paying at the end of November, a few weeks ago, I had nothing left for food or rent."

"And that is why the cards stopped," I said. "You couldn't afford even the price of postage on December 5th."

"Yes." Tears collected on her lashes. "They were the most important part of my year. I had such pleasure remembering those happy times, drawing the little bird somewhere on the pictured side. I thought of what a sweet little boy Mr. Ingoldsby had been, and how well he'd grown up. I thought of him as if he were my own, and now he has little ones of his own. And this year I couldn't even do that – couldn't even send him a card." A tear slid out of her left eye and glistened like a jewel on her cheek before disappearing into the shawl wrapping her to her chin.

"This year you will do even better than that," Holmes said. "This year you can draw little birds in person, for we shall take you to see the Ingoldsbys. I've telegraphed them, and they invited you to tea tomorrow. They suggested today, but I thought you needed to rest for awhile."

Mrs. Hudson agreed, as did I. In her frail condition, Mrs. Beale might be overcome at seeing the little boy she obviously still loved so much. "Her memories of Mr. Ingoldsby were what sustained her through her penury, her hunger and cold," I said when we went back upstairs. "Would that everyone had food and warmth and happy memories. The world would be a different place if that were true. You might be out of a job, and mine might be much easier if people grew up eating well and living in warm dry housing."

"Indeed, yours would be easier. Certainly rickets and other results of malnutrition would abate. Tuberculosis might even disappear. But you can rest assured that greed, malfeasance, and hate would still be with us, driving humans to crime."

"A bit cynical for the Christmas season," I countered.

"For any season, but the heart of man doesn't improve much with the comforts of a fire and nourishing food. Think of the rich amongst us who have everything and continue to commit crimes."

Alas, I had to concede he was correct in his thinking, but I still clung to the belief that many crimes would cease with comfort, and the release of fear of starvation and freezing to death.

Mrs. Beale wore her best dress for tea at the Ingoldsby's, pulled from her trunk and ironed by the maid. It was a soft rose color with a bit of lace here and there. Her hair was carefully pulled up and arranged. Mrs. Hudson lent her a cape with a hood.

"We want to look our best," she said as she tweaked the lace and bustled around us as we were leaving. Finally Holmes said, "Would you like to accompany us? I'm sure the Ingoldsbys won't mind an additional guest for tea."

Mrs. Hudson drew back, aghast. "Certainly not! This is a family affair. With the addition," she amended, "of the both of you who made it happen." Turning to Mrs. Beale, she said, "Enjoy yourself, my dear. And don't worry about a thing. We will make something happen for you."

"Thank you."

Holmes had a growler waiting at the kerb. We settled ourselves in and the cab moved into traffic.

"Such a pleasure to be riding in a cab again," Mrs. Beale remarked. "I was too cold to enjoy it yesterday. Indeed, I believe I must have been half-asleep for much of the journey."

She had actually slept for the entire trip, but I didn't remind her of it, for then she might recall why, and those days were over now. No need to dwell upon them. Mrs. Hudson would find a place for her.

The cab stopped before a handsome Georgian brick house with a black front door under an elegant fanlight, the brass polished to bright shine even on so late of an overcast afternoon. A spray of holly branches held by a red velvet ribbon echoed the design of the fanlight.

"Festive," Holmes murmured as he helped Mrs. Beale out while I paid the cabby with a generous tip for the holiday.

Holmes tapped the door-knocker and it was instantly thrown open by Mrs. Ingoldsby herself, while a butler stood slightly to her left, no doubt in case we proved to be ruffians! – with a disapproving expression on his face.

"Come in, come in! Welcome to our home! We are so excited to meet the sender of those lovely cards. I'm Caroline Ingoldsby. George isn't home yet – he was delayed – but will be here as soon as he can."

Behind her a pair of boys of the same height came into view. Apparently they were the twins although they didn't look alike. With them was their younger sister wearing green velvet, and they all danced with excitement. "Mama let me wear my new dress," confided the little girl, Melinda, when her mother had introduced them. The two boys were William and Phillip.

I thought then that Mrs. Beale would be overcome, but she took to the children immediately as we moved to a large sitting room, cozy with a fire, comfortable furniture, and wallpaper striped in shades of blue. A large brown dog (add - lay) on the hearth and a grey cat slept in a basket.

"What a lovely room," remarked Mrs. Beale as we were seated. A Christmas tree stood in a place of honor, decorated with paper ornaments probably made by the children: Chains, cornucopias of sweets, and a paper nativity scene tucked into a gap in the branches.

Holmes pulled the packet of cards from his coat and handed them to Mrs. Ingoldsby. She crossed the room and placed them on the mantelshelf, along with a number of others already tucked into the greenery. We were immediately served a sumptuous tea fit for a king before Mrs. Beale was drawn into helping the children in making paper birds with horizontal wings for the tree.

"They look like they can fly!" Melinda said.

Meanwhile, Holmes softly explained to Mrs. Ingoldsby what had transpired. "Mrs. Hudson is looking for a place for her – "

"Certainly not!" the lady of the house interrupted. "She must stay here. We shall sort this all out. She shouldn't be working at her age and frailty."

Just then, I became aware of someone standing quietly nearby. Mr. Ingoldsby had arrived so silently that the children and Mrs. Beale hadn't noticed. He watched the scene for a minute. We stepped toward him, and his wife softly introduced us as he continued to observe the lady with his children, engrossed in their task. "We'll put a birdie on every branch," Phillip said.

A change came over Mr. Ingoldsby's demeanor. He stepped further into the room. "Birdie," he called softly.

Mrs. Beale turned her head and saw him there, this tall, handsome man. "George!" she exclaimed, rising and then apologizing. "I mean, Mr. Ingoldsby. You are so grown up."

"If you're still Birdie, then I'm still George," he said. "You made a lonely orphaned boy feel loved. I cried when I came back from an outing and found that you had gone. No one would ever tell me where you went or how to find you. I didn't even know your name beyond 'Birdie'." He looked toward his children and said, "She taught me to make those same birds,"

"Is that why you called her Birdie?" Mrs. Ingoldsby asked.

"I think so."

"My husband called me that," Mrs. Beale explained. "My given name is Ava, a form of *Avis*, which means '*bird*' in Latin. You spent time at our cottage at the estate, George, helping me peel apples and putting cores out in the trees for the birds."

"How ever did you find her?" Mr. Ingoldsby asked, looking toward Holmes.

Holmes repeated some of what we'd just related to Mrs. Ingoldsby, omitting the sadder parts of the story, and instead concentrating on how we'd located her. "And now our work is done. We must take our leave."

"Please – let me know your fee," Ingoldsby said.

"Certainly not. This is my gift to you for Christmas."

"It's so generous of you!" Mrs. Ingoldsby said. "I can't thank you enough."

"Nor I," Ingoldsby said. "I suspect this story will become an oft-told tale at bedtime."

"One with a happy ending," I added.

"But we haven't reached the ending," Holmes informed me a few minutes later, after we had taken our leave.

I nodded. There was the matter of the toughs who'd robbed Mrs. Beale . . . but that could wait until after the holiday.

Mrs. Hudson had been busy in our rooms. Holly, mistletoe, and pine greenery sprigged every picture frame and the mantelshelf. She was waiting in her traveling clothes to hear how our meeting went. We told her as briefly as possible.

"I'm so happy for her. I wish more stories could end this way. And I wish you both had somewhere to go for Christmas. I've left you a joint and trimmings. I trust you can take care of yourselves, but if you change your mind, my sister will welcome you at her house tomorrow."

"That's kind of you, Mrs. Hudson."

"Wait – I have a gift for you." I rushed upstairs to my room and brought down the blue vase clumsily wrapped in brown paper. Holmes gave her a small package from his room as well.

"I believe I'll open them here." She removed the brown paper and exclaimed over the blue glass vase.

"It matches your eyes," I said. I noticed that it looked small. "Sorry it isn't larger."

"Why, thank you, Dr. Watson. It will look lovely in my sitting room and will be perfect for small bouquets which are my preference when my other vases are either too small or too large. It's perfect. Thank you."

Holmes gave her a crystal candy dish already filled with boiled sweets.

After our perfect dinner we relaxed by the fire, but I was called out on a case. Mrs. Cummings' baby decided to be a Christmas present. After I delivered her baby, Mr. Cummings thanked me for coming out on Christmas Eve.

"It's no bother. You saved me from a boring evening by the fire, and now you have a little one to celebrate with."

"My wife wants to name him Noel, so we've decided to name him after you. John Noel, it is."

Childbirth is a miracle whenever it happens, but on Christmas Eve it's a special miracle. When the family wasn't looking, I slipped a sixpence and an orange from my bag into the stocking that Mr. Cummings had hurriedly hung by the chimney for John Noel.

Snow passed us by that Christmas, despite earlier flutterings. Snow is beautiful, but I don't care for the mess that we humans have to deal with. We should retire to a snug cave somewhere in snowy climes and sleep off winter.

The streets that were busy with carol singers and last-minute shoppers earlier were silent now. Since the weather was cold but not vicious and I was in the area, I decided to stop and see Lucy Meers. I found her address in my pocket and decided to walk, as it was only one street over and a little way down.

The Meers family was surprised to see me. Their daughter Lucy had been too feverish to come to her appointment. I listened to her chest. The rales had subsided and her fever was almost normal. "Whatever you are doing works. Continue doing it," I instructed her parents. "Give her plenty of liquid and whatever food she can keep down. Let me know if she worsens."

As I repacked my black bag on the table in a dark corner of the room, I surreptitiously slipped fruit into an empty bowl, apples and oranges. Perhaps they would think Father Christmas paid them a visit in the night when it came to light in the morning.

No cabs were about in that neighborhood so late, so I walked in the clear night back to Baker Street, overlooked by stars of a particular brightness.

I slept late the next morning. Christmas Day was quiet. With Mrs. Hudson away, Holmes and I did for ourselves from the ample dishes that she'd left for us. Around eleven o'clock, a private messenger brought two parcels to the door, one for each of us. The contents were identical, very old fine French brandy.

"Calvados," Holmes said unwrapping his first. "From Normandy. Cider brandy distilled by Gilles de Gouberville in

1553. How fortunate it was called after the region and not Gouberville. I don't fancy sipping e*au de Gouberville.*"

I laughed. "I suspect people would sip this under any name."

"Your romantic streak holds sway, Watson. Or is it because of Christmas? '*A rose by any other name would smell as sweet.*' Let's hope this doesn't have the same result as what occurred in *Romeo and Juliet.*"

He brought out a package wrapped in brown paper and handed it to me. I removed my identically wrapped gift from my black bag and gave it to him. "Hmm," he murmured. "Can it be?"

Yes it could. We had each given the other the identically-wrapped same box of Habaneros from the nearby tobacconist shop.

We lounged by the fire. The day was snowless, but still very cold. I was content to listen to the sounds of the fire and hoped that no more babies decided to arrive on this day.

Holmes left around two to pay some calls, but he didn't specify as to whom. I suspected he would drop by Scotland Yard to see Gregson and Lestrade, if not others who might be on duty this day.

I caught up on professional reading and one or two yellow-book stories of derring-do, and dozed periodically after my long night out, and was much the better for it. Holmes returned around nightfall. We decided to save our gift bottles for the end of the year.

"I'm glad Mrs. Beale's case ended well," I remarked over ordinary brandy.

"Oh, it isn't ended. Indeed not. Mrs. Beale's part was merely small beer, albeit devastating to her. No, much more is to come."

He drifted off in a smoky reverie and would say no more. I decided to turn in.

Mrs. Hudson returned late on Boxing Day and insisted on cooking. "I brought back a fine gammon, fresh from the country."

The next three days saw me busy with diseases of winter and broken bones at Barts, several trying cases in which overeating had been a factor, a matter of poisoning from a green dress, and other of the sundry disasters that man is heir to.

I received a note from my relative Millicent Watson, who was still alive and well. She was quite appreciative of the exotic – to her – assortment of teas, and also to be remembered by her great-great nephew. I saw little of Holmes during those days except in passing, and once or twice breakfast or dinner. I wasn't in the habit of asking him about his plans, but took his activity to mean preparations for the next-to-last day of the year were going forth.

As we sat down to dinner on Thursday, Holmes said, "The thirtieth is upon us on tomorrow. I hope you'll be available from nine in the morning to accompany us to the bank."

"Is that the time Mrs. Beale usually goes to pick up her annuity?"

"It is."

"Will we be her only protection?" I wasn't sure that I was up to taking on toughs yet after my battle injuries and long fever bout.

"No. She wrote down all details of her walk to the bank and back, and where she was accosted both times. We'll have men in those areas, and also stationed along the route to the bank. Lestrade and his men will be out in force, albeit discreetly placed."

I was comforted by that, but the next morning after a quick breakfast, I slipped my Adams into my pocket and hoped I wouldn't have to use it.

I busied myself with some of my patients' notes for an hour or two. Mrs. Hudson provided a light lunch which Holmes declined to partake. I'd noticed this was often the case with him when something was about to happen.

"Holmes, you do know that food provides energy and keeps us going."

"I can't spare the energy to digest it and wait for the transformation to that energy. I already have sufficient for the task at hand."

At half-twelve, Holmes picked up a satchel and hurried me down to the street where a hackney awaited us. "I ordered it earlier," he explained.

"Surely a hansom would be sufficient."

"We're stopping for Mrs. Beale. I wanted her to ride in comfort."

I refrained from saying that anything on wheels would be a comfort to one who had walked for the last ten years. Mrs. Beale deserved her comforts.

George Ingoldsby escorted her to the cab and to my surprise, though possibly not to Holmes's, he insisted on accompanying us. Mrs. Beale wore her old cloak, and under it her best old clothes that she saved for bank days. Holmes insisted that nothing must be different today from her previous trips to the bank.

As we drove through the crowded streets toward Mrs. Beale's old neighborhood, Holmes went over the plan with her again. "You must not be emboldened and try to resist them. We want them to take possession of your property."

"We'll have them in the act," Ingoldsby added.

Holmes stifled a laugh and I looked away. The man seemed to be living an escapade from *Boys' Own Paper*. Perhaps he read stories of that sort to his own sons.

Holmes stopped the cab out of sight of Mrs. Beale's former abode. He opened his bag pulling out a different coat, which he put on. Then he did a few things to his face and hair before clapping a battered hat onto his head.

Ingoldsby and Mrs. Beale stared at the transformation. "Whatever are you doing?" Ingoldsby asked.

"I can't follow Mrs. Beale dressed as a toff without being taken for one, can I?" He spoke in a rough accent.

Ingoldsby could scarcely understand him. Then he laughed. "I say, Holmes, you're a corker!"

Holmes smiled faintly and replied in his own tones. "I leave no stone unturned, nor anything to chance."

I saved that away for future remembrance. It fit with my observations, but I hadn't yet framed it in that way.

He gave us our final instructions. He helped Mrs. Beale from the cab and loitered around the corner while she entered her former lodgings, only to immediately exit and begin her walk to the Shadwell Bank. The cab carried Ingoldsby and me to the bank by another route, and we were inside the sturdy red brick building when she arrived. She went about her business as usual, while we looked over a sheet containing printed figures at one of the tables close to the entrance. When she left, we concluded our imaginary business with one another and, with a handshake, we followed her – first me and then Ingoldsby.

Outside, we pretended to bump into each other and, with animated gestures, conversed as we followed the route back to Mrs. Beale's former lodgings. I didn't see Holmes or the Scotland Yard detectives, or even the duty constables. I assumed that they'd been sent to the farthest reaches of their beat in order to give the thieves a false sense of security. As we neared the meaner streets, the crowds roughened, and I suspected Holmes must be in the middle of them, but invisible as he blended in. He'd even rubbed dust and dirt on his clean shoes and trousers before we separated, lest they give him away. As he said, he left nothing to chance.

From a distance we followed the brave little bluebell that stood upright on Mrs. Beale's straw hat. As she passed a dark, dirty alley, even worse than Wirthy Lane, three toughs suddenly burst from it, dragging Mrs. Beale out of our sight. We weren't close enough to hear what they said, but could imagine them saying something along the lines of, "Your money or your life!"

We sped to the corner where we heard her reply querulously, "Please – this is all I have! I'll starve!"

One of the men laughed, but the other didn't because his laugh was suddenly choked out of him when he was grabbed from behind by a rough fellow with dust on his shoes. He could only made slight gagging sounds, as a baton of some sort was now tight across his throat. At that moment, two other rough fellows came down the alley toward us. They were disguised constables, but they stopped short, for Mrs. Beale had a knife at her throat.

"Back up!" the tough who had seized her ordered. "This is *my* pigeon!"

"Not much meat on them bones," one of the constables said.

"Naw," added the other. "We don't 'tend to share. Give over."

"I said get back!" the knife-wielder snarled. "Covy Joe won't take kindly to you muscling in."

"That's who you work for?" the first disguised constables asked with scorn.

"Yeah," came the reply as the knife was brandished. "He's smarter'n whoever you dungs are workin' for!"

Mrs. Beale gasped, but stayed on her feet.

"I doubt that," one of the constables said, but they started to back away slowly.

Meanwhile, Holmes had allowed the unconscious partner to collapse in a quiet heap, and then he slid without sound along the alley wall and closer behind the attacker. No one else moved. Something had to be done, or the attacker would soon become aware of Holmes.

"I say there," I interrupted in my plummiest English accent, with apologies to my Scottish forebears. "I believe that I'm lost. You fellows wouldn't happen to know where the Shadwell Bank is located?"

The tough's attention was drawn my way for a moment as he weighed the seriousness of my presence. At the same time, Ingoldsby shrank back as if he wanted no part of this scene, a typical response of the upper class, and perfect for this occasion.

Holmes took advantage of the situation and struck the criminal a hard blow to the head with his baton. The constables were quick. One snatched Mrs. Beale out of harm's way while the other cracked the attacker's knife arm with another baton that appeared in his hand. Holmes took care of the third one. "You're under arrest," he said, turning him over to a constable.

Ingoldsby came closer, and Inspector Lestrade joined us. Mr. Ingoldsby reached Mrs. Beale first and took her arm. "Are you all right, my dear Birdie? That ruffian didn't hurt you?"'

"No, I'm quite well, thanks to all of you." She righted her brave little straw hat, with the upright bluebell quivering somewhat.

Lestrade ordered the police wagons brought up. I gave each of the criminals a glance. The one that Holmes choked was waking up, while the second had a nasty bump on the back of his head, and the third's right arm below the elbow might very well be broken. I informed Lestrade that they would need medical attention, but I wasn't prepared to provide any without my medical bag.

At the inspector's nod, the constables loaded the three thieves into separate wagons and gave instructions to have a doctor at attention when they arrived. Ingoldsby then invited the constables and Lestrade over to his house for a libation, but unfortunately they had to decline, as they were all on duty and had the business at hand to complete. "Come tomorrow, then," Ingoldsby offered. "At anytime. We want to think you for taking three more criminals off the street."

Holmes and I had nothing there to further occupy us. With Ingoldsby and Mrs. Beale, we adjourned to the waiting cab where Holmes pulled off the old coat and cleaned his face, using a rag from his satchel. He wiped his shoes as well. Then he drew out a small clothing brush and returned his trousers to their former state. The old hat and coat went back into the bag.

The three of us watched him with fascination. This was the first time that I'd seen him make such a transformation in front of me.

"You are presentable again," I remarked when he donned his own coat, Inverness, and fore-and-aft cap.

"He is always presentable," Mrs. Beale said, "as whatever the occasion calls for."

"Well said." Holmes favored her with a smile.

The entire story was told again for the benefit of Mrs. Ingoldsby over a celebratory tea and libations. When Holmes seemed to reach a saturation point in conviviality, we made our farewells. Before we left, the children presented us with a stack of paper birds. "For your tree," Melinda said.

I hadn't the heart to tell her we had no tree.

"I can't thank you enough," Mrs. Ingoldsby said.

"Nor I," Mrs. Beale echoed.

Back in the flat, I placed the paper birds in the mantel greenery where they perched festively, and then I sank down in front of the fire while Holmes dumped more coal on the embers and worked the bellows.

"That went well," I said.

"Indeed. But I wonder: Will we hear more from this Covy Joe? And how many toughs does he have on his string?"

"Let's not borrow trouble for the future," I said. "Let the old year end on a high note."

"It has, but we must keep in mind that those three toughs are mere sardines in the swill of the River Styx."

"How poetic of you. And literary."

Holmes snorted. "Facts, my dear Watson. I deal in facts only."

NOTE

*   See "The Persian Slipper" *The MX Book of New Sherlock Holmes Stories Part XXV – 2021 Annual (1881-1888)*

The Case of Blackmailed Manor

"'Tis not a fit night to be abroad, Watson," Holmes remarked as he turned away from the window and sat in his customary chair close to the fire.

From my vantage point on the left of the fireplace, I could see beyond his silhouette to the swirling yellow fog.

"Excellent choice. I concur."

Holmes opened a journal he had been perusing off and on all day while I rooted through medical journals piled beside my chair.

The night promised to be a cozy one with early retirement but we were interrupted by the knocker at the front door and the murmur of voices. I put down my journal but Holmes remained absorbed even when Mrs. Hudson ushered in our visitor, a man of medium height with a commanding presence, swathed in a dark enveloping coat, a scarf the color of sepia ink wrapped around much of his face as protection against the rank-smelling fog.

He stood erect and looked as if he spent a deal of time upon a horse. His sandy hair and brows framed a bony face with a high-bridged nose and pale blue eyes. A lord, no doubt.

Mrs. Hudson took his hat and helped him with his overcoat. When he threw off the scarf, I could smell the rank fog on his garments as Holmes put down his journal. We stood to welcome the visitor.

"I am-"

"Lord Creighton, I believe," Holmes said with a slight tilt to his head. "Do sit down." He indicated his chair and to my amazement brought over another from the table. Not even the King of Bohemia rated Sherlock Holmes's chair.

"Thank you," Lord Creighton said with a slightly puzzled look.

If one is not familiar with Holmes, one is amazed by his seemingly prescient knowledge and, even though it is now familiar to me, I never grow accustomed to his insights drawn on so little as a hair or a twig or a twitch. I wondered what had revealed his lordship's identity.

"I apologize for the lateness of the hour but I had to wait for my wife to retire."

"No matter. My associate, Dr. Watson."

I am not exactly an associate. At the time of this case, I was only helping Holmes when it was convenient while attending to my medical practice.

The peer of the realm looked at me, a great honor, I supposed, and quite the reverse of the cat looking at a queen. I nodded and at his slight nod, I returned to my chair. We listened to the crackle and hiss of the fire while waiting for him to state the reason for this late visit on so foul a night.

Finally Holmes spoke. "Since this is not a social call, you must be about to suffer a loss and you have come to me to try to prevent it."

All learned response left Lord Creighton's face. His mouth opened though I was glad to see his jaw didn't drop as it might've on a lesser mortal. "How did you know?"

Holmes waved his hand. "It does not signify. Now tell me the details of your request."

"I –I made some mistakes. Stupid mistakes involving a young woman –"

"Who turned out not to be what you thought and now she is blackmailing you in some way that does not involve only money."

This time Lord Creighton merely flushed and nodded. "I – yes that is what happened more or less."

We waited for him to tell us which was more and which was less.

He seemed to consider one beginning, then another. "It-ah - was foolish of me. I believe now I was the target from the beginning of a scheme to lay hands on my property."

"You are being blackmailed but not in the usual way?" Holmes lifted his eyebrows.

"That is correct. How did you know?"

"A peer would not come out on so foul a night still dressed in his dinner attire for mere ordinary blackmail. What are the demands?"

"How did you-"

Again Holmes waved a hand. "Blackmailers always make demands, some more impossible than others. If this were a straight-forward money demand, you would've paid the blaggard and hoped that was the end of it. Black-mail is seldom easy but often one finds this out after the screw has already been turned."

Lord Creighton grimaced. "No doubt. This woman wants more than my money. She demanded I auction one of my properties, Wyndhurst Manor. She will bid on it and win. Then when I give her the deed she will take it but not pay me for it. I can't let this go out of this room."

He looked from Holmes to me and back again.

"Your secret is safe with us," Holmes assured him. I nodded my agreement.

Holmes steepled his fingers. "What do you wish me to do for you?"

"The auction is tomorrow. I wish you to outbid her. No matter how high she goes. I will cover it. She will be thwarted and I will retain my property at no cost other than the auction fees. And yours."

"Will she not then bid higher?" I asked.

"I do not believe she will have the funds or the nerve to continue bidding. She will expect to get it at a good price as it has not much land, merely ten acres."

"Will she not then ask for another one of your properties?" I asked.

"Apparently she wants that particular one." He spread his hands to a length as if limiting the blackmailer's powers.

Holmes nodded. "She and the one who wants the property sought to involve you in an embarrassing liaison in order to force the sale of the manor. She has not asked for any further monies?"

"No. Only the deed to the manor."

"Very well then. I will buy Wyndhurst Manor for you," Holmes said.

"Excellent." Lord Creighton removed a sheaf of papers from inside his coat. Here is a bank draft. The amount can be filled in at the time of the sale." He gave us the particulars of the auction and left.

We didn't hear the slamming of the coach's door. Surely Lord Creighton did not walk here. Nor had we heard horse's hooves when he arrived. He must have walked around from the side street. He doesn't know who is involved in this scheme and doesn't want his coachman to know he's consulting Holmes. I was pleased with my deduction. Clues were there for the noticing. Knowledge was often a matter of noticing and deducing.

"If he had come to me sooner, we could have avoided the auction charade. It is obvious that someone wants the manor badly for whatever reason. The blackmail is arranged so he will not be terribly discommoded and will not involve the police. It should not be too difficult to find out the person behind this scheme."

"How did you know his lordship's identity?"

"He was pointed out to me once."

I laughed.

"What's funny about that?"

"He isn't memorable." No way would I let him know I thought he had some abstruse method of detecting his lordship's identity.

Holmes returned to his chair as the distinct clop of hooves sounded in the street below our windows and a hansom cab stopped at the door.

We didn't hear the cab resume its journey down Baker Street. Holmes raised his eyebrows as we waited for our caller to reach our door and in a few minutes Mrs. Hudson ushered in our second visitor of the night, this time a woman. She refused to allow Mrs. Hudson to divest her of her outer garments.

Holmes rose and offered her his seat. The chair he sat in earlier was still in place. He took it. "Good evening, Madam."

She wore a long enveloping cape and hood the color of shadows, well-worn and with at least one small rip I could see. Her face under the hood was covered by a veil. She wore black gloves. Black boots peeped from under the cloak.

When she didn't speak, Holmes tried again. "Good evening, madam. How may I help you?"

She sighed and threw back her hood. She removed the veil which had either been worn to protect her face from the yellow fog or to hide it or both. Her hair was a rich chestnut that gleamed as if polished. Her face was a perfect cameo of pleasing features and her eyes were the color of a Scottish summer afternoon.

"I hardly know where to start," she began in a hesitant voice.

"Start anywhere, my lady," Holmes said.

"How did you know?"

"You must have sent a servant to buy that cloak in Monmouth Street since I am certain your retainers are paid well enough to afford better. Your boots are polished and of fine quality but your gloves were the main indicators."

"My gloves?" she said in a faint, disbelieving voice.

"Yes. They are black and not noticeable in the dark but they are the finest kid. Dent's?"

She nodded. "I-yes. My mistress —"

"Your cloak does a good job of covering your dress but I can see the edge of grey China silk below the hem."

Her face pinked up prettily but she recovered. "I see you live up to your reputation, Mr. Holmes. Where did you learn so much about the apparel of ladies?"

"Disguises are part of my business, Lady Creighton."

She stared at him but he didn't tell her how he knew her name. I, too, had begun to suspect she was Lord Creighton's wife. How many peers would be out on a night like this?

"Do you also know why I am here?"

"Something dire to bring you out on such a night in a hansom cab awaiting you in the street to take you home instead of traveling in the family coach. Obviously it is something you wish to keep secret from family members. Your husband, perhaps?"

"Yes, yes, it is my husband." She cleared her throat.

"You have done something you don't wish him to find out?" I ventured.

She noticed me as if for the first time.

"This is Dr. Watson, my associate," Holmes told her. "He is as discreet as I am."

She nodded. "Yes, well, it is not something I have done. It is something I overheard. I wish you to act as my agent in a property sale."

"My lady, I am not a property agent."

"I don't know where else to turn. I do not want my husband to know what I know. He would be most – chagrinned."

"Indeed," Holmes said to encourage her.

She looked about to cry. I started to search for a handkerchief in case it were needed but she pulled herself together.

"My husband is selling one of his properties!" She almost cried the words that came from deep inside her and had to be wrenched out.

"Is that all?" I expected something serious and life-threatening.

"Indeed, that is not the worst that can happen to a man," Holmes said almost soothingly.

"No, no it is not but it's so unnecessary. The Manor is dear to us, well to me. It is where we spent our honeymoon and lived for a time until my husband's father died and William assumed the title."

"Do you know why he is selling this property, my lady?"

"No. I have my suspicions. I followed him one night to an assignation. He met a woman near the Serpentine in Hyde Park. It is near our town house and I know the area well. I concealed myself behind shrubbery."

She faltered and bit her lip.

Holmes raised his eyebrows at a lady going out alone in the night. "And what did you hear?"

She had risen in his estimation for such an act. Not a missish lady, this one.

"I heard her tell him she would bid on Wyndhurst Manor at auction which will be held tomorrow according to his calendar but not pay for it and they would be quit. I hope he doesn't believe that. She is obviously blackmailing him for an affair. It is not necessary to pay her off. I know about the affair."

"I see. What would you have me do for you?"

"I wish you to buy the property." She reached inside her cloak and drew out a silken pouch which she handed to Holmes. "You will need to sell these. I cannot. The buyer would know I desperately need the money and offer me far less than their value. And I cannot risk anyone recognizing me. Words of detrimental flavouring fly quickly around London."

Holmes loosened the drawstrings and removed a quadruple choker of flawless perfectly-matched pearls. They gleamed in the firelight as if each held a secret of its own wrapped in the lustrous curves. The catch was a large ruby like a great square of blood surrounded by flashing diamonds of serious quality.

Holmes ran his thumb over the large stone. "A pigeon's blood ruby, I believe, from the Mogok Valley in Burma. The finest in the world."

"These pearls are worth far more than the Manor. The ruby alone is worth a king's ransom. You should have no trouble selling them in the morning and getting to the auction at eleven to act as my agent."

Holmes returned the choker to the pouch. "I will do as you ask but if you know about the affair, why not tell your husband there is no need for the auction?"

"It is not a matter of just my knowing. My husband has a sterling reputation. He has the trust of the Queen. If this sordid affair were made public, I do not know what might happen. His standing in the government would be compromised."

Holmes nodded and she rose. "After it is done, the deed will be returned to my husband without explanation."

He accompanied her to the door, perhaps because she was a member of the peerage or perhaps because he admired her. With Holmes one could not always tell. When he returned I couldn't resist a dig. "I thought you weren't a property agent."

He laughed. "This promises to be of more interest than a play, Watson, and we have the best seats in the house."

At eleven 0'clock on the following morning, we presented ourselves at the auction rooms on King Street. The crowd wasn't large. I'd never attended an auction before but I would have thought more would be interested in the estates and lands being sold. We found seats in the middle and sat through the auction of several small farm holdings until a buzz went around the room which had filled during the earlier auctions. Up to now the crowd had been male but several women joined the company including a ladies' maid swathed in a veil near the back. She looked familiar, maybe the way she held her head. I pointed her out to Holmes as discreetly as I could.

"Ha! I knew she wouldn't be able to stay away. She's wearing black bombazine instead of silk under her cloak and cheap, mended gloves and somebody rubbed dust on her boots. She's here to make sure I carry out her wishes."

"But you didn't sell her pearls. We came straight here from Baker Street."

"I never had any intention of doing so. Is Lord Creighton here yet?"

"Yes, he's just arrived. Which one of the ladies do you think you'll be bidding against?"

"The one in the back left corner."

I craned to see which one he meant. A woman sat in the seat Holmes had indicated. I couldn't see her face. Her black mourning garments included a dense veil that blurred her features beyond recognition. Only the rich fabrics differentiated her dress, shawl, and cape. This was indeed a day of opposites. The tart dressed like a lady and the lady dressed like a servant. I pointed this out to Holmes who laughed. "One would hardly disguise oneself as oneself but as far from one's true self as possible. Not exactly opposites, however. A lady could hardly be expected to wear tart's clothing as a disguise."

The auctioneer cleared his throat. Instantly the room fell silent. An assistant held up a photograph of a medium-sized manor house in the late Tudor style, unmodified from the front though no doubt the living areas had been modernized.

"We offer this Elizabethan house, Wyndhurst Manor with its surrounding ten acres. Bidding will begin –" he named a price. The widow raised her program.

I waited for Holmes to bid but he did not. The bidding continued with various raises around the room but as the numbers went up, the bidders began to fall silent. When at last it looked like the widow had won the bid, Holmes raised his hand.

The widow turned her head to examine this new interruption. He didn't look at her but waited for her to raise the bid which she immediately did.

Holmes nodded at the auctioneer.

"Any more bids, ladies and gentlemen? Anyone?" The auctioneer checked the room.

"Very well then, going once -," he began but the widow bid again.

The amount hardly left her lips before Holmes snapped out a raise.

A current of excitement ran through the room as the crowd realized this was a duel between the tall bony man and the widow swathed in black. They peered at both of them as the bid went back and forth. No doubt bets were being laid.

The widow's anger showed now in the jerk of her head. This was not supposed to happen. She sat upright and almost hissed her bid which Holmes raised. I couldn't spare a glance at either of Holmes's clients to see how they were reacting to his duel. I, like the entire room was intent upon the bids.

Beside me Holmes appeared to be enjoying himself. He slouched in his seat with one hand along the back of his chair to turn slightly sideways with a view of his opponent while she stared straight ahead. Once I thought I heard him laugh under his breath but he kept his demeanor serious until the widow named a sum that was, by any judgment, astronomical.

A constable entered the auction room. Perhaps this was to deter theft with so much wealth on the premises. He looked at all the faces, especially at the veiled widow. He turned toward Lord Creighton and nodded. He stood almost at attention at the back of the room.

The auctioneer repeated the last bid.

Holmes did not hesitate. He raised the amount. A murmur traveled through the crowd. What was going on? This almost landless estate could not possibly be worth that much.

The widow seemed to glance around the room but did not reply. The auctioneer mopped his face with a handkerchief and said going once but not in a positive voice. He looked from the widow to Holmes then back again.

"Going twice."

Again he perused the two faces, the inscrutable black-veiled lady and the tall man.

"I say, Watson, this is fun," Holmes said under his breath.

"Going three times." The auctioneer looked almost pleadingly at the widow. He would get a hefty sum for his efforts this morning without another bid but one could not fault him for trying to make more.

"Sold to the gentleman."

The widow rose to her feet, snatched her cape and walked away with swift strides.

"The game is afoot now, Watson. Follow her. See where she goes and whom she meets but stay out of sight. This game could prove dangerous before it's done."

The room erupted in talk as Holmes stood to claim his estate. I slid through the crowd unnoticed. All eyes were on this mysterious man who had bought the paltry estate for such a lofty sum. Someone was bound to recognize Holmes though he was not as known then as he is now.

No doubt the widow hadn't noticed me either, but I kept back as she strode through the hall and made her way outside.

She hesitated on the street and looked around as if expecting someone. When no one materialized to her satisfaction, she hailed a hansom and climbed in. I took the next one.

"Follow that cab," I directed the driver.

"Aye, sor."

The street was crowded with every manner of conveyance plus pushcarts, barrows, riders on horseback, big-wheeled penny farthings, and pedestrians. I was exposed in the half open-fronted cab but the widow could not see me following close behind her. We entered a shadier area of London somewhere near St. Giles and stopped in front of a little house in Nottingham Court which opened onto a lane. It was in slightly better condition than the houses around it. The woman exited the cab and paid the driver. I sank back into the shadows in case she recognized me from the auction but she didn't turn my way. She stomped up to the house and swerved to enter through the rear. I took note of the address and asked the cabbie to return to the auction hall where I'd forgotten my case.

Holmes was finishing up the paperwork on the property he'd won. I gathered Lord Creighton was pleased. We all left the hall separately to converge around the corner. Holmes gave him the paperwork.

"Gentlemen, the matter is done. May I offer you a ride home in my carriage?"

Holmes inclined his head. I hoped he would get a considerable fee for this morning's work.

In the carriage Creighton confirmed the widow was the lady in question.

"How could you tell?" I asked. "I never saw so much as the tip of her nose through that veil."

"By the way she moved and her voice. She was extremely angry when she left. As I anticipated." He sounded well-satisfied at besting his blackmailer.

"Let me see if I have this straight. You wanted Holmes to outbid this woman who wanted your manor, an old house with only a small amount of land around it. And now you are quits with her?"

Lord Creighton's pale blue eyes were mildly surprised at my summation. "Why yes."

"The blackmail is done?"

"It is indeed. I have foiled her."

I shook my head. "Strangest blackmail I've ever heard of."

"There have been one or two cases that were stranger perhaps, remember the Black Pearl and the German pincushion settlement?" Lord Creighton said.

I could not agree. "They were unusual but not this strange. The purpose of blackmail is to get something. The widow didn't get anything."

"The blackmailer succeeded in forcing the sale of the property. He does not know Holmes bought the manor for me. He thinks it was sold to someone other than myself.

"I abided by her rules. I auctioned off Wyndhurst Manor. It is not my fault if she dropped out of the bidding. The blackmailer behind the widow did not get the property but now thinks I no longer have it and maybe that was his intention."

"Indeed I hope you're right."

"I'm sure I am," Lord Creighton replied as the carriage drew up in front of our stoop.

"Let's hope so." The client was happy and luncheon awaited.

Before exiting the coach, Holmes asked, "Watson, what was that address again on Nottingham Court?"

I gave it to him.

"Does this sound familiar to you, Lord Creighton?"

"No, should it?"

"Perhaps not."

"I'm sure I've heard the last of that woman," he said firmly. Lords were accustomed to settling matters to their satisfaction.

"No doubt," Holmes said.

"I fulfilled my part of the bargain. It's not my fault the woman left a loophole. She outsmarted herself. She thought she could bid higher than anybody but even she was afraid to go as high as I was prepared to." Lord Creighton looked well-satisfied and that was all that was necessary on a case.

"And it was his money," I said as the carriage drove away. I started to open the door at 221B but Holmes stopped me with his stick.

"Not just yet, Watson."

"It is well past time for luncheon, Holmes. You may be able to exist on the word but I cannot. I need sustenance."

"Oh very well. The afternoon is free."

We ate a sumptuous repast without conversation. As the dishes were cleared away, I eyed my comfortable chair by the fire but Holmes had other plans.

I donned my overcoat and followed him downstairs. We found a hansom on Baker Street and took it to Nottingham Court. Holmes arranged for the cab to wait for us. "We shan't be long."

"Oi 'opes so, Mr. 'Olmes."

When we were out of his hearing I asked Holmes what we were looking for.

"The owner of that house."

We separated and asked around. I pretended to be looking for investment property. The denizens of that area of London seemed intent on showing me other properties for a fee. "I am interested in that one," I told one toothless grizzled old man who took hold of my coat and tried to lead me away.

"Let him be, Jonas," a man in an army coat said. One sleeve was pinned up.

Jonas scuttled away.

"He's harmless," the sergeant said if that was what he had been and he hadn't found his coat somewhere.

"Maiwand?"

He nodded.

"I also took a Jezail bullet. 75 caliber. Perhaps you can help me. I'm searching for the name of the owner of that house."

"That's not a difficult one to answer. He uses the house as a bordello from time to time."

And no doubt other nefarious activities. The name he gave me was a street name. He didn't know any other. "I'm sorry."

"Thank you." I gave him a generous tip and returned to the cab. Holmes met me there.

"The Hark!" we said at the same time. The Hark was a man behind many criminal endeavors, a member of the upper class fallen into disrepute.

"To be more specific his name is Jerrold Harkin," Holmes said.

"What, I wonder, is his interest in the blackmail scheme," Holmes said.

We returned to Baker Street and had no sooner removed our costs when the knocker sounded at the door. Mrs. Hudson showed up the same visitor in the tattered cloak.

"Lady Creighton, Mr. Holmes."

"Indeed. Please, take a seat." He indicated his chair by the fire and again took one from the table. I sat in my facing chair but she turned to speak to Holmes.

"I came to thank you for representing me at the auction but I cannot believe my necklace brought such an exalted sum on short notice. Might I not owe you some monies?"

"No, Lady Creighton, you do not. On the contrary I have something to return to you." Holmes took a parcel from the bookcase and presented it to the lady.

She opened it and withdrew the same silken pouch that held the pearls the day before. They spilled onto her dark cloak and caught the firelight. The ruby flashed its blood sign. Her perplexed expression spoke the question.

"It was not necessary to use the pearls," Holmes explained.

"But how did you know that before the auction?"

"I am Sherlock Holmes." He smiled briefly.

"Oh. Oh I see. Then we have lost Wyndhurst Manor."

"No, not at all. I said it wasn't necessary to use the pearls. The manor still belongs to Lord Creighton. He bought his own property and retained the funds used for the purchase. I paid for the property with a bank draft he supplied to outbid the blackmailer. I have not told him of your visit. In the interest of the transaction, I deemed it prudent that the fewer who knew about it, the better chance of the ruse working."

"My husband came to you?"

"Yes. He waited until he thought you'd retired last night to spare you the worry of this business."

"He wanted to keep the Manor? Did he say why?"

"No my lady. He did not confide in us but I presume he wanted to keep it for the same reason you gave."

Her face flushed with happiness and her eyes shone like stars. "Mr. Holmes you have made me so happy. I thank you for all you have done for our family. May I imburse you for your services?"

"That will not be necessary. Your husband will see to that." Holmes said.

She had an anxious moment then. "Please don't tell him-"

Holmes held up his hand. "Say no more. It was as if you had never been here."

I accompanied her downstairs and saw her into a hansom.

Holmes was deep into Debrett's when I gained my chair. "Are you looking for Harkin in the peers?"

"Yes I am."

I was taken aback. I was joking. "Surely no one in that house could be a peer. Are you finding anything?"

"I am. Jerrold Harkin is a cousin of Lord Creighton on his mother's side. He has no doubt turned to crime when he didn't inherit property."

"He must've thought he could get a lesser property from his well-propertied cousin."

"No doubt that was a part of it but I suspect he also wanted to take it from his cousin. The taking was maybe more important to him than the gaining of the property."

"Will you be informing his lordship?"

"I shall send him a cryptic telegram. Perpetrator identified."

"One question I have wondered about. What brought the good constable to the auction room?"

"I did, of course."

"What prompted you to do that?"

"This was a crime in the process of being committed. I suspected the woman was all too familiar with the constabulary. I sent Lestrade a telegram asking for the loan of a constable for a transaction to prevent a crime from involving a peer. No further explanations. No questions asked."

"The power of the peerage," I said.

"Indeed."

"I hope he appreciates his wife."

"I hope she thinks he appreciates her."

"Isn't that the same thing?"

"Certainly not, Watson, but it should be."

***

The Crimson Trail

"Tha' must mind out for that 'un," Peters said. "He's a right bad 'un."

"Aren't they all bad 'uns?" asked Biggins.

"Some may be, but most in the big house ha' mental problems and can't help tha'selves," Peters nodded at the imposing metal door, located deep within the Fairfield Asylum. "That 'un knows what he's doin', an' likes it."

"You mean killin' an' all?"

"Aye. And robbin'. His kind don' want to work like ordinary folk. They feel like the world owes 'em sumpin', and woe to him who gets in his path." Peters opened the small peephole door.

Biggins peered inside. The prisoner lay curled on his bed facing the wall. He didn't react to their voices or give any sign he heard them.

"Is he breathin'?"

"He's breathin', all right," Peters said. "Nobody down here is as bad as this 'un, or as smart. He's a right brain, he is.""

"Not smart enough not ta get caught," Biggins said with a grin.

"Tha' won't believe what he did ta get caught. I heard he's a' 'arch-criminal', as they say, an' a admitted murderer. He killed eight people in Lunnon alone!"

"What's his name?"

"We don't say his real name, you understand, but down here he goes by 'Roy Smith' He's some kind of kin to the Royal Family. He's right royal, he is – but keep that ta yerself."

"Kin to the Queen?" Biggins' eyes widened.

"Aye. Sumpin' like that, he sez.

"What's he doing locked in here then, 'stead of with other criminals?"

"He's more dangerous than those. He's a real cold-blooded killer, he is."

Biggins looked thrilled. "Do you think I could get his autygraph?"

"Ask him – but be polite-like. He don't like people making fun at him."

Biggins opened the larger observation door. "Mr. Smith, sir," he said, his voice louder, "my name's Biggins. Could I please get your auty-graph?"

No reply. Mr. 'Smith' didn't move.

"He isn't in a good mood," explained Peters, "but then, he never is. Just shove the tray through the slot and let's go now.

*Woodyard can pick it up in the morning. We got work ta do . . .
."*

"You are the worst patient I have ever encountered," I said as Holmes leapt from chair to table to chair again, looking for entertainment in the form of a monograph, a newspaper, a chemistry problem, anything to pique his interest.

"I need a case."

"You won't find any in this room. Stop moving around. It jars your ankle. Sit down and stay in your chair. You're to rest until that ankle heals."

He had awakened me in the early morning hours when he hopped up the steps to our sitting room. I then spent the next few hours alternating cold and warm packs on his ankle, wrenched on dark ice when he returned from an investigation. "Take a nap. You must be sleepy after traveling all night."

He slapped a newspaper off the table. "I'm not tired. On the contrary, I'm full of energy and bored. I need something to distract me. You know how I hate to be mentally idle."

"Well, you're not going out on that ankle, and that's that." I tried to loom menacingly, but only made him laugh.

"I don't have any weight on it, see?" He crouched on one leg over a tangle of newspapers, his injured leg stuck out behind him while his right leg bore his weight, which wasn't as much as it should be for his tall frame.

He teetered and would've fallen had I not grabbed his shoulder and strong-armed him back into his chair. I propped the damaged limb on an ottoman and tossed a plaid rug over his legs as he settled his features into morosity. "Now you look the proper invalid," I said with satisfaction, "but remember to move your toes to keep the circulation going."

We were interrupted by the sound of the doorbell downstairs. Holmes perked up.

"You aren't going out of this house until your ankle is healed," I reminded him. "And don't think you can sneak out if I leave to see a patient. Mrs. Hudson will take over. There is no eluding her. She wields a mean broom."

As if in reply to her name, Mrs. Hudson knocked on the door. "Inspector Hopkins and two other gentlemen to see you, Mr. Holmes."

Holmes looked as thrilled as I've ever seen him. "Thank you, Mrs. Hudson. Send them in, please."

She disappeared for a moment and then returned with three men whose coats and hats had already been deposited in the downstairs hall. "Go right in."

"Come in, gentlemen. Hopkins." Holmes nodded at the inspector. "What can we do for you?"

The two strangers were well-dressed and bore the marks of the middle-class in their speech and manner. Hopkins was his usual self, with his thrown-together look in a brown suit, maroon tie slightly askew, and his narrow face home to a sharp nose and a sharper pair of eyes.

"This is Mr. Ogden-Truitt, Director of the Fairfield Asylum in Yorkshire, and Dr. Bennet, who is the – "

"Your famed prisoner has escaped from the asylum," Holmes interrupted.

They looked surprised, more so than Hopkins who was accustomed to Holmes's astounding powers. The inspector tried, but couldn't contain his snort.

Dr. Bennet recovered first. "How did you know?"

"Why else would you have come here at this time of day? Your special prisoner has escaped, and you believe him to be headed to, or perhaps already in, London. I can think of no other reason for your visit. Eliminate the impossible, and whatever is left must be the solution. Gentlemen, sit down and tell me about your concerns."

As they were being seated, I explained what happened to Holmes's ankle. They looked disappointed.

"We were hoping you could help us," Hopkins said.

"Because William Maugham has escaped," I said. It wasn't a question. I wasn't surprised it had happened. I don't have Holmes's powers of deduction, but after working with him, I've learned something of his methods.

Ogden-Truitt nodded. "We're trying to keep it quiet. We don't want to give the situation any more publicity than we have to, but we can't find a trace of him. It's as if he disappeared from the earth."

Recalling how Maugham's trial had been covered in the newspapers, I asked, "Does anyone know how many murders Maugham has committed?"

"Not for sure," Bennet said. "When questioned, Maugham just laughed."

"Scotland Yard attributes eight in London alone to him," Hopkins said. "No doubt that's a conservative figure. We have no idea what he may have done in the Shires."

"How long has he been missing?" I asked.

"Two days," Hopkins said.

"Two?" Holmes said, with not quite a sneer. "And you're just now seeking help?"

"We notified police in the area of the asylum," Ogden-Truitt said, "but they've turned up no traces of him. It's as if he's vanished."

This time Holmes snorted.

"We're sorry we took up your time," Ogden-Truitt said, his porcine features stiffening. He was about my height, but of considerably more weight and with large protruding blue eyes. The doctor was taller with dark hair and eyes, and an air of understanding that many in that profession acquire from observations of their fellow man.

"You're incapacitated," Dr. Bennet said. "We didn't know."

The party stood to leave, but Holmes stopped them. "Wait!"

They turned back to him in puzzlement – hoping, no doubt, for words of wisdom from the famed detective. I didn't expect him to give them much. How could he know anything from just now hearing about the escape? He surprised me.

"Just a run-in with a bit of ice," Holmes said. "I can manage with a cane – "

"You will not," I said.

"Watson, this is a gift! I'm between investigations, gentlemen. I shall be glad to take it."

"You're staying right here. Walking on that ankle now will only worsen the wrench and lengthen the healing time."

"Then I shall solve it for you from this room," Holmes said with certainty.

"Holmes . . . ." I warned.

"How can you?" Bennet was skeptical, and didn't try to hide it.

"I'll not leave this room. Watson, you'll see. Now, gentlemen, please be seated again." They returned to their chairs. This time, Ogden-Truitt took mine directly across from Holmes. His knees almost touched the ottoman bearing Holmes's blanket-clad feet.

"Watson," Holmes directed, "a spot of brandy for this cold, dreary barely April morning."

I poured brandy into four glasses and handed them around. Then I poured one for myself and pulled up another chair to listen to Holmes spin a tale on this blustery London day. I was confident he wouldn't be able to do more than give the men direction, and wished I'd made a wager with him as Bennet recounted the little they knew about the escape.

When we were all settled, Holmes said, "Tell me everything. Leave out nothing, no matter how trivial or inconsequential you may think it."

Dr. Bennet cleared his throat.

"Two days ago – the day before yesterday – the guard delivered Maugham's morning meal and found him lying curled in his bed, facing the wall, as was his habit of late. He removed the evening meal tray and slid the breakfast tray through the slot. When he returned with the noon meal, the morning tray was untouched. Maugham hadn't moved, and he was unresponsive to commands. The guard returned and reported Maugham's condition. I called on another guard to accompany us and we went to examine the prisoner.

"I unlocked the door and we entered. Still no response from Maugham. I reached and felt for a pulse and, finding none, turned him over onto his back. His face was covered in blood that spilled onto the front of his nightshirt – or what we took at the time to be blood. Our first thought was that Maugham had been attacked with a cudgel of some sort and bludgeoned to death. I sent a guard to bring the director as I searched for wounds. I hadn't found any when they returned and, using the prisoner's carafe of water, I cleaned his face. That's when we made the discovery."

"The face didn't belong to the prisoner," Holmes said.

Ogden-Truitt looked surprised. Hopkins smiled and nodded to himself.

"How, sir, can you know that?" Ogden-Truitt asked.

"It is my business to know that."

Bennet nodded. He understood now he was in the presence of a razor-sharp intellect. "The dead man was the night guard," he explained.

"And the blood?" I asked.

Bennet consulted his notes as if to assure himself. "The blood on the face and the nightshirt proved to be dye of some sort, and didn't come from any wounds on the body."

"A theatrical touch consistent with his personality," Holmes said with a nod.

"I determined the cause of death was strangulation," continued the doctor.

"*Petechiae*?" I asked.

"Yes," Bennet confirmed. "His face exhibited *petechiae* due to manual strangulation."

"I questioned the guards," Ogden Pruitt added, "and assured myself that none had given the prisoner anything to aid in his escape. We can only surmise at this point what happened when the guard took the evening meal on the previous night. Maugham must've been lying in his customary position, but respiration couldn't be discerned. Against training regulations, the guard entered with his key to check on the unresponsive prisoner. As he turned him over, Maugham must then have clamped his hands around the man's throat and strangled him. It would've taken about three minutes.

"He then exchanged clothing with the guard and smeared his face with the red dye," Bennet concluded.

"And put him in the curled position in which you found him," Holmes added.

"He must have consumed the contents of the evening tray," Ogden-Truitt said, taking over the narrative. "It was clean the next morning when the guard brought the prisoner's breakfast. Then Maugham, using the dead guard's keys, walked out unnoticed."

"Wasn't the evening guard missed?" I asked.

Ogden-Truitt shook his head. "It was his last duty of the day to deliver the prisoner's meal, so if he didn't return afterwards, he wouldn't have been missed."

"And what happened when the escape was discovered?"

"There isn't much more to tell," Ogden-Truitt said. "We searched the buildings and the grounds and found nothing. We spent the rest of that day, and yesterday as well, hoping to pick up some sign of the man, but with no success. This morning we came to consult you."

I leaned forward. "Did you use dogs?"

"We did," Ogden-Truitt said. "The hunt continued with the dogs, but the problem was that Maugham had donned all of the guard's clothing and left his own on the dead man. They were about the same size. Some time passed before we could procure something of the guard's. The dogs were confused by the double scents and couldn't find a trail."

"There is also some indication," Bennet added, "that Maugham had saved pepper from his meals in order to put it outside the cell door so that the dogs' noses would be confused."

"And you informed the local police?" Holmes asked.

Hopkins glanced at Ogden-Truitt and said, "They did, and then in turn called in the Yard, but to prevent any public panic, we've simply put it about that a lunatic has escaped. We announced that it was '*Roy Smith*'. No one knows yet that it was Maugham who escaped."

"When the public perceives the massive efforts made to recapture him," Holmes said, "it won't take long for them to guess who is really at large. Was it wise to hide the fact that such a man is on the loose?"

Ogden-Truitt flushed. "We also let it be known that this man is dangerous and may be posing as royalty." He glanced toward Holmes's ankle. "And we had hoped you might help us catch him."

"And so I shall," Holmes promised once again.

"But how can you say that?" Ogden-Truitt said. "You're confined to your chair!"

"I repeat, I shall solve your case without leaving this flat." Holmes waved his hand. "Now continue. Tell me more about Maugham, beginning with his stay at Fairfield, from the beginning."

"He arrived six months ago, almost to the day," explained Dr. Bennet, "William Maugham, clad in women's garments to prevent any public knowledge that he was there, was brought to the institute as 'Miss Joanna Cane', dangerous and delusional."

"How was he conveyed to the asylum?" I asked. "By closed coach or by train?"

"Coach," Ogden-Pruitt said. "He wouldn't have been able to see much if any of the countryside, so he won't know a great deal about his surroundings."

"Upon his arrival," Bennet continued, "Maugham was issued men's clothing, *sans* belt, suspenders, or necktie. His shoes were carpet slippers. He was lodged in a part of the building formerly used for storage of things that needed to be kept cool. This was decided because the only way in or out is through a separate entrance. A grated stone fireplace along one wall is the only heat source. The room is furnished with an – " Bennet pulled a little book out of his vest pocket and turned several pages. " – iron bed against the far wall, horizontal to the door, a deal writing table, and chair on one side, a necessary with a basin and ewer on the other, and a rug on the floor. A narrow barred transom over the door is the only light source besides the fire. Coal was doled out to him through the slot where he receives his meal trays, a few small pieces at a time."

"Meals are served three times a day," Ogden-Truitt said. "At seven in the morning, at noon, and at five in the afternoon, and a pitcher of water daily."

"He also seemed to use a lot of soap," Dr. Bennet added. "More than the usual pris – er, more than the usual *patient* in the asylum, and he's asked for a second pitcher of water of late."

"Shaving apparatus?" Holmes asked.

"A razor contrived in a box attached to a chain held by the guard was allowed every other morning," Bennet said. "His hair was cut once a month on the first, while he's shackled. He'd last shaved the morning before his escape."

"And today is the third morning," Holmes said, "so his hair won't be disheveled from length, and he was freshly shaved and won't look to the untrained eye like a mental patient. Maugham thought of everything. All he had to do was await his opportunity."

Bennet nodded.

"You mentioned a deal writing table," said Holmes. "Was he allowed books and writing materials? Be specific," Holmes leaned back in his chair and closed his eyes.

"He was allowed books, periodicals, and newspapers," Ogden-Truitt answered, "and a few pieces of writing paper at a time, along with a soft stub of a pencil."

"I approved his reading lists," Bennet said. "The tomes all seemed time-consuming. They would keep him occupied."

"Did you choose the books provided to him?" Holmes asked.

"No," Dr. Bennet replied. "He made requests."

"And this consisted of – ?"

"Well, there were no lurid yellow books, I assure you," Bennet replied. "His list was most edifying: Historicals. A few novels – Dickens mainly."

"I need a specific list of the books in his possession at the time of his escape," Holmes stated, "and a drawing of his cell as it was when you found him. Show everything in it, including the vessels in which his food was brought, and the tray."

"Is that necessary?" Ogden-Truitt asked with obvious skepticism.

"Everything is necessary if you wish to apprehend him before he kills again," Holmes said neutrally.

Dr. Bennet looked slightly exasperated, but he consulted his notebook and spent a moment scribbling before he tore out several pages. He handed them to Holmes.

"This is everything?"

"Yes, it is."

"These are the books he requested?

"Yes."

Holmes scanned the list. "Ah yes, Fitch's *Castilian Conquest of the Canary Islands*. Can you tell me if the edition of *Romola* was published in 1891?" he asked.

"I don't have that information," Bennet said flipping through his notes. "Is it important?"

"Yes," Holmes said, controlling his sibilance.

"Come, come, Mr. Holmes." Hopkins was impatient. "What difference does it make which edition the man read? The book didn't have information in it to help him break out of his prison."

Ogden-Truitt turned to Holmes. "Did it?"

"Not to the naked eye. Nevertheless, I need that information. Hopkins, please send a telegram to ascertain that fact. In addition, send wires to all the train stations near the asylum and beyond, asking if a man of Maugham's description boarded a train. That information is crucial to determine his route and possible destination."

"We've already done that, Mr. Holmes," replied the inspector. "No one reported seeing a uniformed man purchasing a ticket or boarding the train."

"What does the guard's uniform look like?" Holmes asked.

"Not too different from a police constable's," Ogden-Truitt said. "Dark blue coat and trousers, black shoes, a cap with a bill."

"Any insignias?"

"Yes, the initials of the Fairchild Asylum on the cap, and an insignia of rank on the collar devices – "

"Both of which can be easily removed and the cap discarded," Holmes said. "The uniform then could pass for ordinary clothing, especially if the wearer was perusing a newspaper."

Bennet nodded. "We didn't consider that."

"Maugham would've had no difficulty boarding a train surreptitiously. Ask the station masters you've already queried for descriptions of everyone boarding the trains – women or men – and not just to the south, but in any direction on that evening. And send telegrams to the next stations on the line as well."

Hopkins nodded and slipped downstairs to send the messages by way of a waiting constable.

"Did Maugham have the means to purchase a ticket?" Holmes asked as we awaited the inspector's return. "How much money would the deceased guard have carried with him?"

"Very little," Bennet said. "He hadn't been paid. The guards are discouraged from carrying more than a few pence with them in case some of the patients have light fingers,"

"There is one way that Maugham may have obtained some money," Ogden-Truitt said. "He charged one of the guards fifty pence for his autograph. He may have done the same for others we don't know about."

When neither Bennet nor Ogden-Truitt offered more, Holmes prompted them to continue.

"It seems that to the guards," Bennet explained, "Maugham was something of a celebrity – particularly to two of them named Peters and Biggins." He went on to explain how Biggins had, on several occasions and against all the rules, begun to pester the prisoner for an autograph. At first there was no response, but apparently Maugham finally agreed.

"Several days ago," explained Bennet, "Maugham agreed to sell an autograph. Biggins left the payment, and when he next delivered the prisoner's food tray, an autographed piece of paper was stuck in the slot."

"And which of the two guards was found dead in Maugham's cot?" asked Holmes. "Peters or Biggins? Surely it wasn't Biggins, who had requested the autograph. Or perhaps it was – with Maugham's twisted mind, he might have considered it an honor for Biggins to be known as one of his victims."

"No, it wasn't Biggins," said Bennet.

"I'm glad of that," I said.

"Nor was it Peters," Ogden-Truitt added. "It was a new fellow – Woodyard was his name – who went to the cell by himself before he was checked out to do so. New guards are to be accompanied by a seasoned man for a month. This man was cocky from all accounts. And he paid for it with his life."

As the afternoon progressed, Holmes by way of Hopkins sent and received various telegrams as ideas occurred to him. Bennet completed his drawings of the cell and the countryside around Fairview. Meanwhile, time passed slowly as we awaited answers.

The mantel clock seemed to tick louder than usual. I poured another round of brandy for everyone. Holmes asked Hopkins what else had been done to capture Maugham.

"The nets are fixed, Mr. Holmes." The inspector rubbed his hands as if he'd been working in china clay. "Figuring that he'd head this way, officers are stationed in pairs all over Paddington Station. Maugham will not get past them."

"How long have they been in place?" Holmes asked.

"Since we were notified of his escape," Hopkins said.

I glanced at Holmes. I could, for once, tell what he was thinking. "If the escape was only discovered the next morning," I said, "then Maugham already had ample opportunity to go in any direction. You don't know the exact time he made his escape or the direction he was traveling, or his destination, or by which station he might enter London. Guarding Paddington isn't enough. If Maugham took a fast train immediately after his escape, he could have hidden himself anywhere in London long before your men positioned themselves."

Holmes gave me a nod. "Excellent assessment, Watson."

"The job now is to recapture the criminal," Hopkins argued. "The route he took can be established after we have him. Do you agree that London is his mostly likely destination?"

"Indeed," said Holmes, "but knowing the route he took could help us recapture him before he harms anyone – if he hasn't already done so. We have to consider his targets. In the past, they have always been members of the upper classes, but he was never averse to killing anyone else who got in his way."

Holmes asked me to retrieve the relevant scrapbook from the shelf behind my chair. He flipped through it until he found his entry for Maugham.

"In London he has killed a coachman, a baron, two elderly widows, an admiral, the niece of a member of Parliament and her maid, and Lady Tillson. I don't see much pattern there, but he seems to prefer members of society and their servants. The guard's death was necessary to cover the fact of his escape as long as possible." He looked to Hopkins. "No new reports of thefts or murders outside of the asylum grounds so far, I assume?"

"None reported as of noon today by the local constabulary."

Holmes nodded. "Then I think we can rule out his hiding in the local countryside or forting up somewhere on the moors." He turned to Ogden-Truitt. "Has he any relatives who would aid and abet?"

"None that we know about," explained Ogden-Truitt. "There is some truth to his claims of royal blood. The Royal Family has never acknowledged his existence publicly and wants him to go away and stay away – hence the Fairfield Asylum cell. They can't stop him from claiming royal blood, but many criminals have been known to do that. They don't want him hanged because then his royal status would be revealed. The publicity would be damaging to the Crown.

"They also don't want him housed with common criminals or mental patients for much the same reason. Hence his solitary cell. The staff hasn't specifically been told that he is a royal. They have heard rumors, of course, but only Dr. Bennet and I have this knowledge with certainty.

"The crimes and murders he has committed are known, but he is 'Roy Smith' at Fairfield." Ogden-Truitt finished his brandy.

"More?" I asked him.

"Not now, thank you."

Fortuitously at that moment, Mrs. Hudson – sensing, no doubt, the urgency of the situation without knowing the facts – brought us trays, with Daisy, the temporary maid, assisting her. They poured tea for all of us and left us replenishing ourselves with scones, sandwiches, and biscuits – a welcome respite after so much brandy.

I poured a cup of tea, buttered a scone, and topped it with jam. Meanwhile, our visitors also helped themselves. Holmes's appetite was also hearty now that he had something to occupy his mind. Mental activity would speed his healing as he forgot he was staying off his feet. An immobile Holmes was difficult at the best of times.

Holmes continued to study the sketches as he ate whatever I put on his plate, without seeming to notice the difference between a scone or a biscuit or a sandwich.

"Any further thoughts?" Ogden-Truitt finally asked.

"None that I care to share at this point."

"Surely Maugham would've taken the easiest route," Ogden-Truitt theorized, not for the first time as the day dragged on. "And he wouldn't be able to travel far on foot, because he hasn't been exercising during the months he's been incarcerated."

"Not necessarily," replied Holmes. "He would know we would think of that. Maugham is smart, a wily criminal, or he would've been captured long before he was. Also, we don't know what he did at night. He could've lifted his iron bedstead a hundred times a night, run miles in place, and walked the distance to a distant railway station within the parameters of his cell. In short, gentlemen, he most likely has been planning and preparing for this escape since the day he arrived, half-a-year ago. He would have noted the uniforms which, with moderations, could pass for an ordinary man's coat. When he was brought in, did anyone check his mouth for anything he might have carried with him, coins? A small penknife?"

"No," Ogden-Truitt said with noticeable exasperation, as if we were challenging his administration of the institution. "That's never been required at the asylum. I received the procedural manuals when I was named director. We followed them for Maugham, just as for the other patients."

Holmes gave him a sharp look. I knew what that meant: A new manual should've been written for this singular prisoner.

Ogden-Truitt must have understood Holmes's thoughts. "We were cautioned not to put any directives concerning this specific prisoner into writing, as something might embarrass the Queen should they be stolen or copied.

Holmes raised an eyebrow. Obviously something had gone awry, or we wouldn't be discussing the escaped killer.

Holmes continued to study the notes that Odgen-Truitt had provided. "Not much of a life for a man such as William

Maugham," he mused. "I do wish the Royals would take care of their messes." He looked up. "All Maugham had to do in that cave-like cell was plan his escape and decide which of the guards he preferred to kill."

Holmes held up the drawing of the prisoner's cell and the food utensils. "The cups and bowls and plates are tin, you say?"

"That's right," Bennet said, "and all accounted for after every meal."

"The meals are left on trays at the cell and retrieved at the next meal."

"It simplifies the guards' duties. Breakfast is delivered at seven. Then at noon, that tray is retrieved when the noon meal is served, and then that tray retrieved at the evening meal."

"His morning meal tray was still there when the guard went to deliver the mid-day meal?" I asked.

"Yes."

"The tin tray's edge forms a lip?"

"Yes," answered Bennet. "In case of spillage. The spoons he used are carved from pine by one of the guards, as well as a crude fork."

"No wooden knives?"

A smile twitched at the corners of Holmes's mouth.

"None. His meat is always cut before leaving the kitchen."

"That must have been a great trial to the descendant of a Royal Duke," I said with a bit of sarcasm.

Hopkins laughed. He apparently had no great liking for many of the upper class. "Maugham probably told himself that having his food cut up is part of the service to his Royal Highness, like food tasting and embroidered underclothing."

Dr. Bennet turned away to hide his smile.

The doorbell sounded downstairs. "That will be Carstairs with answers to some of the telegrams," Hopkins said.

The constable was admitted by Daisy, who let him come up without being announced. No time for niceties now. I opened the door to the landing as soon as his knuckles grazed it. He held a sheaf of telegrams which he handed to me, and which I then passed to Hopkins.

"Thank you, Constable," he said. "You may wait downstairs." He glanced through them and then said, "These are lists of passengers – all that could be determined. Names, when known, and descriptions."

"Hand them around." Holmes said, and Hopkins parceled them out to the five of us.

"What are we looking for?" Ogden-Truitt asked.

"Anything that can give us a clue to the escapee," Holmes said. "Take out a pencil and cross out any passengers that cannot possibly be Maugham. When you're finished, pass them to someone else to double-check."

We quickly scanned the wire messages. I crossed out three short women, a family, and two couples. My possibles were two tall women traveling on a west-bound line.

"Let's report," Holmes finally said. "Watson?"

"Two tall women headed west," I began.

"We can rule them out," Ogden-Truitt said.

"Not necessarily," Holmes said. "The crucial factor is their status as travelers. Were they together or separate?"

"The ticket master says together."

"Dr. Bennet?"

"Three single men, but they were on the short side. Maugham isn't as tall as you, Mr. Holmes, but neither is he considered short."

"Director?"

"None to report."

"Hopkins?"

"Families – Short women, two short men."

"I have none either," Holmes said. "Director, are you sure?"

"Well, there was one tallish man, but he appears to be a Scot headed home on the north-bound train, instead of toward London."

"'Appears to be'?" I asked.

"Red-headed with a strong Scot's burr."

"Please pass me all of the telegrams," said Holmes, "so that I may scan them."

I collected them and deposited them into his outstretched hand. He was silent as he looked at each one, before then discarding each into a pile on the floor. He kept one in his hand. "I don't see a reply about the book edition," he said.

Exasperation flitted across Ogden-Truitt's ample features. "I fail to see the importance of one edition of a book or another."

Holmes curbed his impatience. "It is important to look at everything for clues."

The downstairs bell sounded and the constable returned with another telegram for Hopkins. In the meantime, Holmes scribbled a message on a scrap of paper and bade the constable to send it immediately. At Hopkins's nod, he took it. Hopkins wrote one of his own and gave it to him as well.

When we heard the downstairs door close, Hopkins said, "We have a problem. The Queen has been confined to Buckingham Palace by the weather for four days. She now wishes to go for a late afternoon drive in Hyde Park for fresh air. The departments who protect her cannot stop her, but we have warned her guards that today isn't the best time and to tell her the weather is uncertain – that it may rain or even snow."

"Can't you tell her the real reason?" I asked. "That a killer who likes murdering the upper classes is likely on the loose in London? She seems reasonable for a queen."

"She is also stubborn and has a calm, cool character after surviving eight assassination attempts," Hopkins replied. 'We shall not be ruled by the unhinged,' she is reported to have said. And Maugham is her relative, though publicly unclaimed. Apparently she feels he would not harm her."

"She may actually believe that as queen she is immune to death by assassination," Holmes mused, "but it would be prudent not to drive her carriage into face of it."

"The last assassination attempt was over fourteen years ago," Hopkins said. "And one of her past attackers actually hit her in the head with a cane. She sustained an enormous swelling and bruising of her face and eye."

"We must work faster," Holmes said. "I feel the need for a pipe. Will anyone join me?"

Ogden-Truitt accepted a Cuban cigar, but Bennet declined. Holmes filled his pipe with black shag and soon the room filled with the pungent smoke. I opened the far window an inch or two. Would this be a one-pipe problem? The most I'd seen Holmes smoke when mulling a case was three, but those cases didn't have the consequences this one now promised. While he smoked, Holmes continued to study Bennet's drawings of the cell and the grounds of the asylum, along with nearby railway stations. Once he consulted his *Bradshaw*, but made no explanation. He seemed lost in his musings when the bell sounded yet again downstairs. I met the constable at the door and accepted the telegrams he brought. I gave several to Holmes and another to Ogden-Truitt who opened it, took a look, and passed it to Holmes.

"Here is the further information on those books you seem to think is so important," he said.

Holmes read the telegram, along with his own. Then he stated, "I thought as much. Gentlemen, I can now tell you that the Scot who was headed north was William Maugham."

"Thank goodness the Queen is safe!" Ogden-Truitt said. "Hopkins, you can tell your men to stand down now. Maugham is fleeing the away from the capital."

Hopkins didn't react. He'd worked with Holmes enough to know something was afoot.

"I think not," Holmes said, pulling out one of his own telegrams from the stack. "Last night, a railway porter in his velveteen uniform was waylaid on that line and found locked in a lady's trunk in Berwick. When discovered, he was wearing only his underclothing."

"Did he say who did it?" Lestrade asked.

"He was hit from behind. Maugham didn't go to Edinburgh, but dressed as a porter and, without doubt, boarded a train at the next station headed south to London. Lestrade, you must telegraph the Yard to step up the constables on the grounds of the parks and palace, because the assassin may be headed for the Queen. Have them clothed in ordinary dress as much as is possible on such short notice, and watch for a tall red-haired man, most likely still wearing the porter's uniform – but he could also have affected another disguise acquired on the train or in London:

A chimney sweep, a clerk, even a hansom driver. He may still have the red hair, and he'll likely be wearing a hat or cap."

Hopkins didn't wait around for explanations, but leapt to his feet and rushed downstairs, giving orders to the constable as he ran.

"Let us hope he's in time," Holmes said. "If Queen Victoria is his target . . . ."

The next two hours were excruciating as we awaited word on the capture of the criminal, but at half-after-five, Hopkins returned.

From the look on his face, like a man after a satisfying meal, I knew he'd been in time.

"Come in, Hopkins," Holmes said, "and tell us how it went."

The inspector didn't bother removing his topcoat, but he did take off his hat. He accepted the cup of coffee I poured for him. He was exhilarated by the successful capture, but he would soon begin to fade. I put in extra sugar. He nodded his thanks as he took a long swallow.

"It was just as you suspected, Mr. Holmes," he said. "The red-haired Scot *was* William Maugham. Since his escape, he acquired a pistol from some unknown source and a workman's clothing, but he isn't talking. When the Queen's carriage approached, he took aim. One of the disguised constables, hobbling along with a cane, saw him and raised it, bringing it down on Maugham's arm so hard that the cane cracked. Maugham was immediately apprehended by constables in the area and hustled away to the Yard. I doubt the Queen even knew what happened."

"God save the Queen," Ogden-Pruitt murmured.

"I rather think Scotland Yard did that," Holmes said.

"Tell us, Mr. Holmes," Dr. Bennet asked, "how did you know the red-haired man headed for Scotland was the culprit?"

"It was the two books I inquired about," Holmes said.

"Books!" Ogden-Truitt sputtered. "How could those two books tell you anything?"

Bennet gave him a look. He might have had an inkling of the part those books played. I had a glimmer, but it was far-fetched in my opinion.

"Here is how it had to have happened," Holmes said. "When Woodyard brought the evening tray, he found, as you surmised, the prisoner curled up in a fetal position, apparent blood staining his nightwear, possibly even some on his face. Woodyard entered with his key, which is against regulations for new guards, but he was startled and thought something had happened to the prisoner. He, no doubt, bent over to examine the prisoner, and that's when Maugham grabbed his neck and strangled him. He exchanged clothing with Woodyard and put red dye on the man's face before turning him to the wall to delay his discovery longer."

"But – "

Holmes held up his hand to Ogden-Truitt. "A moment. Those two books are the key. Maugham requested them because the backing of the Canary Island history is *yellow* and the 1891 edition of *Romola's* cover is *red*. Maugham likely poured water onto his tray and used it to soak the backing of the book and make red and yellow dyes. He probably had already used his noon tray to make the red dye and put it on his nightshirt ahead of time. In the evening food tray, he soaked the yellow one while he exchanged clothing with the deceased guard and ate his meal. He mixed the red and yellow and applied the result to his fair hair, thus disguising himself as red-haired. He cleaned the tray and returned the dishes to them.

"He removed the insignias from the coat, possibly as he walked to the railway station, where he boarded the north-bound train, making us think he was a homeward-bound Scot. He attacked a porter, donned his velveteen uniform and got off at the next station to catch the London-bound train. He wouldn't need money for a ticket while wearing the uniform, and if questioned he could say he was on his way somewhere. When he arrived in London, he acquired a gun from some source and his workman's disguise which no doubt included a cap to cover his dyed hair Was he wearing one when you caught him?" he asked Hopkins.

"Yes, he was," Hopkins said, "but it didn't cover all of his red hair, and it fell off in the scuffle."

"He loitered unobserved, he thought, near the palace watching for opportunity. When the gates opened and the carriage drove out, the chance was his to kill the Queen. He is full of rage because the Royal Family won't include him or acknowledge his rightful place as a royal. Unbeknownst to him, the Queen has prevented him from hanging like the killer deserves."

"There's rotten apples in every barrel," Hopkins said.

Ogden-Truitt's face was a picture of amazement. "And you deduced all of that from a book cover?"

"*Two* book covers," Holmes said. "I knew that the Canary Island volume's cover was yellow because only one edition of that tale has been printed. I needed to know if *Romola* was the red-backed 1891 edition to proceed."

"Where will they incarcerate him this time?" Ogden-Truitt asked. "I hope not at Fairfield."

"Perhaps on an island somewhere," Holmes said with a smile. "I hear St. Helena is lovely this time of year."

They took their leave after thanking Holmes profusely.

Hopkins lingered. "A book, Mr. Holmes! This case depended on a book! Who would've ever suspected?" He left, shaking his head.

I refrained from saying *A book! A book! My kingdom for a book!* "This was an interesting afternoon."

"Indeed it was."

"I think Hopkins was wrong about the Queen, however. I'm sure she was aware of what was happening. Anyone who has survived eight known assassination attempts would perforce be acutely aware of what was going on around her."

"No doubt, Watson, no doubt."

A few days later, a courier arrived at 221b Baker Street. Mrs. Hudson brought him up the stairs herself. She was so excited she could hardly speak. "He's from the Palace."

The courier, a footman in Palace livery, presented a small box to Holmes. "With Her Majesty's deepest appreciation," he said and took his leave.

Mrs. Hudson was torn between escorting him down the stairs or staying to see what was in the box.

"I'll wait until you're back to open it, Mrs. Hudson," Holmes said with a smile.

No sooner had the downstairs door closed than she flew back up the stairs. "What did she send you?"

Holmes removed the silk wrapping. He opened the Windsor-blue enameled box, a treasure in itself, to find a small medal with a ruby imbedded. "It's a *Personal Service to Her Majesty* Medal," he said, taking it out.

The ruby caught the firelight and flashed red.

"Most appropriate," I said. "You followed a crimson trail from the Fairfield Asylum to Buckingham Palace, without ever leaving 221b Baker Street."

"Hopkins has called me in seven times, and on each occasion his summons has been entirely justified," said Holmes.
— Sherlock Holmes
"The Abbey Grange"

The Shadow of Malice

The telegram arrived after breakfast: *Boscombe Valley needs our attention. Come armed. Paddington 11:15.*

What in Boscombe Valley needed our attention so soon? A year ago at the request of Lestrade, Holmes solved a murder with his usual efficiency, utilizing clues the Inspector overlooked, as per usual.

With my wife visiting her cousin in Brighton, I left my patients in the care of my esteemed colleague, Anstruther, tossed necessities into a grip, and set off for the station where I met Holmes in his traveling cloak and cap. The day was warm but London weather in early June was subject to change. We'd just enough time to buy tickets and find our compartment. "This will explain everything," Holmes said, thrusting a letter at me when we were seated. The paper was thick and expensive by a lacy, feminine hand with a strong back slant.

Dear Mr. Holmes,

I am writing as a last resort. Since you were in Boscombe Valley last year my father died and James McCarthy was acquitted in the murder of his father. Some in the Valley yet believe him guilty but they do not signify or did not until recently.

After a suitable mourning period James and I were married and have been blessed with a pleasant life until some weeks ago when my normally good-hearted husband became abrupt and taciturn. He will not tell me what is troubling him but spends long hours going over the estate books. I believe he's haunted by the murder of his father and that is wreaking further havoc on us. I'm writing to ask you to find out what it might be and help us bring it to an end.

Several attempts have been made on his life. I feel a strong sense of impending doom hanging over us. I cannot involve Inspector Lestrade. He thought James guilty and might think so again. I know of no one else to turn.

The letter was signed Alice Turner McCarthy.

Holmes busied himself with a volume of essays on the antipodes by some unknown chap while I read. "Really Holmes if you want to know about Australia, just ask me. I lived there in my childhood and retain strong memories."

"I'll bear that in mind, Watson. What did you think of the lady's letter?"

"I think you solved the murder but problems from her father's past are lingering."

"Though his life was exemplary in England until the end, John Turner's was the complete opposite during his youth in Australia," Holmes said. "What in that life could be plaguing this family   now?"
"I remember as a boy hearing stories about the gold fields near Ballarat and the theft of the shipments. Those gangs are admired for their 'roughty toughtyness' now, but in truth they were murderous thugs. It is a credit to him that John Turner changed his ways though I cannot fault McCarthy for his blackmail

scheme. He was grievously wounded by Turner's gang. At least John let him live on the home farm, but when Turner killed McCarthy, he proved the killer instinct still resided in the old gang leader, no matter how genteel he had become. I regret Alice and James must continue to suffer as a result."

"Indeed." Holmes put down his book and steepled his fingers. Some time passed before he spoke again. "Past crimes often have a long reach. James and Alice have suffered quite enough."

"Do they know who killed the elder McCarthy?"

"No. You and I are the only ones who know Alice's father killed Charles McCarthy to try to prevent what he considered cursed blood from marrying into the Turner family. His concern was misplaced. James McCarthy is a sterling young man."

"Why didn't you tell them the truth?"

"I didn't want the sins of her father to taint their lives. I expected their ordeal to end with James's acquittal as it seemed to when Alice married him."

"Two of those involved are no longer living. The present unknown difficulties may have nothing to do with that murder, Holmes."

"They may not, Watson, but I suspect they have everything to do with it. This case may appear difficult but prove to be simple."

"That is directly opposite to the previous case," I pointed out.

"Indeed."

"I wonder about these attempts on James McCarthy's life."

"We shall know more when we have gathered information."

"I know. Never theorize ahead of the information."

"Facts."

Our rooms at the King's Arms in Ross-on-Wye were the same as on our previous visit. Holmes had the foresight to wire ahead for a carriage which took us to Goodrich Court, a gray stone house with dark brooding windows. The house seemed to have taken on the morose habits of the late owner despite deep red velvet curtains on the windows that put me in mind of fresh, iron-rich blood.

We were shown into the drawing room where Alice Turner McCarthy joined us. Her pink afternoon gown seemed to pale amidst these new trials. Her golden curls were somewhat askew and she appeared tired.

"Forgive me, I didn't expect you so early," she said, ringing for tea.

"We took an early train," Holmes said. "I assume your problem is now one concerning your husband but not yourself?"

A cloud passed over her pleasant features. "My husband hasn't been himself for a few months. As he is away at a meeting, we can talk freely."

She broke off when a maid brought in a tray and didn't speak again until we were fortified with aromatic cups of tea.

Mrs. McCarthy did no more than nibble a cake and sip her tea while we ate with enjoyment having missed the midday meal. Holmes was yet a slim lanky man while I was beginning to round out as my mother might have said but I couldn't pass up the sandwiches and cakes, though I did wish the sandwiches were more robust than cress.

Holmes went straight to the heart of the matter. "Tell us of these attacks that have alarmed you."

"Three weeks ago my husband and I were driving to Ross when suddenly we heard a crack. James swerved the horses in time but we were barely missed by a large limb."

She fell silent, remembering.

"Limbs oft-times fall," I observed, helping myself to another sandwich.

"They do though we keep those along the drive well-pruned to prevent such accidents."

"Quite right," I said between bites.

"My husband examined the fallen limb and discovered it sawn almost all the way through."

"Could someone have been pruning and stopped before the job was finished?" I asked as it seemed the most logical cause for the near-accident.

Holmes put down his tea cup. "The pruning would've been done in early spring with plenty of time to finish."

"True," I said.

"Still one wonders how a sawn limb could be timed to fall just when a victim was passing beneath it. Have there been other episodes?" Holmes asked.

"The next week we were walking in the park when we heard someone calling for help."

"Were you not skeptical after what happened with the limb?" I asked, anticipating.

"Yes, of course but this cry for help was coming from the other side of the small island in the river. James jumped into the boat we keep for excursions and started rowing to the islet. Halfway across, the boat suddenly sank beneath him. The Wye was in spate with strong currents. He managed to swim to shore but a cold wind sprang up and I feared he would take a chill."

"I trust he did not," I said.

"No, he has a strong constitution. The boat washed ashore at the next bend and we retrieved it."

"And you found a considerable hole in it," Holmes said.

Alice stared at him. "How did you know?"

"Things often happen in threes." Holmes almost smiled. "With the first, there is doubt. With the second, some doubt and caution comes into play. Hence the need for a request for help. I wish to examine the boat if you have it here but there is more. You have recounted accidents from three weeks and two weeks ago. What is the third event that caused you to write that letter?"

"My husband was riding over the farm when the horse was startled by an animal cry. James was able to control him but the saddle slipped. He would've fallen under the horse to be trampled by its hooves, but he leaped upon Reveille's neck and brought him to a standstill. James retrieved the saddle and discovered the girth had been sawn almost through on the opposite side so the saddler wouldn't have noticed it."

"Someone appears proficient with a saw," I remarked.

"So it seems," Holmes said. "What of this change that has come over James?"

"He spends long hours going over the books for the estate. When I ask if there's a problem, he assures me all is well but some nights he gets up after we have retired and goes back to his desk. I followed a few times to see what was troubling him but I have no clue."

"May we see his desk?" Holmes asked.

She was torn between wanting to find an answer and protecting her husband's privacy but needs must. She led us to the estate office filled with books from over two hundred years and left us to watch for her husband's return.

"What are we looking for Holmes?"

"Bank statements would be helpful," was his reply but we didn't find any. We found sales of sheep, cattle, a travel coach bought in 1667 but no other recent financial papers beyond the sale of a bull two weeks ago. Holmes prepared to open the deep locked drawer at the bottom of the desk when Alice appeared.

"Please come back to the parlour. James has just returned."

Holmes checked to be sure everything was as we found it before we returned to the tea table. I bit into another sandwich as James joined us.

He showed no surprise to find us there and accepted Holmes's explanation that we were spending a few days to get in some fishing on our way back to London from Wales where to my surprise I learned I'd visited a former patient.

"I trust you found the patient in good health," James said.

"Oh yes, indeed. When I cure patients, they stay cured."

"The good doctor is much sought for his cures," Holmes said giving me a merry eye. "And now we must be off. Perhaps we could stop by tomorrow and you could show us your favorite fishing holes."

James assured us he would be happy to dip a pole and supply tackle for us.

We didn't discuss the case on the ride back to the inn but as we passed Hatherly Farm where the McCarthys lived rent-free while Charles blackmailed Alice's father, Holmes observed the new tenant hadn't tilled the fields.

"Perhaps he's busy with other fields," I suggested.

"That Mr. Greeley what took over from Mr. McCarthy be'ant much of a farmer to my extimation," the driver stated. "Him and his wife come here from over to Bristol. Ask me, they never dug a hole in their lives. Real fancy he is. He likes to pull out his gold watch and say I b'leve I have time for another pint at the inn and then he expects some soul to pay forrit."

Holmes raised his eyebrows, whether at the driver's speech or the farm tenant's antipathy to work was not apparent until we'd gained the inn and were enjoying a roast beef and Yorkshire pudding dinner.

"I didn't think I could eat so soon after tea, but this is a most welcome feast," I told the innkeeper as he served us.

I waited until he reached the far table occupied by a man in a tweed sack coat and mustard waistcoat before I spoke again. "Maybe that's why McCarthy is worried about money. The home farm will not be bringing in its share of revenue."

"Perhaps."

Holmes applied himself to the repast and I joined him as the tables filled. The barmaid aided the innkeeper in keeping glasses filled and plates served. She was sprightly despite the grey hair under her cap.

"This must be a popular night at the inn," I observed. Most of the diners appeared to be locals by their rustic dress. When the barmaid brushed by the man in the sack coat, a few drops of ale from one of the pints she carried fell on his sleeve. His outraged "Clumsy sheila," arched clearly over the din of the taproom which fell momentarily silent.

The barmaid turned back.

He pointed to his sleeve. "Look what you done."

"Loiks sir, I'll get a cloth."

Talk resumed as she went to the bar and returned to wipe the man's sleeve during which time he continued to shovel food into his mouth and cram his considerable cheeks.

Holmes returned to our conversation. "Why would a man take on the tenancy of a healthy farm and not work it?"

"Illness in the family or himself. Financial reversal. Fallowing."

"Those are all good reasons but if the tenant were ill, the driver would have mentioned it. And it is usual to plough and harrow in a cover crop when fallowing the land."

"Perhaps that field is due for a winter crop."

"Perhaps but a good farmer wastes not the growing season."

The excellent meal was followed by a flummery before we retired. I amused myself with a yellow-backed novel I found on a shelf in my room but the heavy repast soon had me in the realm of Morpheus despite the excitement of the novel containing every vice known to man and some perhaps not known. I awoke once to some noise but hearing no repeat, I fell back asleep.

After a hearty breakfast attended by only Holmes and me, we returned to our rooms to prepare for the morning when a scream tore into the morning. It came from the room across the hall. The barmaid doubling now as a chambermaid rushed into the narrow hallway. "Ee's daid! Ee's daid!" she screamed and threw her apron over her face as if that would block any further horrors.

Holmes and I stepped through the doorway expecting to see a man overcome by a stroke or heart thrombosis. Instead, a most gruesome sight lay before us, one I had not often seen since my days in India. The complaining diner from last night lay sprawled across his bed, the covers flung athwart, a look of horror on his face and blood everywhere from multiple strikes. A knife stuck out of his chest at a slight angle, as if the victim tried to sit up before falling back from the killing thrust.

The innkeeper rushed up the stairs. "Send for the constable, man," I told him. There's been murder done."

"Murder?" The innkeeper fell back as if the word could attack him. "There's never been murder at the King's Arms."

"Go, man," I said.

When we were alone with the corpse, Holmes said. "Quick, Watson, search the room before he returns."

He ran his hands over the outside of the man's bag, a worn Gladstone with the initials ACD stamped on it but found no secret compartments inside or out.

I examined the victim's clothes. Finding nothing, I slid my hands beneath the mattress, careful not to dislodge the corpse. Again, nothing. Holmes had no better luck despite examining the bottoms of the few bits of furniture in the room. .

The constable's boots sounded on the stairs. Holmes glanced at the door, leaned over and snatched something out of the man's right shoe lying next to its mate under the bed. He pocketed the object, a corner of an envelope with Bal written on it in rough hand and turned to the young constable. "Ah, Johnston is it?"

The constable's normally pink face turned red. "Mr. Holmes, sir. Is this yer case?"

"No, indeed. We are visiting Goodrich Court on our travels. We were just leaving for some fishing when we heard the chambermaid scream. We waited for your arrival but now we will be off. Our carriage is waiting."

"But sir, I could use your help."

"Nonsense man, perfectly straight-forward case. The victim was stabbed in his sleep no doubt by a robber. Come, Watson, we mustn't be late."

The barmaid sat in a corner of the taproom crying into her apron. Another woman in a mobcap tried to comfort her. "Tain't yer fault, Lizzie."

"They'll blame me cuz I was the one what found him." Fresh sobs shook her shoulders.

"Start with her," Holmes told the constable.

"He'll never solve it," I said in the carriage.

"He can contact his district inspector and after that Lestrade. We found no money. The position of the knife shows the victim woke up during the robbery and was stabbed with what could be his own knife. For now we have another case to solve. A wronged young man's life may be at stake."

Holmes did not customarily pass up a case we were on the periphery of but he was correct that our attention was better spent on the case in hand. We dismissed our cabman as we would be late leaving and the McCarthy's coach would convey us back to the inn.

By the morning light James McCarthy was a changed man, his face thinner and the area beneath his eyes smudged with shadows. He was dressed for fishing but Holmes told him about the murder at the inn and steered the conversation to the matter at hand. "Your wife told us about the attempts on your life."

"They were surely accidents."

"Nonsense," I said. "Girth straps don't cut themselves, nor limbs."

James's face paled at hearing this voiced by another.

"Be so kind as to show us the places these accidents occurred," Holmes said.

"There's nothing to see but I will show you." He called for a cart and the three of us drove down to the river. He was correct. The scene was peaceful with the Wye Purling between the islet and the bank. Holmes examined the boat pulled up under a willow.

"I expect the boat was damaged in the storm," James said.

"Not unless the storm had a chisel."

"Someone is familiar with tools," I observed.

"And caulking," Holmes murmured. "No trace is left but I suspect paper and glue were used which the rower's weight would submerge. The plug would stem the flow until the rower was about halfway to the island."

Birds in the park suddenly stilled and I felt the shadow of malice present in the valley.

Holmes next asked to see the fallen limb and James drove us there. Holmes cast farther afield and found a bit of rope where it shouldn't have been in a low-hanging branch. "A bowline, the king of knots," he remarked as he placed it in the cart. I gave him a quizzical eye but he was busy mulling and pretended not to see.

"And yes, finally the saddle."

We drove back to the barn where James left the cart and led us into the tack room. The saddle had not yet been repaired. It straddled a rail, its girth strap sawed across on the right side.

"Satisfied? My wife worries about me too much after what happened to my father. She fears the killer is still out there. I've told her whoever murdered my father couldn't possibly want to kill me, too."

"In that, I totally agree with you," Holmes said. "However, that does not preclude another killer trying for an entirely different reason."

James stared at Holmes. "Surely not? I have no enemies."

Holmes made no reply. Had he not heard the question?

As we started up the path to the house, James turned around and spread his hands. "Who? Who would want to kill me and for what reason?"

"That remains to be discerned. How much have you paid the blackmailer?"

James gaped at Holmes. "How – how did you know?"

"You sold a prize bull. You've been worried about money and preoccupied but your estate is in good shape both financially and in appearance yet you have lost weight and look as if the world were about to fall on you."

"Not me," James muttered. "Onto my wife. She does not deserve this."

"No, she does not, nor do you. What did the blackmailer tell you?"

"He said he was in Australia with my father and knows that Alice's father was the murderer. How could that infirm elderly man have done murder and got away? He was hardly able to walk."

I glanced at Holmes to see if he would tell James the truth.

"We don't know that he did. We only know that the blackmailer told you he did. Did you believe him?"

"Yes. I did. I was afraid not to. Please don't tell Alice. Her father never liked me and opposed our marriage. I've loved her since we were children. I don't want her hurt."

"And yet you married another," I said.

"Yes, I'm sorry for that but I was told Alice would never marry me against her father's wishes. That marriage wasn't legal due to

Elizabeth's previous marriage being viable. My father had been murdered. I was alone. Elizabeth was comforting to me."

"Why did you pay the blackmailer? You know they never stop once they have your money coming in," I said.

James looked away as if he couldn't bear to see our reactions. "I – I didn't know what else to do. I couldn't let him tell the world that my dearest Alice's father killed my father."

"It was the one thing he could tell you that would force you to pay," Holmes said. "The blackmailer knew this. Tell me, did you ever meet him face-to-face?"

"No. The initial letter was in the post. After that he instructed me to go to a certain tree that had a hole not readily visible to the passerby."

"Show us," Holmes directed.

James stepped off the path just as a shot rang out barely missing his head. A bullet thudded into a tree behind where James stood not a moment before.

"Quick, behind this wall." Holmes pushed James behind the boundary wall for the kitchen garden. More shots struck around us as we dived into a bed of lettuces.

I jerked my revolver out of my pocket, raised it over the lip of the wall and fired blind just ahead of the direction from which I had heard the shots. I didn't know if the shooter had left or was reloading and lying in wait for us to emerge but I wanted to give him pause and make him take cover.

We listened for a moment. I heard nothing but Holmes said, "He's going in the direction of Hatherley Farm. After him but stay behind trees in case he tries again."

Behind us Alice called, "James, are you hurt?"

"Go inside, Alice, it's not safe out here," James said.

"It's not safe for you either," she replied.

Holmes took the lead sheltering behind the trunk of an enormous oak. We followed zigzagging from tree to tree but no more shots rang out as we closed on Hatherley Farm. Holmes stopped before we cleared the trees. The farm lay before us, a picture of tranquility with pink roses climbing a trellis over the enclosed porch door, smoke drifting from the chimney.

"We must have missed him," James said.

"He had no other place to go," Holmes said. "He hasn't had time to make it to the out-buildings. He must be inside the house. What do you know of this man Greeley?"

"Not much. He was in the navy. Seemed like a regular chap."

An alertness came over Holmes when James said navy. His lip twitched in a faint smile. "Ah. Then let us beard Mr. Greeley in his cabin."

Hooves clattered behind us as Alice drove up in the pony cart we'd used earlier. "I demand to know what is happening."

"Mrs. McCarthy, can you please remain here? We shall have need of the cart presently," Holmes said.

The look that passed between them was one of understanding and she nodded.

Holmes strode to the door with James and me following. He raised the owl knocker but before he let it fall, the door opened and a slender blond woman stood there.

"What is happening?" She looked beyond Holmes and saw McCarthy. "Why James, whatever is happening?"

James looked dumbfounded. "Elizabeth?"

"Is this the woman you married who was married to another?" Holmes asked him.

Confusion clouded his face. "Yes, she is, Elizabeth Markson, but what is she doing here at Hatherley Farm?"

"You will find that her husband is the one who has been trying to kill you, the engineer of the accidents. Is that not so, Mrs. Greeley?

"What?" Mrs. Greeley's face registered shock. "That can't be true."

"Indeed. Why did you come here to this farm?"

"My husband heard it was to let. He applied and was accepted."

"You didn't know the farm belonged to James McCarthy?"

"No, he said it belonged to John Turner. We were only in Bristol when I was married to James. I didn't know this was his home. He never talked about his past and I never came here." Tears welled up into her eyes and she fumbled in her sleeve for a handkerchief.

"We need to come in now, Mrs. Greeley. We must see your husband to clear this up," Holmes said.

"That won't be necessary. We can clear this up right now. Step aside, Bessie."

The voice came from the stair landing where a man stood holding a shotgun pointed at us crowded in the foyer, Mrs. Greeley, Holmes, and James. I was behind them somewhat and might not be visible from the height of the landing.

The man was red-faced with a jutting brow whether from anger or ancestry I could not tell. He was dressed in browns and grays which would have blended into the trees and with a hat pulled low, made him all but invisible to us. He gestured with the shotgun. "Step away, I say again, Bessie."

"No, Bert. I will not. Put that gun away and tell them it was all a terrible mistake."

"The only mistake made was you marrying him."

"I thought you were lost at sea."

"So you said."

"I left him the minute I found out you were alive. You left me with nothing, Bert. He was kind. I had to take care of myself."

"Get out of my range of fire, woman." He raised the gun and aimed.

My Adams was in my hand. I was partly behind the door, not altogether inside the foyer. I raised my right hand and fired. The man must have sensed my movement for he pivoted left and took the bullet his in his right shoulder.

Mrs. Greeley screamed. "No, Bert!"

Before he could switch the shotgun to his other hand we were upon him. James pinioned his arms. "Need something to bind his hands."

"Here, this will do until we can find better." Alice, summoned by the shot, handed him her scarf.

Bessie collapsed in sobs as we took Greeley to the pony cart. We left her to her tears as we could not fit another in the small cart. Alice insisted on going. "I will not let James drive away with a man who has tried four times to kill him," she said giving Greeley a look that would have sliced a ship in half.

Bessie Greeley stood in the doorway wringing her handkerchief as we drove away. I examined the man's wound and put a compress on it using my handkerchief. He made no sound but glowered at James. The bleeding stopped by the time we reached Ross-on-Wye and I was able to dress the wound properly at the inn. We delivered the miscreant to the constable who locked him in the cell in the small constabulary and joined us back at the inn.

"We need you to look at the man stabbed in the inn last night," Holmes told James.

"Me? Why would I know anything about him?"

"We need to make sure of that," Holmes said.

The corpse was laid out in the inn's cold room pending the arrival of Inspector Lestrade from Scotland Yard. The constable called him in because he was involved in the previous murder in Boscombe Valley. He arrived looking as he had the last time we saw him, sallow in his brown suit with bright ferret eyes, just as we entered the cold room.

"What is this, Holmes? Watson, Mrs. McCarthy, Mr. McCarthy." He nodded at each of us.

"This man was murdered in his sleep last night, stabbed in the heart. McCarthy was about to see if he recognized him," Holmes said.

"Get on with it, then."

The constable pulled the sheet back to reveal the man's face, pastier than our morning's view of it. His lips were thick, his nose bulbous with dark eyes under graying brows and hair. His chin had sunk in on itself.

"He looks somewhat worse than the last time I saw him," James said. "His name was Frank Harbuck from Ballarat. He knew my father in Australia and visited us when he was down on his luck. My father always gave him a few pounds. What was he doing here? He had, I believe, a problem with cards and drink."

"The innkeeper said he's been here for three weeks. Is that when you began to receive blackmail letters?" Holmes said.

James gaped. "How did you know?"

"Ha. I daresay the pony pulling that cart has figured it out by now. You've been worried about money. Your wife wrote to me this week asking for my help in determining the problem. We believed you were being blackmailed for something Harbuck threatened to tell the world and the attempts on your life were meant to remind you to continue to pay. That was not the case at all." Holmes fixed his gaze on James. "Perhaps he planned to accuse you of murdering your own father again. You couldn't put Alice through that a second time. Just the threat of it was enough to send you scrambling for money to pay the blackmailer. You were under duress from the attempts on your life which at first seemed to be accidents but with the attack this afternoon proved to be a deadly assault."

"What led you to suspect Greeley?" Lestrade asked.

"With Harbuck murdered the attempts on James' life couldn't have been done by him," Holmes said. "When you remove the impossible whatever is left, however improbable must be the answer. In this case it wasn't difficult to figure out who was left.

"The farm's fields have not been planted. Why was this man here if not to plant the fields? This tenant's agenda didn't involve the tilling of the soil but planting of another kind. He'd no intention of harvesting any crop but murder. He came to kill McCarthy out of insane jealousy."

"But why?" James protested. "I didn't know him."

"An examination of his navy record will show, no doubt, he is a man of volatile temper and rashness of judgment. The anger became a raging beast in his mind that only the death of his rival could assuage. He scouted the area and learned the tenant farm was to let since McCarthy married Miss Turner and moved into Goodrich Hall. He presented himself to the unsuspecting James and was accepted. It seems he can give a good account of himself albeit not a truthful one." Holmes glanced at McCarthy who nodded.

"He was enthusiastic about his plans for the farm. I agreed to take him on for a year."

"He wanted to kill the man his wife married. We see that," Lestrade broke in, "but what has he to do with the murdered man?"

"We'll get to that but meanwhile if you could send the constable to bring Mrs. Greeley to the inn, it would be most informative to hear her story."

"Tell him to take our pony cart," Alice said. "I want to put an end to these events in Boscombe Valley now."

"Quite right," Holmes said.

McCarthy ordered tea brought for all of us in the parlor. Holmes asked the innkeeper how long the barmaid had worked at the inn. "

"Lizzie? About a month."

"What was her surname?"

"Uh, Cabell, I think. Yes it was Cabell. I remember thinking it were similar to call bell."

"What were her duties?"

"She served in the bar and came back in the mornings to do the chambers when we had guests."

"Where does she live?"

"Dunno. Didn't ask. I think she stays with some relative or other. That's what these women do if they don't have a man."

As Mrs. McCarthy poured tea, we helped ourselves to ham sandwiches and wine cake. All of us were in need of nourishment after the activities of the afternoon without stopping for lunch, I realized. Alice sat close to James and murmured to him low. We couldn't hear her words though once I saw Holmes almost smile. No doubt she was commenting on him.

When we were refreshed, Holmes stood in front of the fire and faced us. "Now we come to last night's murder. Harbuck received money to keep him quiet. The barmaid last night heard him call her sheila and realized he was from Australia. She, no doubt, thought he'd made money in the gold fields of Ballarat. I found this in one of his pockets." He held out the corner of the envelope with Bal written on it. "She may not've known about his blackmailing. She schemed to steal his money but he must have awakened during the robbery. She'd armed herself with a knife and used it. She returned to her duties this morning to find the body and feign innocence. She went home at the usual time but I doubt she will return for bar duty. She will be far from Boscombe Valley by now and I daresay will look entirely different."

The constable returned with the news that Mrs. Greeley was nowhere to be found. "She must've gone to relatives, sir. I found evidence of preparations for a journey."

"Good work, constable," Lestrade said.

"It would be well to check on Greeley," Holmes told Johnston.

"You didn't recognize her when she came to the farm with her husband?" Lestrade asked James in a suspicious tone. He still seemed to think James was a murderer.

"I never saw her, just her husband in passing. When I called at the farm, no one was home."

"The name didn't give you a clue?" Lestrade was still skeptical. "Elizabeth Greeley?"

"She was Elizabeth Partman when I knew her," McCarthy said.

"She returned to her maiden name when she thought Greeley was lost at sea," Lestrade said. The words were hardly out of his mouth when Johnston raced in. "He's gone, sir. His cell was unlocked."

"Perhaps his wife followed us and released him," I suggested.

Lestrade was not happy about that. "The man will be far from here and dare not show his face in the Ross again. Maybe this'll remove the stench from Boscombe Valley."

"Indeed, perhaps it will," Holmes agreed with him.

Charles and Alice McCarthy were happy with the outcome and thanked us effusively. Holmes and I had the train compartment to ourselves back to London. After we were settled, I said, "Do you think Lestrade will find them?"

"Mrs. Greeley is a woman of means now, however ill-gotten. That along with her great ingenuity will make her difficult to run to ground."

"Interesting two crimes were both attendant on poor James McCarthy."

"The two were branches of the same one. Everything stems from John Turner's past. He harmed Charles McCarthy in Australia, McCarthy made him pay. He killed McCarthy and let the blame fall on James who married Elizabeth when he thought Alice would never have him. Elizabeth was still married to Greeley whether she knew it or not. When he learned of the situation, Greeley wanted to kill James out of extreme albeit mistaken jealousy. Elizabeth disguised herself and worked at the inn so they would have money to live on while Greeley effected his plans."

"So the murder attempts on my husband and the blackmail were two separate crimes committed by two different men?" Alice asked.

"Correct. Greeley didn't know Harbuck was blackmailing James and Harbuck didn't know Greeley was trying to kill James. Harbuck's murder was a crime of chance. Elizabeth thought Harbuck was wealthy because he came from Australia's gold country. She hid herself in the inn and in the night robbed Harbuck. When he woke up and caught her, she killed him, the blackmailer."

"Sounds convoluted to me," I said.

"It's not. Greed drove this case from beginning to end."

"How did you reach that conclusion, Holmes?"

"Motives, Watson. Motives. When Harbuck learned of James's marriage to Turner's daughter, he figured out who killed Charles McCarthy and blackmailed James who paid to prevent further scandal. I don't know if James believes Turner killed his father, but he'll make sure his wife and the world will never know. We've removed the shadow of malice from Boscombe Valley. James and Alice can live free of the past and I hope we will receive no more calls for help from Boscombe Valley however pleasant the fishing may be on the river."

"Do you think the Greeleys will try again somewhere else?"

"Elizabeth's motive for the robbery was to escape from her marriage. I strongly suspect one member of that pair is no longer with us. Care to wager which?"

I remembered the look on Lizzie's face as Greeley threatened us. I suspected he'd not been the most exemplary husband. She mentioned James's kindness. She'd likely seen little of that in her marriage. "My money would be on Elizabeth."

"However did you reach that conclusion?"

"Motive, Holmes. Motive."

***

The Scourge of Scorrhill Moor

When Holmes returned from the dead on the fifth of April in 1894, he expected two things to happen. First word would get out on the street that he was alive and cases would appear. Second, I would move back into my old room kept intact by his brother Mycroft with the other rooms of the 221B Baker Street flat. I was happy to do so. Life had been lonely for me since the loss of my dear Mary. I quickly found a buyer for my Kensington practice, a young Dr. Verner who met my price without a murmur. Family money, no doubt. I remembered how long I worked to save enough to buy my first practice. By June I moved what I needed to Baker Street and once again was ready to assist Holmes with his cases.

"Are you surprised I accomplished my move so quickly?" I asked Holmes after I had settled in and taken my place on the left side of the fireplace in the sitting room.

"Not in the least from an old military campaigner such as yourself." He poured celebratory brandies to toast our new partnership.

Mrs. Hudson was delighted to have us back. "Oh it's as if you had never gone away," she exclaimed as she served us a superb meal.

I slept better that night than I had since the onset of Mary's illness.

Holmes's first expectation had not been as forthcoming as I had. No one knocked on the door with a case. In the past idleness had plunged Holmes into despair. I hoped he'd acquired some equanimity during his sojourns in the last three years.

I suggested he place an ad in the newspapers but he refused. "That is not my modus operandi," he said. "I need this time to catch up on the criminal world's business while I was away."

I was glad he didn't say while he was dead. Death had been too close to me of late. He busied himself with newspapers his brother saved for him, cutting and pasting articles into his various scrapbooks, seemingly unperturbed by his anonymity.

I continued to see my patients as was my habit in the mornings thus leaving afternoons free for cases that might arise. On the tenth afternoon after I'd moved in, I paced the sitting room while Holmes calmly read a book.

I stopped at the window and watched a man with a peculiar gait make his way through the crowded street. "I wonder what disease he suffers from." I said aloud.

Holmes stood up and glanced out the window. "We shall know soon enough. I expect he is coming to consult one of us."

The door knocker sounded as Holmes returned to his chair on the right of the fireplace, within easy reach of the Persian slipper that held his pipe tobacco, usually Navy cut.

With an air of relief that the client drought was over, Mrs. Hudson announced our caller. "Mr. Judson Jacques to see you."

He was a young man around twenty-six I reckoned with a somewhat awkward air about him as if he were not accustomed to what he was about to do. He was of medium height, long-limbed but with a hint of muscle under the blue serge of his coat and trousers. He was clean-shaven but the pallor of his face didn't match that of his hands which had seen a goodly bit of sun.

"Do come in and have a seat," Holmes bade him.

I observed his gait as he did so and decided it was caused by a small hesitancy before putting each foot down. Not a disease then. I'd just started on the cause when Holmes asked him a peculiar question.

"India or the Antipodes?"

"India, sir." He looked from one of us to the other. "Mr. Holmes?"

"I am he. This is my colleague, Dr. Watson. Not long off the ship, are you?"

He stared at Holmes in amazement. "No sir, but how did you know?"

"It is your gait, the maritime roll. You wait to make sure the deck is where it's supposed to be before committing to placing your foot. An admirable practice for a naval man. And you have recently shaved your beard as well as worn a hat giving your face a paleness lacking in your hands."

He glanced down as his hands and curled his fingers as if they needed protecting.

"What brings you to me, Mr. Judson?" Holmes asked when the young man hesitated to speak.

"It's my fiancé, sir. This were my last voyage before taking an office job. Helen, my fiancée, Miss Cole took a governess job until my return. We were to be married next week and I can't find her." His voice broke on find but he recovered.

"Where have you looked?" Holmes asked.

"I sent a telegram as soon as I arrived in England. No reply but the place where she's governess is isolated so next I took a train there and went to the house."

He paused again as if putting off saying it could prevent her disappearance from being real.

"And she wasn't there," Holmes said it for him.

"Yes, sir. I mean no sir."

"What did her employer have to say?"

"He said she left to meet her fiancé at the end of March. Went to India, he said. I were well over halfway back by then and she knew it. She wouldn't have gone to meet me. We were saving to buy a little cottage," he wailed. "Sir."

"Did you report the matter to the town constable?"

"Town doesn't have one."

"Does she have relatives she could have visited?"

"None, sir. She were an orphan, as am I."

"That answers my next question of whom in your family she might have visited."

Jacques gave Holmes a mournful, beseeching look. "That's just it, sir. Neither of us has anyone."

"Please give Watson the particulars. We shall take the first train in the morning." Holmes said. He stood and shook hands with the young man, then donning his coat he was down the stairs and away.

I wrote down everything Judson Jacques told me and confirmed the departure time of the London and South Western Railway to Exeter. We were headed for the moor country of Devon which should be lovely this time of year. Jacques wanted to return with us but I convinced him to wait a few days until he heard from us. He agreed with reluctance.

"Please find her, Dr. Watson. She's all I have."

"We will do our utmost," I assured him as he turned to go.

I didn't hear Holmes return as I retired early to pack and get a good night's sleep. He was already at breakfast when I went downstairs.

"Ah Watson. Packed and ready, I see."

"I am. Miss Cole wasn't on any of the ships bound for India at the end of March, I take it."

He laughed. "You remember my methods well."

"I had a lot of time to think upon them."

"That you did." He poured another cup of coffee while I tucked into my toast and eggs and ham.

"I must say I have missed Mrs. Hudson's cooking more than I did you."

"Watson, you have grown so witty."

Witty I may not be but I am wary and made sure to pack my Adams at the last minute. We took a hansom to Waterloo Station and spent the journey reading the morning papers. I brought along a yellow book to while away the time while Holmes napped.

At Exeter we changed trains stopping in between for a cold luncheon. In Lynford, we left the train and took the coach north into the part of Dartmoor, that desolate heath land broken by verdant valleys known locally as Scorrhill Moor. We were the only passengers. Our destination was Lyngate on the River Lyn which trickled along until it ran into the River Exe. The coach turned northwest and drew up in front of the Moormaen Inn at the top of a little rise and gave a good view of the little town. The inn appropriately was built of stone which, Holmes informed me, was the meaning of maen.

"Why not the Moorstone Inn then?"

"You'll find that people in the hinterland cling to the old ways and names."

"I'm from Scotland. You don't have to tell me about clinging to old ways."

"Indeed."

In the past Holmes rarely discussed cases until the facts had been gathered and studied and this one was no different.

"Excellent, Mr. Bovey. We will be with you in a moment," Holmes said to the driver of the hired dogcart waiting in front of the inn.

We left our bags in our rooms and settled in for the scenic ride. Holmes queried Mr. Bovey about the area and its inhabitants in particular the Gauldens of Swydden Manor."

"They've not been here long," he said emphasizing his rs in the Dartmoor way. "He's a good enough sort. Inherited it, he did, from a distant relative. Sir Eustace got his title from railroad stocks in London. He grazes grey-faced sheep up on the moor."

"What about the family?" Holmes asked him.

"His wife is often not well. No one's put a name to it. Some say it's imaginary. That leaves the daughter, Emily."

"Does the daughter go to school?" I asked.

"She doesn't. Had a governess but I heard she left, run off with a man, some say but you know how old biddies like to talk and embroider."

"I do, indeed," I replied hoping my dear Mary wherever she might be was not hearing me disparage certain types of ladies though she often had done it herself.

I glanced up and saw an imposing house, almost a castle, somewhat ruined where stones had fallen from crenulations. "Is that the house?"

"Nay. That's Scorrhill Hall. Naught to do with the Gauldens. Or much of anybody else. T'were onc't a fine manor-like castle but has been falling down for some time now."

Swydden Manor was a surprise tucked into an area of trees with fields stretching behind it beside a small creek. The house built of grey stone was not as forbidding as I pictured it, my frame of reference being Baskerville Hall in a previous case on Dartmoor. White shutters and a dark red door gave the house a jaunty air.

As we alighted, Holmes requested Mr. Bovey wait for us. He tipped his hat and drove over to some grass for his horse to graze while he waited. As the day was fine, I didn't think he would need the rolled tarpaulin under his seat.

Holmes had hardly rapped the iron knocker in the shape of a pineapple when the door opened and a small pallid man in butler raiment said, "Yes, may I help you?"

"I am Sherlock Holmes and this is my colleague Dr. Watson to see his lordship." He handed a card to the man who took it and said, "Wait here." He closed the door leaving us on the small covered porch. I noted the boot scraper in the shape of a wolf when the door opened again.

"Sir Eustace will see you sir, come this way." He led us through a large hall hung with all manner of country delights, stag

319

heads on the wall, weaponry hung within grasp, paintings of country subjects such as stags, bleak moorland, game birds, with a chair here and there if one had to wait for long periods in inclement weather and into a library lined with books, similar artifacts and art hanging on the walls.

After introductions and pleasantries, Gaulden, a tall ruddy-faced man who looked as if he spent a lot of time drinking by the fire, said, "I hope you haven't come with your own patented cure to try on my wife, Doctor."

"I have not. I accompanied my colleague on this journey. You have perhaps heard of him?"

"I have but I thought you were dead," he addressed Holmes.

"So did many but as you see that is not the case. I have returned to my practice of consulting detective and I am here in behalf of Mr. Judson Jacques."

"Oh yes. The young man looking for the governess. Well she's not here as I told him."

Sir Eustace stood by the fireplace as was the habit of those desiring to be perceived as a country squire. He had not invited us to sit on the comfortable seating nor had he called for refreshments. We were not guests in his estimation and not worth a splash of brandy or a pot of tea. Parsimony and snobbery came to mind.

"What did you tell him?" Holmes asked quietly.

He glanced at Holmes. "The truth. I told him what happened. We went on a visit to my wife's family. She didn't wish to accompany us but preferred to stay here to work on her needlework. I believe she needed new dresses or some such. Since the trip was a holiday and no lessons would be required, I agreed for her to remain here but she would have to do for herself. When we returned, she was gone. She left a note to say she went to join her fiancé in India."

"Had you heard of him before?"

"She mentioned she had a young man but he was on the high seas."

"Did she tell you her fiancé was en route from India?"

"No. Not to my knowledge. She may have told my wife but she didn't mention it to me."

"Do you still have the note?"

"I doubt it. It probably was made into spills."

"May we speak to your wife?"

"Certainly not. She isn't well. Talking to strangers would disturb her greatly."

Holmes fixed him with a stern eye. "Indeed. Why?" I should think if a young woman in her employ went missing from her house, one that taught her daughter, she would be concerned and want to get to the bottom of the matter."

"Eustace, have we visitors?"

An attractive lady in her late thirties entered from the hall. She was dressed in a dark blue riding habit and looked quite robust to my eyes. A girl of about nine in a similar habit accompanied her. Both bore the healthy look of those who exercise out of doors, and were decidedly unsickly.

"Keeton, bring refreshments, please. Why are these gentlemen still standing? Please, be seated," she directed.

"My dear, this is Mr. Sherlock Holmes and Dr. John Watson from London. They are inquiring about the governess. My wife Lady Gaulden and my daughter, Miss Emily Gaulden."

As we bowed, she said, "Most distressing. We went on a short trip and on our return, she was gone. That was over two weeks ago. I have been trying without success to find a new governess. You don't happen to know of any?"

"I'm afraid not. Was no trace of her left behind?" I asked to see what might turn up.

"Not even a thimble."

"The note. I found a note on her bed," Miss Emily said.

"A note! What did it say?" Holmes addressed her.

"It just said she'd gone to India to be married," Lady Gaulden said.

"Do you have the note?" Holmes enquired without looking at Sir Eustace.

"I do. I put it in one of these books. Now which one?" She stood and walked with a steady gait over to the shelves of books. "Ah, here it is in *The Scarlet Letter*, a dreary American tome that ends badly." She returned the book to its place and handed the note to Holmes before returning to her chair. Keeton entered with tea and biscuits.

Holmes read the note as Lady Gaulden poured and proffered. I accepted but Holmes did not.

"Just as you said, Sir Eustace. Strange that, because her fiancé said he was on his way to England but she clearly says she is going to meet him and be married in India. Most curious."

"I thought so," Lady Gaulden said.

"Is this by her hand?" Holmes asked.

"It seems to be," she said. "Emily have a look. You are more familiar with her writing than we are."

Holmes conveyed the note to Emily who glanced at it. "Yes, that's her writing but why did she sign her name, Helena Cold?"

"Indeed, that is what I intend to find out, if possible," Holmes said. "May I keep this?"

The thought occurred to me Miss Cole might have another interest and was using this method to remove herself from her fiancé's influence. "Did she have any friends in the area she might have stayed here to say goodbye to, that sort of thing?" I asked. "No friends with handsome brothers? No single young men in the area?"

"No," said Lady Gaulden. "I should certainly have known if she had. We are isolated here and almost islanded by topography. We attend church regularly in Lyngate and a few village events but other than that we're alone here. Miss Cole was a companion to my daughter as well as a governess."

"You've not neighbors you dine with?" Holmes asked.

"None beyond the vicar and his wife and the doctor and his," Lady Gaulden said.

"Nobody from Scorrhill Hall?" Holmes asked. "We saw the house above us on the moor."

"Prendick? Of course not," she said. "We invited him when he first moved there a few years ago. He came but had little to say. He measured his words with teaspoons and I've only seen him in passing in the village."

"The man's a hermit," Sir Eustace said.

"He has that boy living with him," Emily reminded him.

"What do you know of that boy?" Sir Eustace said sharply.

"Nothing. He seemed to want to play with us. Helen – Miss Cole said he looked wild like Heathcliff in *Wuthering Heights*. She ran him off by threatening to send the dogs after him." Emily giggled. "He didn't know the dogs would only lick him to death."

"So you never met him?" I asked.

"No. If we saw him when we were riding or out walking, we hurried away home. Sometimes he trailed behind us. Sometimes he ran off on the moors. I remember Miss Cole said she hoped he didn't fall into a bog."

"No doubt he knows where these bogs lie," Holmes said. "We'll have a word with him. Thank you for your hospitality, Lady Gaulden. Come, Watson. We must be off."

I hurriedly swallowed the rest of my biscuit and wished I could slip a few into my pocket but didn't want to appear greedy. "Thank you for the lovely tea."

Holmes was halfway to the door before I caught up with him.

"What's the hurry? We could have finished our tea."

He opened the door ahead of the frowning pasty Keeton. "Get some fresh air," I told him as I passed him.

He blinked. "Yes sir."

"There's no more to be learned here," Holmes said as we climbed into the dog cart. "This may be a dangerous case with more to it than a young woman running away from a marriage she no longer wants." He bade Mr. Bovey to drive us up on the moor to Scorrhill Hall.

"Dark'll be dropping down on us if we go to Scorrill Hall, Mr. Holmes, sir. You don't want to be up there when that happens. Many's been lost in the pools and rough tors of the moor." He pronounced the name of the moor by its local name, Scurrill.

"We'll not be long. I hardly think we'll be invited to tea at the hall. If you think we stay too long, you have my permission to return to Lyngate. I'll not think ill of you and the walk will do us good after the long train journey."

He was agreeable to those terms but as we climbed out of the dog cart, said, "Mind you don't tarry. Rain is likely in a bit."

I glanced at the mounds of clouds on the horizon gradually closing on us like a lid overhead. Something darted on the moor behind the house. Too large for a rabbit? Deer? Sheep?

"Is this wise?" I said when we were close to the great door of what looked like a slightly slighted castle or a pile of rock with evidence here and there of crenulations on what was left of the walls.

"Is what we do ever wise in that there is danger involved for the unwary? I trust you are armed."

"I am."

"Then no more need be said."

Behind that great imposing door with the heavy ring knocker lay a large house still in use from the part I could see.

"Yes," spat the man who opened the door.

He was old at first sight with white hair clubbed at the back of his head in the style of the last century, a tall man with deep-set eyes and a slit of a mouth that gave him a gaunt forbidding look. His clothing was nondescript in color and style, his hawkish grey eyes seemed to belie the aged look of the rest of him.

"Sherlock Holmes and Dr. Watson to see Mr. Prendick."

"Doctor? We've no need for a doctor here and there'll be no remuneration for you coming so far."

The man made to slam the door but Holmes shot out a long arm and blocked it. "Dr. Watson is my colleague. He is not here on a medical case."

"Who are you then?"

"Sherlock Holmes. I am a consulting detective from London acting for a client. May we see Mr. Prendick?"

"Come in then."

He turned and strode down the corridor which proved to be a hall hung with all manner of weaponry and left us to close the door which I did with Holmes's help. We walked briskly to catch up with him.

He led us to a parlor, rock walls punctuated with arrow slits which let in enough light to give the room a grayish pallor, something like that of the man himself. He seated himself in a large cushioned chair and flung his arm toward various other seating. "Seat yourselves. Choose what you prefer."

We hadn't much choice there. Most of the chairs seemed rickety but I found a Romanish chair in an X design and Holmes chose one Queen Anne might have sat on if she'd lost weight. We seated ourselves under the baleful stare of the man across from us. When neither he nor Holmes spoke, I asked him if he were Mr. Prendick.

"I am," he replied without further amplification. His words dropped into the cold silence of the room, fireless, curtainless but not dustless. I felt a sneeze at the back of my throat but coughed instead and the urge passed.

Holmes still didn't speak. The silence widened into a lake. I began to feel uncomfortable, tired, and hungry. Lady Gaulden's biscuits did little for my desire for food. We would not be offered tea in this meager household.

"We're looking for a young woman," I said.

Prendick snorted. "Aren't you all?"

Clearly he was not of that company. He had not even a charwoman unless she only came once a year and tomorrow was her day.

"This young woman has disappeared. She is Miss Helen Cole, the governess for Sir Eustace's daughter, Emily."

"Why don't you ask the people next door then? They would know more than I."

"Did you know her?" Holmes's voice was curt. He was tiring of this man's pretense if pretense it was.

"I did not."

"You seem sure of it," I said.

"I may have seen her from a distance but can't say with any surety because I don't know her, don't know what she looks like.

I have seen a child next door on walks with a young woman if that's who you mean. But I do not know her."

Holmes pulled the photograph out of his pocket and held it out toward the man.

He squinted but made no move to stand up and take a look at it.

With an exclamation that bordered on rude, I retrieved the photograph and handed it to Prendick. He glanced at it. "Looks like the one I've seen."

I took it back and put it in my pocket. "Do you remember the last time you saw her with her pupil?"

"No."

"Have you seen her without her pupil recently?" Holmes asked.

"No."

"Not hurrying down to the road, or across the moor?" I asked.

"No. She'd be a fool to go up on the moors," Prendick said.

"Why is that?" I asked.

"Dangerous for those that don't know their way. Bog pools. Tors. Scorrhills."

"Scorrhills? Is that what this hall is named for?"

"Could be. I didn't build it. Or inherit it. I bought it but the condition was so run down I finally gave up on it."

"Do you live here alone?" Holmes asked opening his eyes in a penetrating look.

"No."

"Who lives here with you?"

"My son. He's been away at school but he's home now for awhile."

"What school is that?"

He named one in the far north near the Scottish border, a good school. I suspected Holmes was surprised this curmudgeonly hermit had the means to send his son to a school of excellent standing.

"Where is his mother?" I asked.

"She died."

"May I ask how?" I asked.

"In childbirth."

"May we speak to your son? Perhaps he saw Miss Cole leaving Swydden House."

"He went to the village."

"When will he return?" Holmes asked.

"He has no set schedule." Prendick shrugged as if it was no concern of his what his son did. "You may show yourselves out."

As we neared the door of this cavernous room, a young man stepped inside. "I shall show them out, Father."

"You do that," Prendick said slowly. "This is my son, Julian Prendick. Julian, these gentlemen are Sherlock Holmes and Dr. Watson from London. They are making inquiries about a young woman missing in the area."

I must admit young Prendick was a surprise. I was expecting a half-wild creature and what I beheld when I turned to the door was a young man dressed in the latest London clothing, clean-shaven, hair cut neatly and combed, an immaculate white shirt, dark coat and trousers, polished boots, necktie with a perfectly executed knot in large blue and thin navy stripes, no doubt from his school. "How do you do," he said as he bowed to us.

I tried not to gape but instead offered my hand which he took in a firm handshake. Holmes made no movement to shake but watched the young man intently. Julian stood aside gesturing to the hall, saying, "This way, gentlemen."

After surviving a vicious war in the East and practicing medicine all over London, I am often surprised by humans but seldom as much as I was that day at Scorrhill Hall on the moor. "Your father tells us you have been at school until recently. Do you miss it?"

"I miss the camaraderie, the games, not so much the studying." He smiled and his face became even more charming.

"Any plans to continue your education?" I persisted. Inane questions for the young but good for winkling out a personality.

"Not at the moment. I have an interest in botany and shall continue with that on the moor." He swept an arm outward toward the door and the land beyond it.

"I wish you the best with your endeavors then," I said.

"Thank you, sir." He opened the door and we saw to our surprise the night had descended.

"If you remember anything about Miss Cole, we shall be at the Moormaen Inn for a few days. I bid you good evening," Holmes said.

The door didn't close behind us as we left Scorrhill Hall. I sensed young Prendick watching us from it as we walked away. "I see our conveyance has gone ahead of us," Holmes observed.

"Just as he said he would," I said as a few drops fell from the dark sky. "He didn't want to be driving in the rain. Can't say I blame him."

"Nor I," Holmes agreed. We turned up our collars and strode away at a brisk gait.

We met a herdsman with his sheep heading for lower ground. "To escape the storm?" I asked him.

"Nah. What's a storm to sheep? I'm taking 'em to lower ground for safety. Lost a lamb last night. No trace of it but a little blood."

"That could be tiresome taking them up and bringing them back down," I said.

"I'm going to a different part of the moor. Parkins lost two last week. Can't chance that."

We wished him well. As the road descended the rain drops grew sparser until they stopped. We found Bovey waiting around a turn on the downhill side of Scorrhill Hall.

"I were about to give you gents up as lost on the moor I didn't want to leave you in that accursed place in the dark but I couldn't risk my horse."

"No of course not," I said. "Very sensible of you."

"Anybody pass you on their way up from the Hall?" Holmes asked.

"Nary a soul."

Holmes nodded as if that was the expected reply.

We climbed into the dog cart and set off at a fast walk. Bovey lit one of his lanterns which gave off a cheery glow against the dark. Behind us I fancied I heard sounds, howls, startled cries, moaning, keening. We were some distance from the prison and unlike the time of the Baskerville case, no escaped inmates were about to heighten the danger of the moor which was dangerous enough itself with its rough terrain. Back in the relative civilization of Lyngate, Holmes stopped to chat with the innkeeper while I proceeded directly to table after a quick wash.

After a plain but no less savory meal topped by a splendid pudding in the inn, Holmes and I sat by the parlor fire to enjoy our pipes. We were the only guests and therefore free to mull and discuss the day's fact-finding.

"I find the Gauldens at odds with each other, Sir Eustace and Lady Gaulden. He had no idea the note had been kept by his wife. Indeed, he said he left it for spills. His wife must have found it and put it in the book for safety. Why, I wonder, did she choose that book?"

"The choice was auspicious," Holmes said, "but sometimes a conundrum is just a coincidence."

"Surely not in this case. She could have chosen from any of those books. Why that one?"

"Perhaps she suspected her husband of pursuing the comely young governess. Did he and had he done such before? Did the young lady run away from him and where did she run to? According to her fiancé they were both alone in the world, children of orphanages."

"Could she have returned to her orphanage?"

"I checked with Jacques. She had not."

"Perhaps Lady Gaulden removed the temptation of the governess," I suggested.

"I am not ruling her out because of her situation but because she would have nothing to gain. The governess was leaving in a few weeks to marry her fiancé. Why would she call attention to the situation by putting the note in *The Scarlet Letter*? I think

Lady Gaulden is too smart to do that." Holmes smoked awhile as he stared into the dancing flames of the fire.

Despite the tobacco stimulant, I felt myself slipping into sleep. The fire was almost down to ash the next time I saw it. Holmes shook my shoulder. "Come, Watson. We have work to do this night."

I wanted nothing more than to stretch myself on the smooth sheets on my bed upstairs but Holmes was right. We'd not come here to be comfortable. We came to find out what happened to Miss Cole and to help her if no harm had yet befallen her. I struggled into my Ulster. Holmes made packs from our travel rugs. No doubt they held everything needed for the night. "Any chance of renting a conveyance?"

"No. We'll not be going to Swydden House. The distance will be halved."

In silence we made our way through the sleeping village. People far from London kept farmer's hours, retiring at sundown, rising with the sun. A few dogs looked at us and one insisted on barking until its owner said, "Hush, Nelson," and the barks subsided.

"Well done, Nelson," Holmes said.

On the other side of the village Holmes related to me what he'd learned from the innkeeper while I was napping. "Sheep disappearing all over this area of the moor beginning a few years ago, leaving behind blood traces as if a predator were the culprit. Then the losses stopped. About the time the Prendick boy went away to school. He returned near the end of March and since then three sheep have been taken after killing. The shepherds reported they never heard a sound."

"Do you think he did it?"

"I can't imagine for what reason."

"Do you think the boy killed Miss Cole?"

"We do not know Miss Cole is dead. I fervently hope she is not."

"He seemed a nice lad." His tie was perfection.

"He did indeed. A credit to his father and his school."

"I think we need to look at the Gaulden family more carefully."

"Perhaps. Better to talk to the other servants. See what they have to say about matters. The innkeeper says one of the inn's maids has a sister who works at Swydden House. I shall see her tomorrow. Maybe she can shed some light on Miss Cole's disappearance."

We settled ourselves in a shadowy cleft against the foot of a tor facing the track that led from Scorrhill Hall to the moor. The sky was overcast but behind the clouds a partial moon emitted a meager light. I wrapped myself in the rug and took out a sandwich. The trek made me hungry despite the excellent dinner at the inn. Roast beef with a generous dollop of mustard washed down with a pint of stout.

"Please dispose of those wrappings. People can smell that mustard for a mile," Holmes said.

I swallowed the last bite and rolled the paper into a tight ball. I drank half of the stout and the next thing I remember Holmes said, "It's well after midnight. Nothing will happen this night. We may as well go back to our comfortable beds."

In complete agreement, I stood up, well aware of the hard ground I'd been reclining on. In silence we started down the track, Holmes leading the way with his stick at the ready.

When we reached the road, he suddenly drew back into the shadow of a spindly tree, pulling me with him. In a moment a horseman passed by. The rider's head was drawn into his collar and he leaned into the saddle as if asleep or halfway there. "We need him to turn around," Holmes said as he bent and felt around for a stone. He found one and hurled it after the rider. From the sound of it falling, he hadn't missed the rider by much. The man startled awake but instead of looking around, he spurred his horse into a gallop and disappeared from our view.

"Shouldn't we follow him?"

"I don't think it's necessary."

"Did you see his face? I couldn't."

"No, but I've no doubt it is Sir Eustace."

"Shouldn't we confront him?"

"And what? Hear him say he had a late night of cards with friends?"

"Maybe he was seeing a woman."

"Maybe. If it's a habit, no doubt he has a well-established alibi. I'm sure he's prepared to defend himself."

Holmes was sitting in the parlor reading a newspaper when I went downstairs the next morning.

"Ah, Watson. You missed an excellent breakfast but I procured a pot of coffee and an extra cup for you. Luncheon will be ready shortly."

I don't know how he does it. I could've slept another hour or two but his sleep had been even less than mine and he exuded energy.

"I've had an interesting morning. I'll save it for after you've eaten. Unlike me, you seem to need food first thing upon waking. A tiresome habit."

Fortunately for me we'd not long to wait before the inn served again. I tucked into a solid repast and noticed Holmes didn't' refuse anything either. I raised an eyebrow at him.

"I told you I was busy after breakfast." That was all he would say until we've shared another pot of coffee and left the inn for a stroll along the stone houses. The day was brisk but to be expected after the raw winter, especially up here on the moor.

"Your morning must have included a bit of walking. I've not seen you eat that heartily in years."

"How adroitly you allude to my three-year disappearance. Am I to assume this will be a habit now?"

"I don't have habits."

Holmes threw back his head and laughed heartily.

I stared at him in amazement. "Your jocularity must be due to the freshening air up here on the moors far from the reeking cities."

"No doubt you are correct. Now here is what I learned this morning. Kitty Felton, the barmaid at the inn is a sister to Mary Felton who is Lady Gaulden's maid. She says Sir Eustace has a roving eye and all the girls in the village keep their distance from him including Kitty. He thought he had certain rights but not with the Felton sisters. He has to travel far afield to find a girl who will look at him. He's known to be cranky and a skinflint, two things girls want no part of. It is less and less likely he will find one within riding distance. As for Miss Cole, she never went in a room with him unless Emily or Lady Gaulden or Keeton was there."

"Could he have slipped back and taken her somewhere he could visit her and she wouldn't be able to escape?"

"Kitty said that was entirely possible but Miss Cole wouldn't go with him willingly. Her disappearance may be just that, an unwilling incarceration."

"What is the plan?"

"How do you know I have a plan?"

"I know how you work. You always have a plan."

"You are correct. I do, but often the plan is hijacked or abandoned. We could lie in wait for him tonight and follow him assuming he will be rendezvousing again. Or we can start our search in the daylight. I have horses awaiting us. No rain has fallen since last night. We shall endeavor to follow Sir Eustace's tracks to find out where he went and what he did."

Two sturdy horses were tied in the side yard of the inn. Holmes chose the bay mare while I rode the dappled one. We found the place where Holmes had thrown the stone at the rider. We retraced the prints his horse had made in the road. They led us to a cottage in a tiny town on the other side of the River Lynn called Riverwode. We dismounted and Holmes knocked on the ancient wooden door. When no one answered, we walked around to the back of the house. The place seemed deserted. No livestock in the musty barn, no chickens scratching around the farmyard. No dog, no cat.

"I think it's been deserted for some time," Holmes observed. "No prints of animals or humans in the dirt besides those of his horse. However, we should look inside to be sure Miss Cole is not being held here."

We went over every inch of the cottage and barn but turned up no signs of habitation. "Let's have a pint at the inn," Holmes said.

The Lion and Hare was small with only two customers and the innkeeper. We ordered a pint each and sat at the bar. The two men paid no attention to us or much to each other either. We all sat and drank. The innkeeper gazed out the window.

Finally one of the men said, "Them's Carter's ponies."

"You come from Lyngate?" the other said.

"Yes to both questions," Holmes said.

"First'un wasn't a question," the first man said.

"My mistake," Holmes said. "Innkeeper, a pint for my two critics here."

One snorted. The other said, "Good'un."

The innkeeper put four pints on the bar. The two men each took two. Holmes looked amused.

"We were looking at a cottage at the end of town. Looks like nobody lives there," Holmes said.

"'Z'at what brought you here to this thriving metropolis?" the first man said.

"No, we were riding by and saw it seemingly abandoned so took a closer look. Saw some horseshoe prints leading up to the door and away again."

"That might be Sirrr Eustace. Lives at Swydden House over t'river."

"You think he might be trying to buy that cottage?" I asked.

The men laughed. "He already owns it. Thought he owned the family what was living there but they took off yesterday. Just in time, He has a certain reputation, you see," said the first one.

"Hear tell they went to Plymouth. Or was it Exeter?" his friend said.

"Let me guess," Holmes said. "The cottage family has a beautiful daughter."

No one denied this.

The ride back to Lyngate was a grim one. "Why would he go after this girl if he has Miss Cole stashed somewhere?" I said.

"Two reasons come to mind. He has killed Miss Cole and needs a replacement. Or he doesn't have her."

We rode in silence to the inn.

Our plan for the remainder of the day was to nap and observe the moor at nightfall. We would circumvent both Scorrhill Hall and Swydden House and approach them from the rear but as we reached the inn, our plans changed somewhat. Sir Eustace waited for us in the bar. The locals sat as far from him as they could without leaving the room. His face was red and worse for drink. At our entrance, he sprang from his stool and knocked it over behind him. He strode unsteadily to the door and confronted us. "You, swine, what do you think you are doing?"

He swung at Holmes who ducked, caught his right wrist and twisted it slightly. Sir Eustace let out a cry.

"Is there a private room?" I asked the innkeeper.

He nodded and came from behind the bar to lead us to a room across from the public room. Holmes marched Gaulden into it and pushed him down on a high-backed bench.

"Bring us a pot of coffee," I asked the innkeeper. He nodded and closed the door behind him.

Holmes remained standing as Gaulden slouched over the table rubbing his wrist when Holmes released it. "You didn't have to do that," he whined.

"What is your complaint against us?" I asked.

"You've been all over the countryside making accusations against me." He didn't look at either of us as he continued to rub his wrist. It was beginning to turn red.

"Let me examine your arm," I said as I reached for it.

He lashed out at me with the other arm, his left which did not make contact.

"Enough of that," Holmes said sharply. "Let Dr.Watson examine your wrist."

I took his thick wrist and found it to be in working order. "Nothing here. Stop rubbing it or you may make it fester." That was unlikely to happen but in his state he was not to know that.

He dropped his hands onto the table and began to cry. "I never touched the girl. I swear. I loved her."

"Do you mean Miss Cole?"

"Helen. I know my wife helped her run away from me. I only wanted to see her smile every day."

"What about the girl in Riverwode. And others."

"I never touched any of them. I like to see them smile. They're so pretty, like when I was young. Not like Lady Gaulden."

The innkeeper tapped on the door. Had he listened there?

"Enter," Holmes said and the innkeeper set a tray on the table out of reach of sir Eustace. Sensible man.

The coffee steamed in the pot. The tray held three cups but Holmes and I didn't need any now but would need it later on the moor. I was determined to stay awake this time.

Sir Eustace seemed more awake but not less inebriated when we led him to his horse and helped him into the saddle. "Go home and sleep it off," I said sternly. "Don't use that hand for a week and sleep with it on a pillow to prevent swelling."

"Is that necessary?" Holmes asked when the horse was out of sight on the road to Swydden House.

"Hardly but maybe he won't try to hit anybody for awhile. What a sad wreck of a man."

Rain fell as we made our way onto Scorrhill Moor behind Scorrhill Hall at twilight but it didn't last. I sipped coffee from time to time to stay awake and saved my sandwich for later. I noticed Holmes did the same. We made ourselves as comfortable as possible while the moor settled around us for the night. A light wind sprang up and the clouds sped across the sky interspersed with washes of bright moonlight. I leaned against the hard stone of the tor and thought about the scorrhills or early village remains found here and there on the moor. I could almost feel the ghosts of the long dead if I couldn't see or hear them.

A blob of shadow caught my eye. Had it been there before? I didn't think so.

"It's someone from the Hall," Holmes said under his breath.

We watched as the shadow moved toward us growing ever larger. It must be a man, Prendick or his son, Julian the immaculate? Or someone else? I didn't think the shadow was a woman. It moved like a man as it came straight toward us. I flattened myself against the stone at my back. Holmes did the same.

The shadow dipped behind a rise and didn't reappear. "He's veered away from us," Holmes said.

I checked my pocket for my revolver. I noticed Holmes did the same. We grabbed our sticks and left our sandwiches, coffee and rugs as we ran toward the last place we glimpsed the shadow. Holmes and I saw him at the same time. "Let him go ahead. He's following this track now. We can do the same without keeping him in sight. I think I know where he's going."

"Where?"

"According to a map the innkeeper showed me of the moor in this area, there's a scorrhill nearby. This section of the moor takes its name from the ruins. That must be his destination."

"Unless it's to another sheep herd. What would he be doing at a scorrhill?"

"Looking for treasure. Checking a grave. Or maybe Miss Cole is hidden there."

That jolted me. She had been missing for a little over two weeks now. That would be a long time to be locked up on the moor.

"Better that than dead," Holmes said.

The shadow man skirted some ruins little more than lumps in the moonlight. We stopped in the lee of a tall stone to see which way he was heading. Still northwest. We let him go down the track he seemed to be familiar with. Of course, living in Scorrhill Hall, he would be despite having been away at school for several years. He would have come home for holidays.

The track rose ahead of us but we couldn't see the shadow. Holmes turned and went over a rise and down. He halted above a slight hollow or indentation. I stopped behind him. "A kistvaen," Holmes said like a sigh. "Prehistoric tomb."

The shadow ahead started to turn. Holmes and I dropped to the ground and must have made ourselves invisible because the man continued, intent on his path.

"Get as close as we can and then charge him," Holmes said.

It was as good a plan as any. We crept silently toward our unsuspecting quarry.

The clouds parted and revealed him stopped in front of a square stone in the ground. He leaned over and picked up what looked like an axe handle and used it like a pry bar.

While I was intent on the man, my foot dislodged a small stone. It hardly made a sound above a whisper. The man whirled and we saw his features in the bleaching light. Gone were his young gentleman's clothing, his carefully combed hair, his Victorian manners, his polished boots. He wore no clothing at all. What had seemed a dark shadow was a young male with sleek black fur. He saw us and opened his mouth in a snarl. His incisors were longer than a human's. His eyes flashed and he came for us. I expected him to drop onto all fours and spring but he swung the ax handle at the two of us in the manner of a human. If we hadn't had the presence of mind to duck and Holmes hadn't parried with his stick, the creature might have killed the two of us with one blow.

"Julian," Holmes spoke in a soft coaxing tone, "put down the bar and help us get her out."

Julian looked human again for a moment and then snarled and lashed out with the bar. At that moment, I thought Julian crossed over the line between human and wild beast.

"Watson, use your revolver if you must," Holmes said as he fended off killing blows from the heavy bar.

I pulled it out of my pocket and tried to aim it at the Julian creature without hitting Holmes. One of the mad jabs caught me on my shoulder which had taken a bullet in the Maiwand battle. Long-healed, it suddenly didn't feel healed. The creature flailed again at Holmes who could only protect himself. As dangerous as Julian was in his present guise, I hoped he wouldn't leap upon us like a wild animal.

The creature was unstoppable and untiring. He came at us again and again. I couldn't shoot without possibly hitting Holmes as he ducked and parried. Julian knocked the stick out of Holmes's hand and went in close for the kill.

"Duck!" I yelled at Holmes as the creature reared back to lunge and when he did I fired. Flames seemed to roar out of the barrel.

The creature backed up a few steps, snarled and started for me. I dropped my stick when I fired but Holmes found it and intervened. I raised the revolver again and pulled the trigger. Again I saw flames but I don't know if they were real or in my imagination. Nothing would surprise me this night.

This time I hit the creature high on its arm or shoulder, I thought. It staggered backward roared once and ran away into the darkness. We heard it snarling and then we didn't. Had I hit an artery?

"I suppose we should look for it," I said.

"Our first duty is to Miss Cole," Holmes reminded me. He picked up the pry bar and his stick and bent over the stone in the ground. I retrieved my stick and pocketed my revolver. The moon was hidden behind clouds again but we could make out the edges of the gray stone. Holmes applied the bar while I kept a lookout for Julian.

The stone moved easily. He let it fall backwards. We heard a whimper. The moon came out and looking up at us was a young woman with a face as pale as the moon.

"Miss Cole? I am Sherlock Holmes. This is my colleague Dr. Watson. Your fiancé Judson Jacques sent us to find you."

"Can you move?" I asked her. She had been living in a cramped hole for over two weeks.

"I think so. I tried to flex my muscles at intervals." Her hands were tied with a long rope attached.

"Did he take you out and let you walk around?"

"Yes, he did. I begged him not to put me back but he didn't listen to me. What is wrong with him?" She looked around in the darkness. "Is he coming back?"

"I hope not," Holmes said. "Watson shot him at least once. He will not return. If he still has a mind to think with."

We each took an arm and helped her out of the tomb. Holmes removed the rope while I steadied her. Her eyes darted all around.

"What did he look like when he came every night?" I asked her.

"He looked like Julian Prendick. I couldn't understand why he was doing this to me."

"Did you know him well?" Holmes asked as we started the walk back to the tor.

"No. I'd never had a conversation with him. I just knew him when I saw him. That's what was so strange. We'd never even had a conversation until he did this."

"Did he harm you?" I asked.

"No. He came every night and brought food and water. He didn't talk just watched me eat and then led me around a bit and put me back into that hole." She shuddered.

Maybe she didn't know it was a grave. I didn't ask if anything was in it. Holmes dropped the rope in and slid the cover back into place.

"What did he bring you to eat?" I asked.

"Roasted meat. Mutton. Rabbit once. Sometimes a roasted vegetable, a-a beet or a potato. I didn't like it but I ate it to stay alive as long as possible."

We rested at the tor and wrapped her in rugs to stop the shivering. We gave her our sandwiches. She ate both and drank all the coffee and water.

"He had no food with him when we caught him," I said to Holmes as she ate.

"It seems we caught him in the act of transitioning."

"Into what?"

He didn't reply. Presently he said, "If you can walk, we should be on our way."

We helped Miss Cole up. She seemed more energetic.

"Do you know what he did with your things?" I asked.

"Aren't they still at Swydden House?"

"No," I said.

"I suspect they are hidden away at Scorrhill Hall. We shall go there and find out. I have more questions for Prendick." Holmes looked grim in the moonlight.

Prendick answered the door at the first knock. He had not yet retired and looked worried.

"This young lady needs hot water," I said. "She would also like her things that will have been stored here by your son."

Prendick didn't question us which I thought was odd. He immediately went to the kitchen and returned with a kettle. "Here it is."

"Come on, man, haven't you a bowl and soap?" Holmes said, aggravation crisping his tone.

Prendick led us upstairs into a small bedroom. He set the kettle down on a marble-topped washstand. A sliver of scented soap lay in a blue glass dish. Miss Cole poured the water into the bowl. Steam rose from the china bowl patterned with pink roses and green leaves.

Prendick returned with a linen towel.

"Can you manage?" I asked her.

"Yes. Thank you."

"And her things?" Holmes said to Prendick.

He opened a cupboard where a valise was stored and removed a cloth from a wooden box that served as a trunk.

We left her to it and returned to the sitting room downstairs. Prendick sat in the same chair with his head in his hands. "He did it." It wasn't a question. He raised his head. "Was she harmed?"

"No," I said. "She seems a sensible young woman but I don't doubt she will have nightmares for the rest of her life."

"I'm sorry. I thought I could save him by civilizing him. It seems he merely used the trappings of civilization to hide his true nature."

"Didn't you suspect when sheep were being killed since he came home?" Holmes said.

"I did the first time. I caught him. That's why I sent him away to school. I didn't know sheep were disappearing again here."

"Three. Last week and this week," Holmes said.

Prendick shook his head.

"How did he become this half animal?" I asked.

"I was shipwrecked in the late 1880's. Rescued, I ended up on an island where a man who called himself Dr. Moreau was doing experiments on people turning them into animals and turning animals into people."

I couldn't believe what I was hearing. "Was he insane?"

Prendick looked at us. His blue eyes were filled with pain and sadness. "I don't know. I think you would have to be to carry out those experiments. The results suffered and I realized I was on his agenda. One night pandemonium broke out amongst the beasts. They were in pain and confused. Moreau was killed by one of his creatures. I escaped to the beach where I had found a boat of sorts. On the way I found a beautiful puma woman dying in childbirth. I delivered the baby, a girl. 'Moreau's,' the woman told me. Her other child a young lad was playing in the sand by himself, oblivious to his mother's plight, the burning buildings, the screams. I took them into the boat with me and brought them to London. We resided there for a few y ears until the girl was four. One day about four years ago she slipped away from us in the park. I searched but couldn't find any trace of her. I dared not go to the police and call attention to the children. Julian seemed normal but I was wary.

"The lad was distraught. I brought him here to this abandoned house where I set up my own laboratory to try to make sense of what I had beheld and to reverse any symptoms that might appear. I thought the quiet of the moors where he could roam and experience nature would be a calming influence against whatever Moreau caused but when he was twelve, sheep began to be killed in this area. I sent him to the school and he seemed to adjust to it well. He liked the games and playing with other boys. He even liked learning, especially botany which he excelled at. All was well, I thought, but when I visited him in March, I learned of sheep going missing or being killed in the area and I brought him back here. He seemed unperturbed on returning and intensely interested in the family next door. They had employed a governess while Julian was away at school. He spent hours watching Miss Cole and her charge when they took their exercise out of doors. The child is about nine, I believe. I've wondered if Julian thinks she is his sister."

Holmes and I stared at the man. This was the most far-fetched story I'd ever heard and absolutely horrifying.

"Why would he take Miss Cole?" I wondered aloud.

"We do not know how his mind works. He may think when the family returned, Emily would play outside by herself and he could snatch her. He may have been preparing a place to take them to live. Emily would be his sister and Miss Cole could continue as her governess. What did he tell you?" Holmes asked.

"Nothing. I didn't ask him anything. I just hoped it was all a coincidence, that Miss Cole had run off with another man or to escape the lecherous Sir Eustace. I can only surmise that what you posit is what he had in mind."

"If he was in his mind. He may act more on instinct that processed thought at this point," I said.

"Was Moreau the father of both children?" Holmes asked.

"Most likely. Puma woman was quite beautiful in any guise. I know Moreau was the father of Julian's sister wherever she is but I don't believe she is Emily. Did you kill him?"

"No. I hit him in the arm but it was painful and frightening enough to stop him from killing Holmes. He ran off on the moors."

"It seems nature has won over nurture," Prendick said.

"That cannot be accepted. Nature was interfered with in this case," I said.

354

"Horribly interfered with," Prendick said.

Miss Cole was in better spirits after the change of clothing. We decided it was best to take her straightaway back to London to her fiancé and say nothing of her ordeal. Her reputation needed to be protected and we didn't want the story of Julian to become public. We retrieved our bags from the inn and Prendick drove us to the next town where we took the train to London. I didn't envy Prendick's burden. From time to time we heard from him. He scoured the moors for signs of Julian but found none though the sheep-killing stopped abruptly with the rescue of Miss Cole.

Some months later Prendick thought he'd traced the boy to a ship bound for tropical French islands in the south Pacific. He took the next ship to Tahiti. Holmes received a postcard of a tropical scene from Pape'ete with only a cryptic 'Paradise Found' written on it, signed Prendick.

"Who wrote the note left at Swydden House?" I asked Miss Cole on the train to London.

"I did. I put in clues that I was under duress."

"Emily noticed your name was spelt wrong," I said, "but they all believed you had gone to India."

The reunion of Judson and Helen was heart-warming. We attended their wedding in the registry office and Mrs. Hudson made a wedding feast for them. As they were leaving for their new life, Miss Cole, Mrs. Jacques now leaned out of the cab and said, "I shall be writing my story. Do you think it will sell?"

"All that trouble to protect her reputation and she's planning a book?" I said after the cab had joined the traffic in the street.

"Come, come, Watson. Everyone will know it's fiction."

I wasn't so sure. People love those lurid stories. Look at Robinson Crusoe.

Do you think that's what he did? Or will we find his body on the moor someday?

Oh he rides home in worse wear than this.

MX Publishing

MX Publishing brings the best in new Sherlock Holmes novels, biographies, graphic novels and short story collections every month. With over 500 books it's the largest catalogue of new Sherlock Holmes books in the world.

We have over one hundred and fifty Holmes authors. The majority of our authors write new Holmes fiction - in all genres from very traditional pastiches through to modern novels, fantasy, crossover, children's books and humour.

In Holmes biography we have award winning historians including Alistair Duncan. Brian Pugh and Maureen Whittaker who have all won the Sherlock Holmes Book of The Year Award.

MX Publishing also has one of the largest communities of Holmes fans on Facebook and Twitter under @mxpublishing.

MX is a social enterprise that has raised over $130,000 for good causes including Happy Life Mission (Kenya), Undershaw School for children with learning disabilities (UK) and the WFP (World Food Programme).

Milton Keynes UK
Ingram Content Group UK Ltd.
UKHW031846251024
450150UK00001B/8